1-The bite.

Maureen Smith bit her husband on the finger, deep enough to draw blood, on the 15th June 2023. He was caressing her face, uninvited as usual, and rather than smile with fake contentment she realised, at that very moment, that her husband had been touching her for his own pleasure for 40 years. And she hated the very bones of him.

Maureen Smith decided, as he held both her small hands in his large left hand, that this would be the very last time Timothy Smith held her hands, stroked her face and raised his eyebrows, which appeared to be his version of foreplay. She decided that she would not lie down and think about a long weekend in Whitby she might go to with some acquaintances when Timothy was away at the Conservative Party Conference, and let him do whatever he wanted, because she didn't want to go to Whitby or the bedroom. For some reason, on the 15th June 2023 Maureen Smith decided enough was enough. Or rather she decided this wasn't enough. It was nowhere near enough. It wasn't enough passion or joy or laughter or fire in her belly. It wasn't enough dungarees, or gin or swearing. It was far too much small talk and beige and hoovering and keeping quiet in the corner. And Maureen Smith had fucking had enough.

Maureen, at the brilliantly young age of sixty five, had had an epiphany. Her life flashed before her eyes, but she wasn't dying. Her life danced across her brow, and she saw herself marching against the bomb, recalled the feeling of metal against her skin as she chained herself to the perimeter fence of Greenham Common, she felt the scuffs on her knees made by the policeman dragging her across the road to the waiting police van. She felt all of her subdued rage and swallowed down emotion, the years of gentle nodding, and she bit that bastard's finger with a mouthful of regret.

Timothy Smith screamed and slapped her hard across the face. "What the hell was that for?" he shouted, sticking his finger into his mouth to ease the pain and stop the blood. "You stupid bitch, it's bleeding."

Timothy went to slap her again and she stopped his hand, her face still throbbing from the first blow.

"No!" she shouted. "That's enough." She was firmer and louder than she had been in years, she could feel her flame ignite. "That. Is. Fucking. Enough"

Timothy stepped back quickly, his face red with anger and shock. He stumbled over his steps and stumbled over his words and for once he did not know what to say. He stood against the beige wall of the hall and stared at his wife who he momentarily did not recognise, he had foolishly forgotten who she could be.

"What the hell is going on here?" He finally said, trying to find composure in his voice. "What are you playing at?"

"Oh, it's not a game Timothy, I'm not playing at anything. I said no, that's enough." She began walking towards the stairs when he grabbed her arm.

"Have-you- lost -your -mind?" he spat slowly.

"No Timothy" Maureen smiled. "It appears I have just found it, and you will not touch me again. I am going upstairs now and don't follow me, you are to stay out of my way." She was quiet and firm and her youthful power flashed before his eyes

And with that Maureen made her way upstairs and began to pack.

Timothy Stood in the hallway for some time, taking turns to look at his finger and then look up the stairs. He breathed noisily, as if trying to force his bewilderment and frustration out of his slightly too hairy nostrils. He kept thinking about Mother's birthday. It was only in two weeks away, everything was organised and he couldn't have Maureen showing him up under any circumstance. What could have got into her? She had never, ever behaved like this. Granted, she could get slightly over excited at times, perhaps shown her disinterest or disapproval with an eye roll or unnecessary stubbornness, but she had never displayed such aggression.

He recalled the times Maureen had become frustrated, almost raised her voice and cried, but she had always agreed to lie down, or go for a walk to clear her head when she was not her usual calm, amenable self, and he put that down to that dreadful menopause. Yes, he thought, there were a few spicy moments there, when she would change plans or need to be on her own, but he had read all about it. He knew it better than she did. And now this. Biting like she was a common dog.

He had been asking about the final arrangements for Mother's birthday. She had organised everything with military precision, planned the seating, organised the menu and gifts, and he told her so, he told her how grateful he was, how pleased he was that she had a little project to occupy herself with, how pleased Mother would be to have everyone there, celebrating her ninetieth birthday.

He told her he was looking forward to seeing people from the club who would be impressed at the food and music. And had she thought any more about the hair appointment? He had spoken to the hairdresser and said that she might like a shorter cut now she was sixty-five, didn't want to look too much like her mother with that mop of silver curls. What did she think about getting a different dress, something in grey so as to not outshine Mother? And then he thanked her for being his little superstar. He called her that because she was his little superstar, with her organisation and calm, and can-do attitude. The way she kept the house pristine so that he could have anyone over at any time and not have to call ahead to ask her to tidy, or bake, or make herself look presentable. They had come a long way, but she had got there in the end with his help.

He stroked her face and called her his little superstar. And then he suggested that they throw caution to the wind, be wild, have an afternoon lie down. And he stroked her face again, and raised his eyebrows just the way she liked, knowing that they would be lying down and back up in time for early drinks at the club. And the silly bitch bit him, before he knew what was coming. His finger was still throbbing. It was like she had gone crazy. Like William Duncan's wife from the club. She burnt all of his clothes and smashed his car with a golf club after one too many indiscreet moments. Timothy should be so lucky. He had never so much as glanced at another woman. Well, perhaps the odd glance, but that was it. No harm in window shopping, but he knew which side his bread was buttered. He knew there would be no one else for him from the moment he saw her.

He listened to her footsteps moving back and forward across the bedroom, opening and closing drawers, banging them shut as if she was wanting to break them. He heard her march across the landing to the bathroom and then the clatter of bottles and the thud of something dropping. He wanted to go up there and tell her to be careful, to calm it down, stop being dramatic and just have some fresh air, but he had also never seen her speak up so clearly, not for years. He had never heard her say no to him with such gusto, with such anger and force, not since they were very young, and then he would take her ferocity and retreat, but not now, not these days.

Maureen packed as much as she needed, comfy shoes, nightclothes, jumpers, coat, trousers and tops. Toiletries, a couple of books and her underwear, the comfy ones she kept for when she was being left alone. She grabbed the contents of the safe from the back of her wardrobe containing cash and bank books and whatever else was in there and she zipped up the suitcase. She had places to go, no one to see, and she was fuming hot, burning even, from the tips of her toes to the top of her curly head.

She had spent the last few months organising a bloody ninetieth birthday party for a woman who didn't want to celebrate being ninety, for a man who wanted to bask in all of the glory of an event he had nothing to do with, apart from gladly paying for it all at the end. She would have dearly loved to have been celebrating her own Mum's ninetieth, but here at the grand old age of sixty-five, she was already older than her mother had ever been, by exactly two months. And each day, as she looked into the mirror to tame her mass of white curls, her mother looked back at her and there was sadness in her eyes, and she was so fed up of being sad that she could barely catch her own breath. She was so lost that she could hardly see her way forward, and even though she was looking back at the double of her Mum looking sad, seeing her Mum in her own face brought her a joy too.

And he said it, he had booked her an appointment so that she could get her hair cut, so she could cut away her mother so he didn't have to look at the face of a woman who thought he was a joke. In months to come, when she explained to people what had led to this, why had she left, it would be this moment that would play on her mind and it would be almost unexplainable. I left my husband because he booked me a hair appointment so that I would look nice at a birthday party. It would sound absurd. But the truth would be that I left my husband because I was suffocating, as if he had held a pillow over my face for the last few years, and just when he wanted to cut the last piece of rebellion out of me, that I had swallowed down, just when he tried to make me finally disappear into the beige, I only went and found my bloody rainbow, and it burst forth and exploded in ways that he could never imagine, it was beyond holding back, it was uncontainable. And it was spectacular.

2-The exit.

On the 15th June 2023, around an hour after biting her husband's finger, Maureen Smith finally exited the house that she had shared with Timothy for the last fifteen years. They hadn't downsized when the kids went to university, they had upsized. They, or rather Timothy, felt that they had the money so they should show people that they had it, so the three bedroomed house she had grown her babies in had become a five bedroom house, completely full of emptiness.

Maureen didn't know, as she wrestled her suitcases and bags into the boot of her car, whether she would be back a few more times for things that she didn't think she would need, but missed and wanted and didn't want to lose. Not one of those things was Timothy. Whilst she had wrestled the case and bag down the stairs he had growled at her.

"Where the devil do you think you're going?"

"I'm not sure yet, but I'll be away a while." She replied as the thud, thud, thud of the case hit each step .

"I won't allow it." He shouted. "You're my wife, you live here with me."

She sighed hard when she got to the bottom of the stairs. "Timothy, I am going." She said slowly. "I am done."

And there was something in the way that she said it, in the way that her words came out of her mouth so succinctly, accompanied by the sigh, that he didn't say any more, because for now he knew she meant what she was saying. But he was certain she would be back before Mother's birthday. This was a moment of madness. A blip. So he let her go. He silently gave her permission for this as he watched her curls bounce down the drive to the car. Momentarily he opened his mouth to say that the car was registered to him at the DVLA and she was not to take it, but something got the better of him and he kept his mouth firmly shut. The only sound to be heard once the front door had been shut was the gusts of disgust blowing from Timothy Smith's curious nostrils. He had never been more shocked in his life, and it hadn't even started yet. He was in for quite a bit more shock. He had been amazed that he had actually managed to tame the wildness of Maureen, and it turned out he wasn't amazing at all.

Maureen started the car with her usual checks, but omitted to look in the rear view mirror as she drew off the drive. As dramatic as this leaving may be, she did not want to accelerate and skid away. She had spent so many years standing slightly behind, waiting her turn, she wasn't about to race away now and draw attention to herself more than necessary. She might not know who she was quite yet, but she knew who she wasn't.

She joined the road off the long drive, still avoiding the rear view mirror until she knew he would not be seen. She knew he was in the doorway of the house and she knew he would be puzzled. It wouldn't be an excited puzzlement, an almost finishing a jigsaw or a crossword puzzle, it would be frustration and not know what was going on. Not being in control or in charge. She knew he would be frowning, and the furrows in his brow would gather over his eyes making him look angry. His mouth would be ajar, his tongue clacking on the roof of his mouth as he struggled to still himself. He wouldn't know how to stand or what to do with his hands, when to close the door and when he would realise she wasn't turning the car round and going for a lie and begging him to forgive her moment of madness?

There had been moments, moments when she said no, not directly but with subtle tones, not saying no but not doing what was expected. Sometimes she put it down to being forgetful, and he would blame her hormones. It worked better in the years 45-55, but less so of late. Lately she had done less, but not with defiance or rebelliousness, it was more numbness. People would say that they felt tired in their very bones, but she felt sadness to her core. It was a sadness because she felt trapped and she no longer recognised herself. She was a shadow of who she had expected to be, a whisper of her loudness. She was a moulded woman who had been shaped by the hands of someone without regard for the strength of her own character. She had begun to feel like one of those plastic toys with a spring and a suction pad, that you pressed down and waited and watched for the suction to fail and the spring to claim its shape, but she had been pressed down for so long she thought she would never reclaim herself. But holy hell, her spring found her shape today and her jump into the air felt like a very, very tiny glint of magnificence.

So she would not turn back and look in the rear view mirror, because what was the point of looking back. This was not the time for momentary glances. She pulled onto the road and felt for the house keys in her pocket, not the house she was leaving but the house that she was going to. She anticipated that there would be a maximum 4 hour drive ahead of her and she would stop half way for a pot of tea, because there was absolutely no one to tell her that it would be foolish to stop when you could just get the drive out of the way and then it would be done. There was no one to tut and say her name sternly if she happened to mention that the stop was necessary because she needed a wee. Could she not hold it in? Why did she have the bladder of a child? She had sat in discomfort for many miles before she dared say that she needed to stop. And then she would have to shuffle across the car park with thighs clenched together because she had left it too late, she had delayed the admonishment and dribbled on her gusset. There was some let up in recent years when his prostate had become enlarged and he needed the stop more than she did, then there was no tutting about the stop.

By the time she was on the motorway she thought about the feeling of his finger between her teeth and she let out a little giggle, a stifled laugh that made her shoulders shake a little, she looked at herself briefly in the rear view mirror and wondered who exactly she was? She was not an aggressive woman, she was a silent woman who said yes when asked and always tried to help. She was invisible, but she wanted to be seen. Her gentle laughter made way for tears as she cried for herself, for time gone. She had never been forced to do anything, she had just chosen never to rock the boat, she had chosen to let someone else captain her ship until her footsteps were silent and she was without opinion or matter. She really had no reason to be annoyed with Timothy, he had remained true to himself throughout, put himself first and leaned on her shadow. He had not forced her at all. He had just become more and more as she had become less and less. He had enjoyed being her puppeteer, but she had let him pull the strings. She was not cross with Timothy, but she was absolutely fucking livid with herself. She had been feeling so sad for so long that feeling angry was a welcome relief, it seemed to give her energy and spur her on.

By the time she was two hours into the journey the tears had long dried and she was pulling off the M6 into the services for a wee and a hot drink. She was ravenous, it had been ages since she had eaten, if you didn't include fingers, so she got herself a sandwich and some provisions from the Marks and Spencer shop, just a few things to last the next couple of days, milk, bread and massive amounts of cheese. She didn't even have to listen to his voice tell her that the price in those places was daylight robbery, that they should wait, not put up with it. She just scanned her card and ignored the total, they had the money, she had the money, what else were they going to do with it but spend it?

It was her favourite service station, she knew when she saw what the kids used to call the spaceship that she was closer to her destination than him. She walked in without a single clench in her thighs, and used the toilet, accompanied by the gasping breath of the hand dryers as she tinkled her way towards her sandwich. Empty first and make way for the tea, her Mum used to say, and never pass up the opportunity to sit on the throne. She bought the largest take away tea she could get and walked through the car park along the red tarmac strip with stick people on, letting her know where to move safely, cardboard cup of tea in one hand, burning at her fingers, and her carrier bag of provisions in the other. She struggled to get her key out of her pocket, balancing her tea on the roof of the car before swinging her bags into the passenger seat.

Maureen had eaten in some very fancy places, expensive places, she had eaten all over the world, wherever Timothy's work or fancy took him, but the prawn sandwich in Marie Rose Sauce from Lancaster Services, northbound, was one of the most delicious things she had eaten in many years. She ate ravenously, without care and without a napkin to wipe her mouth. She ate quickly, finishing it all before she took her first sip of tea. And when she finished she tossed the cardboard wrapper into the passenger foot well of her car with utter defiance. She did not gather any litter, wait for people to finish before making her way to the grey plastic bin so that there was no sign of anything gobbled in the car, she just left it there, because she absolutely, bloody well could. The 15th June 2023 was proving to be a day of may firsts.

Maureen cracked open the window, it was hot, her cheeks pink with the heat of the day combined with the heat of the tea. It was what they called close, where you breathed in air hotter than your nostrils and where aching headaches spread across your forehead with the pressure of the air. It started spitting big tears of raindrops on the window, before she had even left the service station. The weather was close, but she was close too, and that pleased her immensely, she felt excited and tired at the same time. It was a day of a lot of weather and a lot of emotion.

She re-joined the M6 as the heavens opened, the great drops of rain threw themselves to the road, and then jumped up to make a haze of rain as she drove. Occasionally a spit of it would come through the window and splat on the side of her face, but not often enough to close the window, and she needed the air. At junction 36 she wound off and felt like she had hit the last leg. It was six o'clock and she pondered that most of the rush hour would have dispersed, the summer holidays hadn't quite hit and so she was hoping that she would be at the house within the hour. She felt the keys in her pocket, tapping them every so often to reassure herself that she was prepared. She wasn't sure what she was prepared for, but not sleeping in the car was a start.

She passed buildings and greenery as familiar to her as breathing, she opened her window wider so she could smell home. How was it that she wasn't here all of the time? In her favourite place in the world. How did she end up in a too big house in the suburbs of a city when she craved quiet and green and this. She had gone along with it all, being hours away from where she wanted to be. She visited less often than she wanted because Timothy was very busy with goodness knows what and he didn't think it was the done thing for her to go away without him. He didn't want to be where she yearned for and so she ended up quietly seeking green spaces in the suburbs, trying to find high ground to climb on to look at views, when all she really wanted was to be here, with a flask and a cheese sandwich, a piece of coffee cake wrapped in greaseproof paper to keep the butter icing off the sandwich in the lunch box. It was always so complicated, pleasing someone else and losing yourself. Except, if she was lost, she wouldn't be here, if she had lost herself fully her rebellion would have been swallowed down years ago and she would be in her too big house right now, making tea and being quiet and pleasing and a little star. But she wasn't, she was here and he was there and the distance between them was glorious. She had coughed and gasped and found herself just when she needed it most.

She had a sudden sense of impending doom as she thought that there was the possibility that he might have followed her. Got into his car, fully aware that she was heading this way towards home and freedom. And what would she do then? She had not left the key to the cottage behind. There was the one in her pocket and the one she had hidden years ago in the back garden, so even if he came she did not have to let him in, and he had no means of access. She doubted he would follow through. He had said so many times over the years that he was a leader, not a follower, he didn't even like it if she walked slightly ahead of him if he had become distracted about something, she had to wait, slow down, do it all at his pace. She had run up mountains, ran marathons, swam in lakes, ridden bikes late into the night and slept in fields, and yet she had spent the majority of her life slowing down so as to not cause aggravation. She was capable of so much and she had swallowed it all down until she could barely breathe. Whatever he decided was his next plan, she made a vow then that he would never set foot into her mother's cottage ever again, even if he arrived in a storm, or in the night, or in despair, his feet would not get past the front step .

The sun was bright in the sky with thin, wispy, white clouds dancing in the blue as she skimmed past the top of Kendal and made her way towards Windermere. She was so close she felt an anxious breath catch her chest. It had been over a year since she had been up here. She thought of the dust and the musty smell that would hit her, familiar and not quite fresh, but comfortingly pleasant. This was the longest she had been away, stayed away, and agreed to be somewhere else. It would be the last time she would ever get to the yellow front door and think of it as a holiday, a home from home. This was where she was going to stay, no matter what came her way in the next few weeks. Whatever he threw at her she would not be going back to that too big house, she would be staying in her Mum's old cottage, her old house, her lovely home.

3 -the house.

Twenty five years ago, when Maureen was less of a shadow and more of herself she spent 2 months in the old cottage with the yellow door. She had leaned on Timothy then, leaving him to manage two teenagers, in the middle of the summer holidays, she hadn't asked, she had told him that her mum was dying and she needed to be there. The only child of an only child, she was needed to support her mum as she fought to see the grass, smell the air, and keep her dignity.

"Well how long will you be gone?" He had asked.

"As long as she needs me." She had said, packing up her bag and wondering how she would measure the length of her mum's life.

"But what about the children?" He asked, as if she had not thought about them, about tearing herself in two for the people she loved most in the world. As if she had not thought of all the scenarios of where she could look after everyone all at once.

"Ask your mum to come and stay." She said, not turning to face him. "She'd love to help out, to be asked, she'll love being with the kids." Whether the kids will love it just the same, she doubted very much.

He offered to pay for a carer, someone to look after her mum as she got weaker, "I am the bloody carer." She said, turning to him and looking him in the eye with a fierceness that made him look away, look to the ground and nod, a fierceness that had lessened over time but still caused him anxiety.

It was the longest she had spent in the cottage since she had left for university, the longest she had spent behind the low wooden door for over twenty years . She had laid bedside her mum drinking tea, chatting when her mum was awake and lying quietly, reading if her mum had gone to sleep. She had prepared meals for tiny amounts to be eaten, happy that there was some being swallowed. She had brushed her mum's teeth, gently washed her face, helped her to the toilet and cleaned her up when the toilet became too far. She had talked on the phone, every single day, always the same question, when would she be home? She understood it from the kids, they missed her and needed her too. But from Timothy, every time he asked when she'd be home he was really asking when Coral would be dead, and the thought that her mum would cease to be breathing, would no longer be the soul of the house, was too much to bear.

"Tell the bastard I'll go when I'm good and ready." Coral smiled weakly, overhearing Maureen telling him that she was going to be here for a while yet.

She never knew what it was about him that turned her daughter's head. What did he have that made her daughter settle down? Or just settle? How did Timothy bag such a brilliant human as Maureen? She could never understand. He was decidedly average, trying to act the charmer, assuming everyone was as pleased with him as he was with himself. He was like a dog under threat when Coral was about. "Don't be a dick Timothy" She'd say when he told his tales for too long or mentioned something about how he'd done a brilliant thing, or pleased someone. He would shudder as she said those words or anything remotely critical about him. But his mouth would stay firmly shut.

"Mum!!" Maureen would whisper loudly. As if Coral had said too much, when really she had said nowhere near enough at all. There was so much more to say to that dreadful man, but for Maureen's sake she would say just enough so he knew that he should watch himself around her, but not too much so that he wouldn't be too vile to Maureen once she was back home.

She had no doubt about the fact that Timothy wouldn't mourn for a moment when she was gone. It would all be a dreadful inconvenience to him that she was requiring time, and attention, from Maureen. But her poor girl, her lovely Maureen, her gentle, fierce, diminished, put upon, wonderful daughter. She couldn't stand the thought of her dealing with life without her. Whenever the phone calls came, whenever she heard Maureen saying that she wouldn't be home just yet Coral felt a tingle of life hit her, happy with her daughter's defiance. It was almost worth being in this situation for her son-in-law to be told no. She never knew that this period of time and the long grief after would lead to the constant period of agreement that Maureen would settle into, apart from the issue of the house being sold. Maureen's refusal to sell the cottage was like the last stand. The negotiations, the pleading, the business talk and she never let that house go. It would be good for holidays, adventure for the kids, it would look great for people to know that he had a holiday home in the Lake District, she used every argument going and it was that ego boost that got him, that he could tell people about his holiday home. Maureen couldn't stand the thought of it being sold and it felt like her safe place, her calm place, her mum's place. She negotiated how he could tell people about his bolt hole up north, but it would never be his. Ever.

Coral died not long after her sixty-fifth birthday. Her lovely handful of brilliant friends came to wish her happy birthday, to see if there was anything they could do. They sat around the bed as Coral did her best to keep her eyes open and they cackled about their combined and individual adventures, moaned about husbands, drank wine, held hands and kissed Coral's forehead when they were leaving. It was the tribe that Maureen had grown up with, the community that raised her, and they held her tightly by the front door as they said their goodbyes. Anytime, any time at all they would be here, any call, any need, anything, but Maureen felt that she should do this on her own, that she should hold onto her mum tight and look after her until she was gone. And then she was.

When Maureen let herself into the cottage through the yellow front door, there was the faintest smell, still, of her mum and her home. How bizarre, uncomfortable and unkind of life that she was now older than her mother had ever been. That her mother had never known her children as grown ups was heartbreaking, but it was a relief that she had never had the misfortune to know the shadow Maureen had become. That she had been. Maureen felt that walking into that home, getting into that hall she had become less of her shadowy self and more of who she should be.

The house still smelt of how it always did, but with an empty dampness. It smelt of varnish and sweetness, with a hint of washing left wet too long. She walked through the house to the back door and unbolted the giant locks, wiggling their stiffness until they banged in the right direction. She pushed open the heavy door and looked out at the little garden, overgrown and weedy, but still a bee's delight. She left the door open and let the outside in, heading to the kitchen to open the windows in there. Everywhere looked a little bit dull, no one had been in properly for over a year, the dust was thick and spider webs hung down from the corners of the room like fine, abandoned Christmas decorations.

It was a job to know where to start once she had brought the cases in. She was so used to silently waiting for directions that she briefly couldn't make a decision.

"Come on Maureen." She said out loud. "Get a bloody move on"

She filled the kettle first and then decided she would give the kitchen a good wipe round. She could start here and filter out. It was quarter to seven, she would give herself two hours to straighten up then eat something. She could drink as much tea as she needed to accompany her clean, no one was counting, telling her the amount she'd had, should she really be drinking caffeine at this late hour? She looked under the sink, the mouse traps were still there, unexploded, so she decided to leave them be. She had left the house clean when she was last here, no rubbish, no pots, nothing out of place, it was just time that had reached out and left it's mess, but it was nothing she couldn't handle. She tied her hair up in an old elastic band. She had forgotten how warm it was when it was down, normally she wore the approved bun.

She spread out from the kitchen and before nine fifteen she had most of the house looking like a home, looking like her home, where she had grown up, before she flew away. It never felt more like hers and she was so pleased to be here, pleased that everything had happened in exactly this order this morning. That he had said she was looking too much like her mum, that he had stroked her face, that he had told her whatever else she couldn't recall, but it was enough to detonate the unexploded bomb in her that had been brewing for longer than she realised. She didn't sit on the edge of the bed and cry as she did up her bra after the commencement of post face stroke activities, or smile as she silently screamed, or offered to bring him a coffee as he reclined against the pillow. She just exploded. She got bigger and he shrank. She finally said no. She stopped following and waiting and started feeling and doing.

She knew that after four cups of tea the two pints of milk that she had bought wouldn't last, and she needed more in the house, so she drove round to the little express shop that opened until ten and bought everything she might need for the next few days before she hit up the big supermarkets. Not that she had plans, things to buy for, she just wanted to be comfortable and safe and able to stay at home without feeling she needed to get to the shops for the next few days. She spent the best part of a hundred pounds on things she might fancy along with the staple provisions for someone who lived in a cottage and wasn't planning to live anywhere else. Things that she liked, rather than pleasing someone else.

Once back in the car she watched every figure as she drove the short journey back home. Watched every person's walk and stature to make sure that Timothy hadn't followed her, watched for his familiar gait and movement. He had had enough time to shrink from her and wallow, become infuriated at her and decide that he was having none of this. She held her breath as she carried the shopping from the car to the house. It was still light but it was heading for darkness and she didn't want to have any more unpleasantness today. She was tired out but wanted to stay up for a bit longer, to enjoy the house and find that contented feeling in her stomach that she had when she first got here, that had since been replaced with anxiety and imagined scenarios.

She closed the front door when she was done carrying, making sure that the bolts were across and the latch locked into place. She double checked the back door locks and closed the open windows, then she pulled the curtains closed and flicked the TV on, hoping she could remember how to do the requested channel retune. She left that to do it's technological business and plopped a finest ready meal lasagne in the microwave, opening a can of ready made gin and tonic, she felt like she was a student again.

When she finished eating and she'd had enough of the TV she checked the doors and windows one last time and had a quick peep out of the curtain both front and back. All was quiet, but she wasn't calm. That little ball of anxiety had grown slightly. But her mum always said doing the right thing churned your stomach up, and doing the wrong thing churned your stomach up, but the right thing churn would always pass. She could certainly manage feeling anxious as opposed to feeling sad or numb, feeling something different was a welcome change .

Maureen cleaned her teeth and had probably not her last wee of the night, she pulled back the comfortably slightly musty smelling sheets and laid down with her phone in her hand. She planned to get lost in videos, made by people she would never know, but there it was. One message, one direction, one demand, sent at ten o'clock exactly.

'Be back home tomorrow at noon. We are going to Mother's for lunch'

And so it began.

She hesitated for a moment, and then she was barely aware that any anxiety she felt drifted off and became a feeling of annoyance. 'Don't be a dick Timothy' she could hear the voice of her mum saying. She knew he would be happy never to mention today, and for her to drive back to the big house and just find her steps again. He'd reprimand her in his own way, a bit of belittling here, an accusation there and he'd be happy with his control and her quiet. She wasn't going back home because she was already home. Come hell or high water she planned on staying in the village, in the Cottage. She had to let him know she meant what she said earlier. She was done.

'I'm not coming back tomorrow' she typed. 'I'm at Mum's cottage, I'm staying here for a while. I'll let you know if anything changes'

She was a hundred percent certain that a while meant forever, and that there would be no changes, but she didn't want him to escalate things, or bother her, she just wanted to be left alone for now. She knew he would want to pretend to everyone everything was normal, and she knew that whatever she had put up with was not normal, not happiness, not a partnership and she would not prioritise his needs or feelings, but she just knew a life changing ending was not to be told via text. Although she could hardly have made herself clearer earlier on.

'But I love you" was the reply.

But she was not after a pen friend, she was after peace, so she turned her phone off and settled down for some much needed sleep.

4 – tea and cheese sandwiches.

There wasn't another home that Maureen felt so rooted to. She was born in the house on Ellerigg Road, it belonged to Coral's parents, and it was a house of books, chatter, discussion and adventure. As a child Maureen was different, in a village where difference wasn't embraced, the girl without a dad was the talk of many whispers. Now not a hushed judgement would be made, but 1958 wasn't so gentle with unmarried mothers. Nanna and Grandad said 'it is what it is' and that was that. There was no sending away for Coral, no talk of adoption, no pressure to be married, there was just dealing with how it was, there was a baby on the way and there was a spare box room to house it. Whether there was disapproval in the house, or discussion forged to arguments, Maureen never heard, they were just a slightly different kind of family. When she was small and people talked, Coral told them to ignore the whispers. At the age of eight when someone in the local shop called her a bastard again, and she finally told her mum, Coral quietly left the house and offered several home truths to Mrs Munsey so that Mrs Munsey could barely look any of the family in the eye again. She had a tongue in her that could whip a navy ship into embarrassment, to be used sparingly for best effect, but she was Maureen's greatest advocate, protector and hero. And life to Maureen was the cottage, Mum, Nanna and Grandad.

The kitchen in the old cottage always had home made cake and biscuits, in various tins in the pantry, ready to go with a tall red flask, topped with a dirty cream lid, for any outdoor day. Any walk or swim in the lake was accompanied by hot sweet tea with the lingering flavour of flask, distinct, slightly metallic and absolutely delightful. A chunk of cake and a rapidly made cheese sandwich would be wedged into a tin and nestled into the bottom of a haversack, alongside the flask that you had to be extra careful of, despite its robust appearance, the fragile glass lining was the secret to the heat and was to be carried with care. They never ventured far without food and tea, occasionally cycling past the old farm to buy milk, sometimes still warm from the cow to top the flask up when it became empty.

Empty jars still lined the pantry top shelf, collected for abundant harvests, rosehip jelly and blackberry jam, Grandad's elderberry wine bubbling in the old kilner jars that Maureen was allowed a sip of, with a touch of lemonade. The once tried dandelion wine causing her to gag at the back of her throat. Opening the door of the pantry on arrival Maureen could still smell the sweet mustiness that had been there when she was a child. The rows and rows of jam laid down for the winter, and the apples in their wooden trays, onions tied in long abandoned stockings looking like dead legs gone wrong. This is what she wanted, this smell, this mark of home, the belonging, not feeling like a visitor in your own home, or the cleaner awaiting instruction. Home was meant to be a sanctuary, a place where you could curl up and be safe and not worry about what someone else was thinking or planning. For Maureen home was a place where things could be out of place, higgledy pigglety and mis-matched, comfortable and calm. Where you could stretch out on the sofa and get lost in a book without being accused of inactivity, where you could put your cup down without a coaster because there had been a thousand rings of tea staining the wood before this latest instalment. Home was a place to rest when the fresh air and sunshine had exhausted every inch of your body and your cheeks felt hot with the warmth of the sun, or slapped by the kiss of the cold.

On the 14th June 2023, the day after the great decision, Maureen woke from a quiet and restful sleep in the sheets of her old bed, the sun peeping through the small gap in the curtains, casting a flash of light across the room. She lay for a moment, adjusting herself on the pillow, listening to the birds and the occasional car in the distance. This was it. This was her place and her home. She didn't have to go downstairs and set the coffee off for Timothy, she could please herself, pretend there was nothing more to be dealt with, so long as she didn't look at her phone for a bit, wait for the influx of calls from people who might start hearing that she had escaped. But really she knew that Timothy would not tell a soul for as long as he could as he wouldn't want people to know that he had been left, he wouldn't want anyone to know that he was not a wanted man. He was that predictable and being that he was such a creature of habit gave her some space and peace. Not for long, but long enough.

She popped on the radio beside the bed and made a quick dash downstairs for a glug water, while she made a cup of tea and grabbed 2 digestive biscuits, fresh from an unopened packed, taking them back to bed, without a plate or the thought of a coaster, she just placed them on the bedside table. She opened the curtains to take in the sky and got back into bed with nothing but her tea and biscuits and some thoughts. No book, no TV, just the radio talking gently beside her and birds alerting the world to the new day. She dunked and munched and let the crumbs fall onto her chest and the bed in quiet biscuit defiance, which she would regret later when the crumbs began to itch her, but it was a definite 'fuck you' to the crumb fearful Timothy, he did not even like the thought of someone else dunking a biscuit, he could not bear to think about the mush at the bottom of the cup if disaster struck.

After she had listened to the news she got undressed and got into the old dribbly shower which was warm, but not hot, and which got you wet, eventually. She washed and then quickly dried herself with a hard towel that had seen better days, but then again, so had she. After getting dressed Maureen went around the house opening curtains and windows, she opened the back door to let the fresh air hit the kitchen, rinsing her mug and placing it on the drainer. She stopped at the door of the pantry and opened it, looking for another smell of home. She stood looking in thinking that she could have a good thirty years of opening this door and sniffing at memories, she stood for a moment, if she could be here for years, being and enjoying, she would not feel that she had had a wasted life, half a life, a little life, she would feel that she had done the right thing, eventually.

Maureen felt a rush of panic overtake her as she stood in the doorway, taking in the smells and sights. What if she had to go back? What if this was the briefest moments of a delightful idea but she had to close the door and walk away, be the version of herself she had become and miss this chance and opportunity of striking out and being where and who she wanted to be? She clenched her fists. No bloody way, no bloody way would she get here, make a stand and then dissolve, she was not his clay to be moulded any longer, she was the Maureen who lived in this house and loved in this house. She relaxed her hands and leaned in further to touch the cool, scratched side of the old red flask. How many times had that been carried away and was still sitting on its shelf ready for another outing. She picked it up and walked into the kitchen, setting it beside the kettle. She felt old much of the time, but she wasn't too old to fill the flask and head on out somewhere. She didn't much fancy sitting in coffee shops and watching people come and go, there was bound to be someone watching her too, she was happy with some anonymity and adventure. She washed the flask first, because goodness knows how long it had been sat with the lid tightly on, and she boiled the kettle, rooting through a cupboard to find an old tin to bung a cheese sandwich in as a nod to her youthful self, before putting it all into her rucksack and finding her walking boots in her luggage. She would unpack it all later, it wasn't temporarily here to be zipped up at the end of the week, it was to be unpacked and remain. She had years to be here, and no one to tell her to move her things, although at this stage in the game of her marriage she never waited for criticism, she just did what was expected. This was her house now and she could live out of those bags for a year if she wanted.

It was a hot and sticky day, and it wasn't even ten o'clock. The air was warm, she searched through the kitchen drawers to find an elastic band to tie her hair up, the one she used yesterday having snapped. She found several but some had clearly been there for years and had almost stiffly melted into the base of the drawers and others snapped pathetically as soon as they were stretched. She would get something later from the shops and suffer a sweaty neck in the meantime. She didn't want to drive today, she'd driven more than enough yesterday and just wanted to be out. She grabbed her water bottle and filled it with water, wrapped a fleece around her waist in case it was cool higher up, and headed out.

It had been years since she had walked to the top of Loughrigg, probably the year after her mum died, with disgusted teenagers following close behind, letting her know that this certainly wasn't their idea of a good time. She had walked on ahead to avoid the constant whine and to encourage their pace. They were old enough to moan about not being at home , or with friends, but young enough to want their mum fairly close by. Maureen remembered the joy of the walk chipped away by the annoyance of the kids moaning at her first, and then mocking her enjoyment. They wanted to stay at the cottage with Timothy, go into the village and have hot chocolates and look around the gift shops to buy things that no one needed. She'd promised them a swim in the tarn and Mars bars to go with lunch but they still appeared to think that she was the booby prize when Timothy was at the cottage seeing to some paperwork and calling people for work

Maureen had walked ahead of the kids as their moans ceased and they started chatting to each other, bonding over the awful situation they found themselves in, tortured by this terrible mother. She had a moment of quiet then, her own annoyance at the constant criticism reducing, she stopped thinking what arsehole teenagers could be and there was room in her head for thoughts of her mum, the grief seeped in, always there, always waiting for when a distraction had left and it could take over again. It was like a monster under the bed, the passing of a loud car, an unpaid bill churning your stomach, it was there, it was waiting. She wondered if being at the cottage made it louder, but the reality was, grief was ready to shout at her wherever she was, and she liked being near where her mum had been. Where things felt right and calm, even with the hubbub of others in the house, making their own patterns on the floor.

Some days she thought she was going mad, she'd be busy with something, tidying up, planning a meal, watching the news, and all of a sudden she'd find her face was damp with tears and she was lost in the sea of grief, bobbing about the waves, trying to keep her head up. It was worse now than when it happened because the denial and disbelief had gone, the shock of it all well and truly diminished, although she still found herself asking how this could have happened? But that was just self torture, it had happened and there wasn't a damn thing she could do about it

She walked on with the kids chattering behind her and she let out a gentle sob, her mum was everywhere and nowhere at all.

"Mum, Mum " Lilly shouted, running towards her and grabbing her hand. "Sorry Mum." Ever the gentle one.

"Don't worry love." Maureen smiled, her face damp and pink. "I was just thinking about your nanna."

"I know Mum, I know." Lilly turned round to Marcus who was still a good few steps behind, "Come on snail boy, I'll race you to the cairn."

And with that they were off, racing against the gradient, Lilly's hair dancing behind her in the gentle breeze, Marcus gathering pace to take over for the win. Lilly squealing as Marcus made it past her, ruffling her hair when he was close enough. She watched them steam up the hill, laughing at each other and trading gentle insults until Marcus reached the cairn, grabbing a rock and placing it on the top.

They filled her thoughts when they were with her, distracted her with their laughter and bickering, infuriating backchat and teenage disgust at the world. They filled her thoughts full of their chatter and needs and she needed her thoughts to be full, so there was less room for the sadness and loss and the grief filled gaping hole that was the shape of her mum. It was like every loss she ever felt was in sharp focus next to this loss too, and it weighed heavy on her. Getting up was an effort, making dinner, chatting with people who had no idea that her life had changed forever while they carried on shopping and walking and chatting. How could that be? How many people had she chatted to and smiled at over the years whose life has changed or bent out of shape and she never even noticed? Because really very few people would notice her trying to pretend to be normal, just getting on with it, just getting over it, she deserved an Oscar. Grief was lonely and support was surface deep and so she held it in most of the time

It was ironic that every bit of her yearned for moments with her mum, and her own kids were moving further away, and it wasn't because they were speeding up mountains. They were busy growing their adult wings and getting ready to fly, as they should, as is the plan for any child, to be confident enough to fly, but she needed her mum so much as a forty five year old woman and there wasn't a damn thing she could do about it

She watched the kids standing side by side, pointing at things in the distance, playfully pushing each other and laughing loudly. They turned to watch her make the last few yards to the top, their pink cheeks and glistening faces, brilliant signs of greeting the outside, despite the fact that they had both wanted to stay inside. They both had little rucksacks on with their bottles of squash and sweets stuffed in the back, still able to be bribed on walks with sugar. She'd insisted the Walkman or whatever they were called were left at home so they could hear what was going on, communicate with each other. She missed their chatter.

Maureen wondered what the kids would think when she told them she had left, that she had headed up to the cottage and she planned to stay there. She imagined Lilly would be pleased, there wasn't much love lost between her and her dad, he had become increasingly intolerant of her as she got more forthright, expressed her views more, cared less what he thought, and Lilly found him infuriating and chose not to hide her contempt. She had come home less and less after university but showed up more in the last few years, pleased to see her mum, and Maureen felt lighter in her daughter's company, she felt supported and like someone was interested in her.

Marcus would probably be indifferent to her situation, he'd be off somewhere, on a dig, she was fairly sure it was Mexico at the moment but she wasn't certain. He was hard to reach, but he sent emails seeing how she was, with great long explanations about where he was and what he was doing that she could barely keep up with. He loved his job, wherever he was. But she would have to let them both know, just not today. Today was for fell walking and certainly not for explaining why.

It was so hot she could feel the top of her nose sweating while she was still only half way up, but it was a good heat, a heat that made you feel like you were on holiday and she felt in a sense she was, she was having a break from her normal life. She heard someone say once that you should make a life you didn't need a holiday from, and this could be it, potentially a 30 year holiday laying out in front of her, she just had to get over the massive bump that was coming her way, and as hard work as the fell was, the emotional bump was going to be a bit harder to climb.

She kept her slow rise towards the top of Loughrigg, feeling a slight breeze the closer to the top she got. She lifted her sweaty hair off her wet neck and let the breeze dance against her skin. As she got to the very top she sat down on the grass and drank from her water. She pulled the flask out and poured herself a strong brown brew into the stained white plastic lid. Maureen wondered how many times she had drunk from this cup, how many times she had been out walking with this flask. She wondered what her nanna would think if she knew that when she put her pennies to one side and saved to get this flask that it would still be doing it's job sixty years later, that tea would be slurped from it's plastic cup as people took photos on phones and drove electric cars. Maureen could hear her nanna saying 'who knew?' and shaking her head, which she did every time something surprised her. She smiled at the thought of nanna and her flask. Everyone she ever loved had drunk tea from that great cumbersome thing. Her grandparents, the kids, her mum, and Timothy. Because she did love him once, bloody hell did she love him, he swept her off her feet, thrust great butterflies into her unsuspecting stomach, he was all she wanted once. Just not now, not for so long. The butterflies flew off and she suffocated, but now she had started breathing.

Maureen grew a backbone? Who knew? Maureen thought. Coral knew, she knew that fiery backbone was just lying dormant, but still there and still ready to straighten when the moment was right. If she was here, if Coral had lived to be a good age, like her own mum, she'd have applauded the return of the strength, welcomed the fire in her stomach that she knew had never gone, it was just embers, waiting.

5 – explaining.

In between cups of tea two and three Maureen clicked the lid off her old tin sandwich box and hungrily chomped her cheese sandwich, after which she thought she should have made two rounds, she was still hungry, her snack size flap jack didn't do much to fill her either. She supped her third cup of tea and decided that she had better start walking down the hill before the sun caught her and turned her crispy. She put everything back into her bag and slung it over her shoulders, rolling into her knees and edging herself off the floor with the grace of a woodlouse trapped on its ancient back. She wondered if she should sign up to a yoga class, or something along those lines, so that she didn't feel every inch her age as she tried to get up from her squat position. If she had stopped looking after Timothy she needed to start looking after herself. She would put it on a list of things she should start to do, perhaps, to fill her time with, to distract her from her choices, to enjoy life again, which it seemed had been amiss for some time.

Once she was gracelessly up on her feet she set off walking, stiffly at first, with more movement than necessary. She could hear the last cup of tea gently sloshing up and down in the flask ready to be supped at the bottom of the hill. She could see the tarn far below her, glistening brightly in the hot sun, like sparks flying between the green grassy fields, and she remembered how it felt to drop herself into the water on a roasting hot day, the shock of the cool water, welcome, but forcing a throaty gasp to fly out of her mouth. She remembered squinting at the surface of the water as she bobbed and swam, the sunshine like spotlights on the tiny waves, carefully deciding where to go in to avoid the sharp rocks, which painfully stabbed at the bottom of her feet like it was trying to keep her out, or the mushy mud like cold gravy, forcing its way between her toes as Ginny Green fingers tickled and danced up her legs, ready to grab her and pull her under. Whatever the discomfort, the hot day swim was always worth it, the skin tingle and momentary cold winning against the humid air, the smell of the freshness of the water dancing into her nose.

There were always a few of them dipping in when Maureen was young, squealing and splashing, laughing and seeing who could get in first. Never swim on your own, all the parents and grandparents said it, retelling stories of the summer of 1946 when someone went in and didn't come out again, the little cross at the edge of the water, a reminder to never be in the water by yourself in the days before mobile phones and constant contact.

Except today when Maureen was hot and desperately wanted to feel cool and sweat free, she wanted to smell the glaze of the water and try and feel her youth beating through her veins. She wanted to feel the weight of the world lift off her shoulders like she used to when she immersed herself in a lake or tarn when she was 20 and full of expectation. She turned on the path to the tarn and smiled to herself. What was it her mum used to say? Don't think youthfulness equals power. There's nothing so intimidating and scary as a middle aged woman annoyed. And she was right. Maybe that's what possessed her? She had less to lose. As the years trotted on and mounted up against her she couldn't waste the moments with fake smiles and pleasing someone else above and beyond her own wants.

Maureen hoped that the tarn hadn't changed too much in the last couple of years. She wanted to find the trees on the edge, away from the path that she used to use, climbing into the water, hidden and naked when she was hot with no costume, rather like today. She was getting into that water come hell or cold water, and if she could hang her clothes in the trees and plop in beneath the branches she could swim without worrying about others watching, or perhaps without them even spotting a pensioner in the tarn. She felt a little flutter of excitement in her stomach as if she had just rubbed out the last forty five years and was carefree again. Just for a moment, just to pretend, she would swim before she carried on home and started making the telephone calls back to reality.

The 1978 version of Maureen wouldn't have gone in the water alone, there would have been six of them, giggling and squealing, completely unable to be missed by any passerby due to the noisy talk and laughter, costume clad or skinny dipping there wasn't much shyness or shame to pass between them, just gulps of air and shivers of delight as the heat left their bodies in the water. At sixty five Maureen wasn't quite so brave and she opted, in the end, to play it safe and keep her bra and knickers on. She still went in through the trees and plopped herself into the water with a gasp, leaving her clothes and bag hanging in the branches of a sycamore. She managed to be in and up to her shoulders before anyone could tell whether she was bra or bikini clad, not that anyone would care either way. People were too busy with themselves and their own worries, mostly, than to pause what they were doing to try and work out her bathing choices. Nobody cared. Except Maureen, just a little. She wondered what Timothy would think of her, bobbing about in the water in her underwear? He would probably think that she had, indeed, gone completely mad and possibly needed medical help. They had been in this tarn together before, but he firmly believed adventure was a youthful pass time, and not for them to chase. The thought of his judgement made her chuckle before an anxious reality crept across her body, edging into her mind and spoiling the delight of the swim. She knew leaving was the easy part, staying away, keeping strong, holding onto this new found resilience was the tricky part. She swam faster across the tarn, trying to race away from the thoughts that were pushing away her joy, occasionally brushing past nature's floating debris, feeling Ginny Green fingers tap at her legs reminding her that there was a lot of dark water below her. Her inability to estimate the depth of the tarn made her turn around and begin swimming back to the sycamore tree kindly holding her bag and clothes. She would finish off that tea and then head back home. Home, she only thought of the cottage, forty years of living in other places and it was still her place.

She sat hidden from view at the edge of the water, dappled sun peeping through the leaves and drying her. Her tea was lukewarm now but she felt she owed it to the flask to finish the last drops before she pulled her clothes over her damp underwear and looked at heading the couple of miles home. She could have stayed, sat by the cool trees in her bra and knickers, but thought no one wanted to discover a sleeping old woman in her underwear. It was still a long walk in the heat, but she felt cool with a bit more energy after the swim. Her eyes were tired though, dry and warm from the heat and squinting at the sun, and she was sure she'd sleep well tonight, tucked up in her soft bed. She looked at her watch, it was only three o'clock, she had to force herself to get up and put her shoes back on. Bending and balancing did not seem to be natural for her today, it was good there was the tree to keep hold of and steady herself with.

Maureen tried to remember the last time she went swimming. Any swimming, not deep, black bottomed tarns. She hadn't done that for ages, swimming without paying someone at a desk, swimming where the water smelt of promises of fresh air rather than chlorine. It must have been some spa or something that she'd last swum at, a gift off a friend, or a birthday present, or maybe something from Timothy. It wasn't her cup of tea, it was hot and sweet smelling, where she'd been given an over-conditioned bathrobe and some flip flop things to keep her from being in contact with the floor. It was the sort of place you showered before entering the water and swimming lengths at pace was not the done thing, bobbing about and then reclining on a sun bed with no sun to warm you was encouraged. Stripping to your bra and knickers and gasping and squealing as you entered the water was definitely frowned upon. You could pay extra to be stroked or manhandled by a stranger. It was good for some, but not for her.

It was a hot walk back to the cottage and just before five when she got in, thirsty and ravenous. She gulped down some water and put the kettle on, eating a banana and a small apple pie as she stood up next to the kettle, waiting for the water to start bubbling and spitting. She was stretching time. Picking things to do so she didn't have to speak to anyone or make firm plans. She didn't want a phone call or a gentle knock at the door enquiring how she was, someone sent round because they'd heard something. Heard she'd snapped or lost her mind. She was fairly certain Timothy wouldn't have told anyone yet, or maybe just mentioned her getting away for a few days rather than explaining to friends that Maureen had left forever, to stay in her cottage with a bit of money saved, and a hope that he'd never come to try and get her to go back to his home. At this moment he'd assume there was some sort of residual hormone surge or ridiculous but temporary notion of annoyance towards him rather than what it was. The end of Maureen and Timothy. The end of something that had started with such promise and hope.

Maureen felt it kind of odd that she was the holder of such information. She didn't really know what she was planning for the next few weeks, but she was certain what wasn't going to happen. That she was in charge of her own destiny, or so it felt at this point, was really bloody amazing. That she was standing in her little kitchen with comfy clothes on, not to be asked if she'd be changing for dinner or cooking the dinner or awaiting a guest or making polite chit chat felt exactly right. But if she didn't speak to anyone or tell people why she came to be here, she suspected they would search and ask and assume, fill in their own gaps. And she was done with waiting, to be told someone else's plan or desire, or story. She would have to brave it out and explain herself. Not justify, just explain.

She would start with her lovely Lilly. She would understand and not judge. Maureen carried her tea through to the front room with her phone and thought about making that call, saying all that she needed to say knowing full well she wouldn't get it all out, there would be so many questions, she decided she would email instead. It was cowardly but she'd give Lilly a chance to read and digest then call her for the answers to any questions she might have.

Where to start though? I've left your dad suddenly, yesterday, when he wanted me to cut my hair and erase your nanna from my face. I left your dad when it dawned on me that I had lived two months longer than my own mum and I realised that I wasn't living at all, I wasn't making anything of the extra moments she never got. I left your dad when I realised that he enjoyed my weakness and everlasting grief and I had to live for me and my mum too. I needed my own choices and freedom and peace and adventure, my own house, my lovely home. I needed the constant weight of judgement and the maze of manipulation to be gone, to be lifted, and I wasn't loud enough to stay and say it. So I left. I left your dad because I stopped loving him a very long time ago and yesterday I really realised I didn't like him either, but the fear of being alone or walking away, that kept me in my corner, ceased to be and I found my voice and used it. I left your dad and I can't and won't go back and I am done, and I told him this but I am certain that he has no idea that it is all rather permanent.

She would say that she'd get in touch with Timothy, go through it all again, try and get him to understand, to make sure he knew where the line had been drawn. She knew she left unexpectedly, angrily, violently even. It was out of character for her, out of recent character anyway. Maybe 20 years ago she was less agreeable, argumentative when needed, feisty even, but she had depleted over the years, becoming less. Less sure of herself, less able, managed less, was noticed less. But as slowly as she had lessened over time her awakening explosion had come quickly and had shocked none more than herself. She would explain all of this to him. Tell him that she could not go back, she could not become that less version of herself that he appeared to enjoy. And if he didn't get it, it didn't matter. The end had already happened.

She opened her laptop and began to type.

Hello Lilly.

Hello lovely girl, hope you are ok and enjoying this hot sunshine? I've had a lovely couple of days staying in Nanna's cottage. I came up yesterday, it wasn't planned, but I had to come. I had a bit of a falling out with your dad and decided I needed to leave and just have some space and relax. You don't have to reply, but you can if you like,

It's silly really, I feel like I've been lost for ages and I suddenly had enough. I'm going to stay here for a good while. I've told your dad I'm not going back, but I don't think he'll have been in touch with you?

I had tea on the top of Loughrigg fell today, from your great Nanna's old flask, and I had a swim in the tarn too, looking a great sight in my bra and knickers, I saved the poor tourists from the view of me skinny dipping, I'll save that for another day.

The cottage is clean and nice and cool despite the hot weather. It's scorching outside. I'm going to put the kettle on in a minute and make myself some tea, then I'll get some food sorted. I've plenty in and I'm not short of money. Come any time but really and honestly don't worry. The relief of being here feels great.

Love the bones of you.

Mam. Xxx

Maureen decided against emailing Marcus. He was not the best at replying and then she'd be wondering if he was choosing not to reply as he thought she'd done the wrong thing, or if he just hadn't read it yet. She couldn't manage that much wondering for the time being and he'd be engrossed in his work and he wasn't fond of distractions at the best of times. There would never be a right time to email but it felt like the wrong time at the moment.

Maureen had been ignoring her phone all day, she hadn't even taken a photo of the view from the top of the fell to avoid any intrusive messages questioning her choices. The little doubting earworm edging it's way up country via 4G, straight from the fingertips of Timothy. There were three missed calls from him. One from his sister, but that meant nothing, she rang all of the time. There were no voice messages, but a long text message from him, perfectly written, grammatically right, not a punctuation missed.

"Maureen, I don't know what is going on with you. Everything was perfectly normal and all of a sudden you behave appallingly, like a toddler, getting cross and biting. You have certainly spat the dummy out. What will people think?

I have told Mother you've got a cold and that's why you've not been around, but she misses you terribly. I've had to go round and get her shopping and tidy round and she was expecting you. Her party is in less than 2 weeks and you have to be there.

For Christ's sake, Maureen, just come home, I'll take you to the doctors myself if you're struggling at the moment. You need to talk to someone, this isn't you. I don't know where you've got this silly idea from that you should be up there. Take a few days and get over this, whatever it is, and then get back home. You don't have to talk to me on the phone but let me know that you are fine and what day you'll be back.

Timothy"

Maureen read it three times. She was surprised at his disbelief. That this wasn't her. His memory was short, even she remembered when she was fierce, she was fierce when she met him, when he was the duty solicitor and she was the arrested protester, and he was gentle and full of advice and kindness. He was sitting in his brown suit and spoke quietly, coughing with a handkerchief over his mouth, recovering from a cold. She had agreed to be bound over and keep the peace and she had left through the front door of the police station as he was struggling out with a briefcase and an arm full of files. He had watched her as she skipped down the steps and onto the pavement, her hair swishing and bobbing about her shoulders, dancing in the morning breeze. He watched until she disappeared around the corner and he was left with just the image of her leaving in his mind. He stood watching an empty street for a moment and then hopped his way down the steps and gave chase, finding her not a hundred yards from the police station ordering a cup of tea and a fried egg sandwich from the Six Pence Cafe pavement hatch. She was rooting through her purse for coins when he stepped beside her and with the confidence of a man in a better fitting suit he said "I'll get this" and he took a pound note from his pocket and placed it on the hatch counter.

She was stirring a damp spoon of sugar into her tea as she thanked him, tucking her hair behind her ear with her spare hand and weighing him up. She was free and fierce then, not a follower, not a dweller of quiet places, not destined to go unnoticed at gatherings and parties. She was seen and heard and admired and his mouth was dry and his palms damp when he was around her. He was on edge around her for a long time, worried that she would be gone, that she would see he was not worthy. And then he dropped the ball and he watched her disappear around the corner with a life full of mistakes, and he couldn't catch up with her and buy her an egg sandwich any more because she had her own pound note and her own plan. He was slightly scared of her fierceness back then, he saw it again yesterday and he realised it had never gone away, it had merely been contained, for a long time, a very long time, but she was back and he was slightly scared again. He said this behaviour wasn't her, but really his surprise was that it hadn't come sooner.

'Timothy' she wrote.

' I know you think I'm struggling with something or having some kind of turn and I need to come home and calm down. The truth is I am calm, I have clarity and I am staying here. I will come to your mother's birthday party, I don't mind or care at all what you tell people, but I'm not coming back to stay. You know we are done. We can sort out details after the party. The number for the caterers and the venue is in the kitchen on the notice board. Your sister knows what is organised, ring her and find out if there's anything you need to do.

Maureen'

Short and to the point. The fewer words the better. You can't argue when no one will argue back. She read it three times and then again to make sure it sounded firm but neutral. She knew she had to explain it to him better, with more detail, but that was for another day and certainly not over text message. A face to face needed to be had. But not today, she needed to strengthen a bit more and firm up her roots to the cottage before then. She was probably naïve to think he was going to take what she said and give value to it, but she had all the time in the world to repeat herself. He could tell the world and his wife the terrible way she had behaved, that she was unstable and needing help, it wouldn't change anything at all. If people thought badly of her they weren't worth bothering with. And she knew she had behaved badly, she didn't hurt people on purpose. She hadn't been herself for years, and now here she was, older, wiser and not hiding away and apologising.

Maureen felt like she had been back in her childhood home for weeks, not just a couple of days. Everything she touched was a reminder of her happy place, her childhood, her lovely mum. Some things she glanced at brought her a joyful memory and other things made her feel like she was gasping for breath with loss. She hadn't been in the cottage on her own for a long time. Always with the kids or Timothy or friends who had been invited. Always with a plan to get somewhere or see something, or take people on a planned walk. Never just filling time with thoughts, or sitting and reading, staring at the TV, listening to the radio, drinking that tenth cup of tea, just because. She felt she was always everyone's everything, the perfect host, the organiser, the person who said yes when asked for a favour, baking cakes for events that she never got to eat, organising afternoon teas that she never got to drink, waiting on everyone, looking after everyone, when really she just wanted to be on her own. She didn't want the thanks of something well planned, she wanted the space of nothing to do. And here she was, in charge of her own day, and a bloody lovely one it was too. She could eat whatever she wanted for tea at whatever temperature without being asked to reheat something or wait for Timothy so he didn't eat alone, or rush to pack up a meal for his mother while hers got cold.

"You're like a daughter to me" his mother would say. And she meant it. She loved Maureen, and who wouldn't? Who wouldn't think that someone who was everything to everyone was wonderful. Quiet at the right times, busy when it mattered, putting everyone else's needs before your own, who wouldn't love that person?

But she wasn't Maureen's mother, she was Timothy's. Maureen's lovely mum was twenty years gone and everywhere all at once.

6- before and after.

Maureen's life was separated into several parts, like boxes lined up in a row. There was her childhood in one box, with Nanna, Grandad and Mum, looking back it was hard, but at the time she didn't have a clue it was anything other than lovely. The next part was breaking into adulthood, if a person ever really grows up, but it was full of adventures and discoveries, tears and fears, university first time round, and politics and then love and marriage, then the next box was becoming a mum and having young kids and being less Maureen more Mum. All of these boxes sat with noise and activities and shouting and frustrations and laughter

Then there were the after boxes. After her mum died and the kids left home and she was lost to circumstance. Of all the separate parts of her life mostly and mainly her thoughts fell into before. And then after. Before Mum died and after she was gone. And that was the mark of her. Maureen had a thought that you weren't really a grown up until you were the age of your parents, and because you were always younger than they seemed to be you never quite felt grown, except now she was older than Coral, and that meant something. She couldn't waste any time, couldn't feel sad and uncomfortable when her mum didn't get the chance to get old. Coral always said she would be an old lady with crazy hair, with a swear word on the tip of her tongue and people would roll their eyes at her latest escapades, but she never quite got there. Maureen felt that she should start to live for both of them.

Maureen filled the sink with hot, bubbly water and popped her flask and lunch tin into it to soak. She was starving and decided she would eat her carton of fresh soup for tea, even though it was absolutely not the weather for soup. She wanted to taste melted hot butter on her tongue when she dipped bread into the hot liquid. Her nanna would tut at shop bought shop, but back in the day when nanna was making the soup, the back garden was filled with growing vegetables and a few chickens, runner beans edging up the back wall with their pink flowers ready to spit out little green tongues, rows of peas clinging to homemade netting, their small fat parcels often not making it into the house, the shells tossed over the gate into the chicken run. Hanging baskets of strawberries and tomatoes edged along the side of the house, every space filled. The greenhouse housed tomatoes and cucumbers, Maureen would go in just to smell the leaves, to breathe in the spicy, mouth watering scent. Dotted around the garden, submerged into the soil were old chipped tea cups, handles long gone, filled with home brewed beer, a tasty tipple for drowning slugs, laying like fat sausages at the bottom of the cups. Broken egg shells scattered around the salad patch like tiny crazy paving, to ward off the tee-total slugs who crawled past the beer, uninterested.

Nanna would be out with her little vegetable knife slicing marrows off their stems or pulling up a few carrots for a stew. Sometimes they would be out collecting mushrooms or fishing the lake or river at dusk when prying eyes were settled in for the night and licences weren't demanded. There wasn't much food Grandad couldn't find and there wasn't much Nanna couldn't cook.

Maureen would love tottering behind either of them, helping, she thought, but she was probably more of a hindrance, although they never confirmed either. When neither of them could dig anymore and both Nanna and Grandad were long gone Coral was the maker of gardens, the stirrer of broth, the chief egg collector. Everything was still plentiful, but without the neatness of Grandad's hand, slap dash but delicious.

Maureen looked out of the window as she stood at the sink, the garden as she knew it was gone, but the foundation was there and she knew where things went, she could have it sorted in no time, slightly late in the season but ready for an abundant autumn. Parsnips and potatoes for Christmas. The old apple trees still stood proud, small red apples changing from their bitter summer flesh to autumn sweetness in the sunshine. Maureen felt a slight shiver of excitement at the thought, she could do this, it would be perfect. She couldn't wait to get started, she would head into Ambleside tomorrow and get to the garden centre to start making plans. Start small and move across the garden and all of its neglected wildness.

Her soup started to bubble, whispering to her about its convenience, disregarding her big plans. She took a couple of slices of bread and spread great smears of butter over the top ready to make teeth marks in. The butter would make up for the lack of cream in the soup. She remembered sitting at this very kitchen table as nanna swirled a few drops of cream into fresh leek and potato soup, a good pinch of white pepper floating on the top, next to the cream, ready to stir and disperse into the thick, hot liquid.

Nanna peeled the potatoes with a little wooden handled knife, kept in the front of a wooden drawer, quickly taking the outer peel off, like a thin muddy streamer. For a treat she would wash the skin and put a bit of melted butter and salt on it, and then if the oven was hot she would slide them in on a tray and then pour them into a bowl or a brown paper bag once they were crispy and cooked, topping them with a good shake of salt. They would melt in your mouth, glistening Maureen's chin with their greasy buttered coating. She would slide her finger into the corners of the bag when it was empty, to get the last of the salty grease on her fingers, cleaning them with her tongue. Maureen remembered complaining once when her friends had packets of crisps from the Co-op, not realising then that nanna's homemade crisps were amazing in comparison.

Maureen often sat on the back door step, Grandad sitting beside her, outside on a stool, as they shelled peas or broad beans together, ready to pour into the bubbling ham hock on the stove, filled out with lentils that would force them all to sit around the television later on, shamelessly farting with family familiarity which meant no one really cared, unless they were sat really close to Grandad. Then Maureen would pull her jumper up over her nose and nanna would declare him a dirty animal.

As Grandad got older it was Maureen's job to be in charge of the garden dibber, leaning over the carefully dug soil to plant the rows and rows of onions ready to grow fat and be laid out in the shed to form a skin and then be strangled into an old pair of tights, knotted on the top and bottom and never allowed to touch, hanging in the pantry like bulbous broken legs, always eight of them placed in the cellar like a fleshy spider getting gradually thinner and legless as winter turned to spring. When money was tight, although young Maureen was never aware of money problems, carrot, potato and onion soup bubbled on the stove for several days at a time. Bread would rise by the range, ready to be dipped and chewed.

Several times a month Grandad would return from somewhere or other with a brace of pheasants, a glut of venison, and a couple of big trout. Questions were never asked and he was treated like a hero, the hunter gatherer. Whatever was or wasn't in Nanna's purse, there was always bread and butter, cheese and sweet, home-made biscuits and an eternal supply of eggs. And more importantly they never ran out of tea. The chipped brown tea pot with it's stained inside and cracked glaze was always ready to brew them all a cup of tea, whatever the weather, kept warm by a navy tea cosy that had been washed and mangled many times, knitted by a long gone Great Nanna who Maureen never knew but who would certainly have something to say about Coral being a husbandless mother, she would be disgusted and ashamed and she would not have swallowed any bad thoughts down when she could vomit them on others. As sour as her thoughts and words may have been, she could knit a bloody good tea cosy that may have been indestructible. Nanna had three miscarriages and a stillborn baby boy before she was blessed with Coral, she said from the moment she found out Coral was expecting, that a baby was a blessing and would be loved however it came into the house, and Maureen was loved to the moon and back.

Maureen ate her soup with the back door open, looking out over the garden, the faintest of warm breezes tickling its way into the kitchen, bringing with it the smell of flowers and grass, with the background noise of a mower moaning in the vicinity. The garden looked smaller than she remembered, but it was overgrown with thick bushes that needed cutting back. The apple trees stood tall, reaching up away from the weeds, and the plum and damson trees were heaving with unripe fruit. Maureen thought of Nanna's jam pan resting on the top shelf of the pantry, covered in a thick layer of dust that she would soak off with hot, bubbly water. She was taken back to sitting her ten year old bottom on the back step as Grandad sat beside her on a rickety wooden stool, knife in hand de-stoning plums and throwing them into the jam pan. His big hands worked quickly and Maureen was slow and clumsy in comparison, not quite cleaning the stone with the deftness of Grandad. They would sit together often, in the process of peeling or chopping, stoning or prepping, before whatever they were doing was handed to nanna for the magic to happen. Chipped cups of hot, steaming tea sat at their feet and they both wiped their sticky hands on old towels to begin munching one of nanna's biscuits before supping the tea. Grandad would ask a seemingly innocent question and Maureen would launch into one of her quiet explanations or speeches.

"So tell me." He'd say. "How's this new girl at school getting on?"

The reality was that he probably knew the answer, he knew enough people to be aware of what was going on and why, but he was keen and attentive enough to his beloved granddaughter that he wanted to hear things from her.

"She's a snob." Maureen said. "Said I couldn't go to her house because her mum said. She said Jesus wouldn't be happy with me."

Grandad shook his head. "Now tell me." He said "Who in their right mind wouldn't be happy with you?"

He sipped his tea and looked at Maureen thoughtfully as she smiled, thinking to herself that this really meant that Daisy and her family couldn't be in their right minds. She knew some people didn't want her around because she didn't have a dad, like somehow she was bad luck, or just bad, but she also knew she couldn't do much about that. Charlie didn't have a dad because he had died, but that was ok, because he had been there once. Mary had a dad who was always in the pub and shouted a lot, cursing people who looked at him as he swayed up the street, bumping into things, with his chin and jacket wet with dribble. Maureen knew that was frowned upon but not as bad as having no dad at all. But she wasn't quite sure why. And anyway, how could you miss something you never had? She was probably too young to realise but it was the weight of judgement that was heavy on her shoulders, too heavy for a ten year old.

Grandad looked down to watch Maureen for a moment, her tongue poking slightly out of the corner of her mouth as she skimmed round the centre of the plum. She frowned as she concentrated, trying to get it just right and wondering why people did what they did at the same time.

"Maureen, love." Grandad said gently.

Maureen looked up at Grandad's sun kissed, lined face, his eyes shaded under the brim of his flat cap that he wore all year round, whatever the weather. He smiled and put his knife down.

"Some people will like you and some people won't." He said, wiping his hands on the old tea towel. "Mostly it won't be anything you've done deliberately, and you don't have to dance for folks to change their minds if they don't want to be your friend. All you can do is be kind, but don't put up with other people's nonsense or judgement. You just keep being you because you're lovely. And if Mary's mum doesn't want you round her house it's her loss. And I'm sure whoever this Jesus is who she's going on about wouldn't care if you had five dads or no dads." He smiled. "People like to point out other people's faults so no one will look at their own Maureen. Remember that and be kind because you're smashing, just as you are."

And with that he picked up his tea and took a big gulp, swallowing hard. He couldn't bear that someone had decided that his Maureen wasn't good enough for their child or their house. His good, clever girl who some folk decided had a stain on her because of nothing to do with anything she did herself. He wasn't going to tell Coral about it all, let her get fire in her belly and tell people what was what. He just had to make Maureen know how great she was, so it didn't matter what the idiots thought, because he knew they were fools. He knew his girl was special and he wanted her to see it for herself.

Maureen sat at the kitchen table with her cup of tea, older now than Grandad was when they sat de-stoning the plums. They sat there so many times, chatting and working, drinking tea and crunching biscuits. She knew he was always level, no questioning her, no marching round to someone's house to tell them what was what, just quiet, and ready with some gentle words, for her to digest and remember. Sometimes she would cry into his shirt as he held her tight and told her that it really would be ok, just maybe not today. And he was always right, always fair and always kind.

Maureen's eyes grew warm, wet and itchy as she thought about her lovely Grandad, an unexpected tear made a dash from the corner and rolled down her cheek. She would make that garden look amazing, she would take it back to the soil and let it become what it was. Grandad tended the garden out of necessity, so they had plentiful food right outside the door, and Maureen would tend it for pleasure and for Grandad. She was done with dancing to please others but she would have danced forever for another door step natter with Grandad.

Maureen finished her soup and reminiscing at about the same time. She put her dishes into the sink and decided that she had done enough washing up for the day. The evening midges were keen to get into the kitchen, as the night turned slightly dusky outside and the kitchen light held optimistic promise for the gathering flies. Maureen did not want uninvited guests and clicked the back door shut, turning the lock. It was still light but the brightness of the day had gone. It was early enough for some people to be heading out, but late enough for others to be thinking about bed and Maureen found herself to be one of the others. She felt like her cheeks were glowing from the sun and her limbs ached from walking and swimming, although she thought swimming might be a stretch, it was more breathless bobbing about. Her tiredness was a delight, tired in every inch of her body from activity, muscle tired and sun tired, rather than exhausted by life or the sadness that she had been feeling of late. It was a good feeling. She closed the downstairs windows while the kettle boiled, she was tired but that was no excuse not to have a cup of tea in bed to celebrate the coming sleep. She felt quite joyful at the thought of getting into bed with a steaming brew, settling down in the cool sheets.

The windows were open upstairs and she opened the bedroom curtains that had been closed to the hot sun. A barely there breeze from the cooler, late evening air brushed her face as she had a final look out onto the fading day. This was enough, it was more than enough, she had looked out of this window her whole life and it was where she should end the day every day, despite what was coming. She knew it was only day two and there were battles to come, she wasn't a fool to think it was this easy to walk away.

7-back then.

The last time Maureen had been arrested was the first time she had met Timothy. It wasn't so much that she stopped protesting, she just stopped shouting and tying herself to railings. She had travelled with her usual crew and held hands around the perimeter of Greenham Common in a mark of solidarity and passion with what turned out to be thirty thousand women. She stood beside Coral, mother and daughter together with thousands of mothers and daughters, singing and being and saying 'no we won't tolerate this.' When she was arrested she had knocked off a policeman's helmet as he reached to grab her mum, Maureen had pushed as hard as she could to protect her protector, and she ended up being dragged away across the rough ground, putting holes in her trousers and scraping her knees, a policeman scooping her up under each arm, until she was pushed into the back of a black van and transported to the police station to wait for the duty solicitor who she barely looked at.

Her mum would be singing and drinking tea with the other women, boiling water on someone's fire, offering someone her spare tin mug, the smell of smoke on her clothes and the bitter taste of UHT milk spoiling her tea slightly.

Maureen would drink a weak cup of tea in the cells, pale and flavourless, on the wrong side of warm. She declined anything else. She had been here before, only a couple of times and after the first nerve wracking arrest and quick release there wasn't a lot to be that bothered about. There wasn't enough room for all of the women arrested and they wanted them gone quickly and easily. Maureen was polite, spoke well to the officers and they didn't want to keep her for any longer than necessary. She signed her papers and thanked the solicitor, and then she was out and off, ravenous and thirsty, ready to pay for something to eat from the nearest place she could find. Then as she was feeling free, the young, nervous man in the brown suit was sliding a pound note her way with a look of hope on his face.

"I'll get this." He said, looking at her a little too long.

She was fairly sure he had been running and that this was not part of the legal service. Her previous rotund solicitor had barely carried his own weight up the corridor as she followed him out of the interview room, he sweated from being alive, there was no chasing and money offerings from him. This was extras. She weighed this young solicitor up for the briefest of moments, watching a bead of sweat roll down the side of his face and tuck itself somewhere into his collar. She smiled and thanked him for the offer.

"Are you getting yourself anything?" She asked as he hovered beside her.

"Oh yes, I'll have the same please." He smiled at the women in the window, not exactly sure what he was getting, but it saved reading the blackboard or asking for the menu, which was covered in blobs of food and tea rings from previous diners. He wasn't convinced that there would be a vast choice aside from what could be fried or boiled and although she had just come out of a police station after going in the wrong way, she didn't look like someone who would eat awful things. She looked like the most beautiful person he had ever seen, and he wasn't very good at hiding that. He kept glancing sideways at her as if she might vanish at any moment, or run off, he wasn't sure he had the energy for chasing her again.

They got their food and tea and walked across the road to a small park with benches. They didn't speak as they walked, he just sort of scurried beside her, assuming they would dine together. He didn't normally eat out of paper in parks, he wasn't sure his mother would approve, and certainly not the partners of the law firm who had employed him because they knew who his mother was. But he wanted to sit in the park and eat from paper if he got to sit next to this woman for a little while longer.

"Do you normally buy egg butties for people you've just represented?" She asked, taking a sip from her plastic cup. She smiled at him, sensing his nervousness.

"This is the first time." He replied. "And the first time I've eaten on a park bench." He added.

"Hell's bells." She laughed slightly. "Where have you been hiding to miss out on eating on benches?" She looked him up and down. "I suspect you're used to the finer things though. There's not a lot of fine dining to be had with cold metal pressed against your backside."

He laughed out loud. "Can I take you somewhere to eat with more comfy seats then?" He asked, surprising himself with his own bravery.

She looked down at her muddy shoes, the bottom of her trousers were brown from where the wet mud had seeped up the denim like litmus paper from a science experiment. She wanted to get back home, have a bath, sleep for days, and feel warm. She knew her mum wouldn't be expecting her back, she was only staying for a few days this time and then she was going home again, Mum could be there for weeks and weeks still, as long as it took, she said. Maureen had gone and listened and shouted and thrived, her mind open to the talk and songs, but she wanted to get on the train and get back to her little flat in Oxford for now, light the gas fire and climb into bed.

"I don't think I'm dressed for comfy chairs and fine things." She said, "I'm ready to go back home and sleep."

"Where's home?" He asked.

"Oxford." She replied, pointing in the direction she assumed was north.

"That's never an Oxford accent." He coughed, screwing up his paper bag into a ball, his belly full of salty egg sandwich.

"Nope, that's true." She smiled. "Home will always be Ambleside really, Oxford is where I live at the moment. Where I need to get back to right now before I end up asleep on this bench. I just need to remember the way to the train station."

"I'll drive you." He said, slightly too loudly, not wanting her to go. Then he added, "I've to go to Oxford anyway, so it's no trouble at all."

She looked him up and down, frowning. His shirt collar stark and starched against his brown suit, smart but for a small drop of egg yolk dribbled down the front, by the top pocket. "You're not a serial killer or a pervert are you?" She asked

"Good lord." He shouted, his eyes wide. "Absolutely not." He couldn't tell if it was a genuine question or if she was joking.

"Well then yes please." She said, thinking of the train fare she'd save.

"Smashing." He said. "Excellent indeed." He smiled, thinking of spending more time in her company.

He walked towards his car which was parked behind the police station, she walked beside him, hands in her pockets, the bottom of her jeans scraping against the pavement. She was so tired, these four days staying with her mum in her tent had made her bones tired. She decided it was definitely her mum's thing and she was proud of her for it, she was proud for the cause but she needed sleep and warmth and clean clothes.

He glanced to his right quickly, watching her yawn again. He hoped his sister wouldn't be as keen to get into a car with someone she didn't know, he would call her and speak to her about that later. He was fairly sure his sister wouldn't be arrested or walk about covered in mud, but he'd call anyway. All the Greenham women he'd had to go to the police station for he was happy to never see again, he was almost a bit appalled at their gall. He would never have let them know he had a car, let alone get in it, but here she was. Her hair swished as she walked and when she laughed before, she tossed her head back like she wasn't bothered at all what he thought of her. She wasn't trying to impress him, he was certain of that. And yet here he was, pretending he had to drive to Oxford at the end of the day, like this was normal and he was just taking her out of kindness rather than taking her because he was amazed by her. Because he was, and he wasn't sure why. It also concerned him that she appeared interested in the lift and not him, and he considered himself to be interesting. He could hold his own, had a good job, nice car, a bit of money and was considered good looking by people other than his mother. Eligible they said, whoever they were. At parties or gatherings people were always introducing him to their single friends, 'this is Timothy, he's a solicitor, you know' and there they would be, girls, young women in expensive dresses, satin heels, styled hair, giggling at his jokes, drinking the wine he bought, talking closely to him and resting their hand on his arm for longer than an acquaintance might. Impressing him, impressed by him. And here she was with muddy shoes, dirty jeans with tears at the knees, garnished with obvious stains of dark dried blood, her hair, curly, dark and untamed.

And not resting her hands on him, or asking him questions or wiping her mouth on a serviette between bites of her sandwich. She had eaten like a woman who was hungry and enjoying her food, and she drank her tea like a woman who was thirsty. There was nothing else. She would have behaved no differently if he had never chased her, she would have eaten and caught the train and he would have thought of her often and wondered if he should have run around the corner. And she would never have given him a second thought, of that he was certain.

The car was parked on a back road close to the police station, but not close enough that he might be seen doing something that was probably not the done thing. It was spotless, shiny, looking like new from the outside and the inside. She sat in the passenger seat and worried for a moment that she might get things dirty, she was wearing clothes that did not belong in a car like this. Why on earth would he invite her into such a clean place when she looked like she had been mud wrestling. She didn't dare sit back into the seat, she was more perched on the edge as if trying to sit down with the minimum of touching.

"Oh, really don't worry about the car." He said, watching her perch. "Just sit back, I knew how muddy you were before I offered you a lift." He chuckled, like he was really not bothered that she would smear something on somewhere.

She nestled back into the seat and smiled at him. "Thanks," she said. "I am aware I look an absolute state, you know. I don't normally go about so muddy, but it's a dirty business saving the world."

"I've had worse in my car." He said, smiling. But he hadn't. He didn't really care either. Not much. Not so he'd say. Not now anyway, he'd throw that back at her at some point in the distant future when the situation required it. When he'd made the story in his head into him being a rescuer.

She gave him her address, Upper Fisher Road, and gave him rough directions, then she laid her head against the seat and watched out of the window, her eyes closing with the motion of the car and because she had barely slept in four days. She was out for the count as he drove the forty five minutes to Oxford. He glanced at her when he could and wondered what Mother would think. And he actually didn't care. He was just pleased she was here in his car, comfortable enough to sleep. He wondered what was wrong with him? This was not normal Timothy behaviour, he was a measured man, weighing up options before he did anything, and a planner, not impulsive in the slightest, not someone to drive an unnecessary journey. He felt slightly exhilarated, to throw caution to the wind, and be spontaneous. Maybe this was him? He certainly liked the feeling, except perhaps the thought of having to sponge down the seat in case Mother noticed any mess. He wouldn't tell her about the park bench meal either.

They arrived in Oxford, Maureen still fast asleep and Timothy still exhilarated at his sudden rebelliousness. He pulled up outside a corner shop and wondered what the etiquette was for waking up a virtual stranger that was fast asleep in your car. In the end he decided that the shoulder shake was the least offensive after saying her name a few times failed to stir her. Maureen woke with a sudden gasp, she had been in a deep sleep and her neck ached. It took her a couple of seconds to join all the dots and remember where she was. "Oh hell, I'm sorry, I am absolutely knackered. Not the best company, you were probably expecting a bit of a natter."

"You're fine, totally did not snore or dribble." He chuckled at his own joke. "Am I anywhere near your house?"

She gave him the final directions and he pulled up outside the front door. "I'd offer you a cup of tea but I've no milk or anything, it'll be rancid now." She said, thanking him for the ride. "And I really want to have a bath and get changed."

He paused for a minute wondering how he could just spend a bit more time with her. "How about I go and sort my meeting out and then pop back with some milk, and you can make me a cup of tea and I'll be on my way?" he hoped he sounded like he was genuinely travelling for business.

"Sounds good." She said, opening the car door and fiddling in her pocket for her house keys. She opened her purse and thrust a pound note towards him for the milk.

"I'll get it." He said.

"No." She put the money on the car seat . "You got the last tea, and you've driven me all the way up here. Number seven, just ring the bell." And with that she closed the door with a bang, thinking that she would just like to have a bath and get into bed, but it would save her popping to the shop for milk herself, and she couldn't not have a brew. Plus he seemed reasonable, if a little keen.

It was less than a week since she'd been home but their house had gathered its unfamiliar scent without her presence. Like when she first looked round and it smelt of new carpet and bleach, without the cheap aftershave of the letting agent punching it's way up her nose this time, though. There were a couple of letters on the mat, one a hand written envelope with nanna's left leaning swirly writing singing her address on the front. She would read that when her bath was done.

She threw her clothes in the linen basket, they were so crusty they kept the shape of a human about them even when they were person free. She was tempted to just throw the jeans away, to save the hassle of the amount of washing that would be required to make them respectable again, but they were her favourite pair so she'd try for the clean.

She turned on the power shower so that it was uncomfortably hot and she let it spray into the bath. Her eyes burned with tiredness, and. with the constant stream of smoke she had endured from the camp campfire, for warmth and tea making. She had volunteered to look after the making of the teas so she could make it exactly to her liking. She boiled water and poured brews for what seemed like hours, as the women sang and beat drums. Oh for the quietness of her little flat.

She climbed into the bath, feeling like she was eighty rather than twenty five. Her cut knees stung with the warmth of the water and she felt like a child again, taking the first bath after falling over, saddened by the sting. She washed herself slowly, devoid of energy, drained by her adventure, wondering how her forty something Mum managed to stay there week after week. She said she had finally found her tribe of like minded women and she seemed genuinely happy and wanted to stay while there was work to be done. While there were fences and weapons she would stay, she said. She knew her mum felt a sense of belonging that she had missed out on from her peers at home.

She could have lingered in the bath for a while, but she didn't want him returning while she was half dressed or still in there. She dried herself and put on an old cotton dress that she could comfortably sleep in, which she hoped she would be doing fairly soon. She hungered for chips, but a tin of soup and bread heated in the oven would do. She opened the windows of the flat once she was out of the bath, towel drying her wet hair and waiting for the doorbell to ring. She was excited for the milk. He seemed nice enough but she wasn't sure why there was a 'but' there, but it was there all the same. She put the kettle on the stove, making sure it was full of water, hoping that he would bring enough milk until she got to the shops in the morning.

The sound of the doorbell made her jump. It was too loud, but she never heard anyone knock when she took the batteries out so she ended up being startled every time she had a visitor or a parcel, which wasn't that often but often enough to annoy. She walked down the dark corridor, past the kitchen and bedroom, opening the door to him. He had taken his tie and suit jacket off, opened his top button and looked less like he might be in a courtroom and more like he might be heading for a pint. He smiled nervously but she knew it was genuine and she let him in, leading him up to the kitchen. She lit the stove with a long match to get the kettle to sing again as he rested his carrier bag on the little square table, pulling out two bottles of milk and two wrapped up portions of fish and chips.

"I hope you don't mind?" He asked. "I had to walk past a fish and chip shop and the smell was amazing. I felt starving so I thought I'd get myself some, but it would have been rude to just buy one."

"Oh my god you're a lifesaver." She smiled, pouring hot water into the teapot. "I was just thinking how hungry I was and it was going to be a tin of soup for tea!"

Maureen stirred the tea pot and leaned over to the draining board to pass him two plates. He opened the newspaper and as she poured the tea he sat down on the stool, helped himself to a knife and fork and began to munch his chips, his lips looking greasy as he chewed. Maureen took the towel off her head and threw it by her twin tub. He watched her flick her hair back over her shoulders, picking at her food with her fingers as she poured more tea. She had felt tired to her bones, yearning for her bed, but suddenly she was slightly excited to have company and something warm in her stomach. She watched him as he ate, he wasn't self conscious, just looking round weighing up her flat. His five o'clock shadow gave him a different appearance to the fresh faced suited youth of this morning. His hair was no longer groomed and the open collar of his shirt made him look less like a maths teacher and more like someone who ate fish and chips off paper, albeit without using his fingers. He sliced at the fish with cutlery as she happily tore at it with her fingers, her hands becoming shiny with grease making her cup of tea slip slightly in her fingers.

"Do you want a gin?" she asked

"Best not." He said, "I've got to drive home in a bit."

"Just a small one?." She smiled, pulling out two glasses from the cupboard and sliding one over to him, leaving fingerprints of chip grease around the bottom of the glass.

They finished their food and cups of tea and started sipping at the gin and lemonade. By the time they were drinking their third large glass they were sitting side by side on their sofa, the window wide open beside them, blowing in cool evening air, making the curtain dance and whisper as they tapped against the wall. The gin felt warm in her stomach and she talked easily, aware that he was looking at her too often for too long. He looked warm, his cheeks flushed pink with the temperature and drink. He watched her closely as she talked, expressing herself with her tales, moving her arms and hands as she spoke, flicking her head back and laughing every now and then, her curls bouncing as her head moved. He didn't want to leave or stop listening to her for a moment. She got up and poured them another large drink, each one getting bigger than the last. She handed him his drink again and this time sat closer to him, so their knees touched and arms knocked against each other as she told her elaborate tails of who she was and where she had been. He just wanted to keep listening, to drink it all in, being here with her. He felt like he was alive and daring and he knew he shouldn't really be here, given how they had met, but he was transfixed. Possibly a mixture of tiredness and gin, but here he was, watching her talk and wanting more.

She drained her glass and he felt his stomach heavy, thinking that the evening was coming to an end and he would soon be heading for the door. He tackled the maze that was his head trying to think of his own tales to tell her, but he wasn't able to match her story telling, his tales normally thought about and digested. He was used to people listening to him, he could command a room, but she wasn't waiting for him to speak, she had her own things to say.

Just as he was wondering whether his lacking was bringing the evening to a close she put her glass down on the coffee table and slid herself over him, straddling his lap and leaning in to kiss him. And there he was, holding on tight to this woman who didn't wait for him, who wasn't sat smiling so she seemed demure, or laughing when he laughed, she was just taking him because she wanted him right at that moment. She was the wrong side of a bottle of gin and he was the right side of what she needed and she didn't wait to be asked.

She undid the buttons on his shirt and touched his warm skin gently as he gasped and caught short breaths, and before he could think of the next thing, she pulled her dress over her head so she was sat across him in only her knickers, and she didn't care what anyone thought, not even him.

8- falling

They lay on the bed together but with a distance between them. The sex was done with a gentleness of a man who possibly normally took the lead but was keen to impress. She moved away from him afterwards, facing him, covered by a brushed cotton sheet and an eiderdown that had seen generations before her, relations who would tut at her evening if they were here, question her choices, wonder at her actions and pass her a good amount of judgement. But they weren't here. They had left genes, some ornaments and their eiderdown and they only people that mattered to her, nanna, Grandad and mam just wanted her to be happy, drink a bit less and visit them more.

Probably not pick up men in brown suits who gained favour with fish and chips, but they didn't need to know who was lying under great aunt Mary's eiderdown.

Finally after fighting the heavy weight of sleep for most of the evening Maureen's eyes flickered shut and her breathing became heavier, slower, her body still with fatigue. Her hair was splayed across the pillow, some stray outer strands moving slightly with the breeze from the window, the street light outside giving the room an orange glow. Timothy watched her breathing become slower and her mouth drop open slightly. Lying on his side, surprised by his evening. Surprised by her, her boldness, her voice, her confidence, her body. He was called to the police station for legal services and he was here lying beside her. He didn't know the etiquette, was he meant to leave? He wanted to stay so badly, lying beside her feeling impressed and unimpressive. Just feeling. Not doing what he thought someone wanted, or saying what he thought she wanted to hear, not telling a story to wow or dropping something splendid into the conversation, he just followed her lead and heard her. He thought she wouldn't be particularly bothered about etiquette anyway. You didn't straddle the solicitor that got you bound over to keep the peace the afternoon you met him and then worry about what fork to use.

He just wanted to lie here, and be in her room and presence, and then worry about how to manage the morning when he woke up. Sleep would find him eventually, once the amazement had subsided. It would take him as he thought about her smell and her skin, as he watched her face, utterly relaxed, in the blurry orange light of the lamp post outside. Sleep would take him as he lay in her sheets and hoped he would be able to lie here again. It would take him all through the night to the awkwardness of the morning where gin was a distant memory and he would stumble over his words.

He was used to being introduced to women at events or gatherings where they would be trying to gently impress him. People were always trying to match him with someone or other sense it would be a slow conversation, listening to him talk, laughing at his jokes, talking around the perimeter of anything that really mattered to a person, then if it went anywhere it would be the rule of slowly revealing parts of yourself that were less desirable, anxieties, failures, worries, drip feeding them once the hook was set. Except the hook was never set as he was never invested or interested, but he did so love the attention. And then here she was, not caring whether he was impressed or pleased, not waiting for him to fill silences or gently chuckling at his jokes. If she found something funny she would laugh loudly, tossing her head back. She wasn't waiting for him to fill silences or anything, and he didn't even realise he had been waiting for her for so long. She slept soundly and gently and the anxieties were all his.

When sleep eventually found him and allowed all thoughts to cease, he snored gently, dreaming things he would never recall. At 6: 30 he woke, his mouth dry and his head beating to the sound of gin. She was still asleep, lying with her back to him but close, her curls springing across the pillow. He needed water and coffee. He slid himself out of bed, locating his tossed aside underpants and pulling his shirt on. He felt like an intruder as he found the bathroom and after using it made his way to the kitchen to drink the tap dry. He put the kettle on but his search for coffee came to nothing so he decided to make do with tea, making two cups and taking them back to the bedroom, fairly certain that she took a tiny tip of sugar to his heaped spoon. She was stirring as he put the tea on her bedside table and she opened one eye to look at him.

"Hell, tea in bed, you can come again." She whispered as she edged herself up the pillow, covering herself with the sheet. "Are you getting back in?" she asked as she tapped the pillow beside her.

They sat up in bed together holding their tea. "Well, I bet that's not your usual call to a criminal." She chucked, breaking his attempts to try and think of things to say.

"Oh yes, it's a weekly event." He laughed, thinking of all of the people he had dealt with and how he would never want to be drinking tea with them anywhere, let alone in bed. "I don't normally do this." He added, as if she needed telling.

She laughed out loud at his awkwardness, spilling drops of tea on the sheets, trying to slurp hot tea to make it less likely to spill. He laughed at her laughter and they chuckled together, sitting up in bed as the sun shot its light through the curtains. He didn't know the etiquette of being at someone else's house who wasn't impressed by the pre-story of him. 'Come and meet Timothy Smith, he's a solicitor you know, studied law at Cambridge, old money'. He was an eligible bachelor, being introduced to the daughter of someone who knew his mother or the granddaughter of someone in the city. And now he was lying in bed drinking tea with a woman who didn't give a shit whether he had anything.

She liked his company. He was slightly pompous in an innocent way, because he'd possibly always taken the lead. She didn't need to be anything she wasn't ever, and more so here. Fellow students on campus were sometimes impressed by themselves and she was always slightly surprised she was here. She earned every bit of it. She had a small but trusty group of friends and really enjoyed her own company too, enjoying hours lying on the bed as the sun poured through the window, reading a book with a brew, how could that not be a delight? It reminded her of home. As much as she enjoyed being in Oxford it was never home. Home was the smell of baking and the waft of sweet peas from the garden, the crinkly smile of Grandad who would catch his breath when he saw her, so pleased to be chatting to her. She suddenly remembered nanna's letter.

She jumped out of bed and scurried to the toilet, making way for another cup of tea. She quickly brushed her teeth on the toilet, as it was offending her, let alone him. "I'll make a brew." She shouted from the bathroom.

She got back into bed, handing him his cup of tea, her letter in her mouth and a packet of unopened digestive biscuits under her arm. She climbed back into bed and plopped the biscuits in the valley between them.

"Help yourself to biscuits." She said, "I forgot I got a letter from my nanna, I got a little distracted." She glanced sideways at him and winked before tearing open the envelope, watching a five pound note float gently onto the eiderdown. She read it out loud

"Hello lovely girl. Just a quick note to see how you are doing? I think you said that you might pop up over the bank holiday weekend and we are home the whole of it. Don't worry if you're tied up at the university, we know how busy you are.

Grandad sends his love, he said there's a massive glut of veg and eggs and if you did come up he'd send you back with bags of the stuff. The freezer is full and the house smells of vinegar with all the pickling I have been doing.

We got a letter from your mum. She's still at that bloody camp saving the world, but she seems happy enough. She said you were going to see her so I hope you've had a nice time and enjoyed the camping if you've been. It's rained something terrible up here so I hope your didn't get too wet

You will be starting your teaching soon. You'll be brilliant. We always said you were a genius and you are. Grandad has been telling everyone you're going to be teaching at the university and he slips it into the conversation wherever he can. He's as proud as punch.

Get yourself something nice with the money and if we see you it'll be brilliant.

Loads and loads of love

Nanna and Grandad."

Maureen smiled and kissed the letter, putting the money on the side table by the bed. She knew the money was really towards train fare so she could go and see them if she wanted. She looked at her clock. It was 8: 30 already. She knew there was a train at 10 and she could get some things together quickly.

"You know, I'm going to catch the train." She said out loud. She thought of the few days off she still had left and knew she should travel home and see them. "Unless you've got a meeting in Ambleside you need to get to?"

His face dropped and he began to cough. "You knew I just wanted to drive you?" he eventually said.

"Of course I did, daft lad." She laughed, and he caught her laughter again, laughing as the warm glow of embarrassment hit his cheeks. She really didn't care so he really shouldn't be bothered.

"You're going to go and see your grandparents then?" he asked, smiling. He had never had the urge to go and visit his when they were alive, any time he went was for a long pre-arranged formality. A dinner or a party, or some dull family event. Not just a visit because you wanted to.

"Do you want to come?" she asked, like it was something normal to do, to travel to the grandparents of the person you got off a charge and then slept with. "On the train, you don't have to drive or anything."

"Yes." He said quickly. "Yes absolutely, and I'll drive." He sounded keen, too keen, but he was past trying to pretend he was nonchalant. "But I've no clothes or toiletries."

"We could nip to Burtons and boots in town?" she suggested, like it was a normal thing to do.

They took it in turns to shower, making it to the shops for quarter to ten. He bought two t-shirts, a pair or jeans, his first ever pair, underwear, soap and a toothbrush. She said he could share her toothpaste and there was a whole under stairs cupboard full of old jumpers and waterproofs at her grandparents if the weather was bad. Which it very well could be in late August in Ambleside. She gave him the fiver and insisted he take it for petrol.

By 1030 am they were speeding up the A34 listening to the radio whisper in the background as they chatted. He had nipped into a phone box in town and quickly called his mother, telling her he wouldn't be going for his usual Sunday dinner as he was popping up north for a couple of nights with a friend. His mother had asked as many questions as she could fit into the very short phone call and he kept things very brief. Yes it was a woman, no it was not serious, no they would not come and see her before they left, no he was not home. Thankfully the pips went quickly and he was able to shout that his money was running out and he would have to go, leaving a hundred unanswered questions and a rather frustrated Mrs Smith.

Maureen had made a flask and grabbed some crisps and biscuits from her flat. She felt so excited that she was heading north, and pleased to have company. She hadn't told them she was bringing anyone but she hoped it would be fine. She brought friends all of the time, just not male friends she'd known for twenty four hours.

"Right." She said as they joined the M40. "I'm just going to say that you're my boyfriend and we've been going out for a couple of months. Is that ok? Just to save too many assumptions"

"Yep." He nodded, glancing at her and then back to the road. He was more than happy that she was calling him that.

"So now we need to have a massive information sharing so that it looks like we've known each other for a while. I'll go first, but also just so you know I don't normally lie to my grandparents. Or anyone. But I can't go up saying I met you yesterday."

He nodded at her.

"Right then, I was born in Ambleside, I'm twenty five, my mum got pregnant and I've never met my dad." She looked at him to see if there was any reaction. He didn't move or change expressions. It really didn't matter these days, she'd had all of the comments when she was younger.

"Me and Mum always lived with my nanna and Grandad, Mum went to teacher training college in Ambleside but we just stayed put with them, I didn't move out until I went to university. I read history and then did a masters in modern history, so I will be doing a bit of teaching and research in September."

"Nanna is amazing, really lovely and forward thinking, but will put you in their spare room I should think. She's an amazing cook and baker. Grandad grows veg, reads loads, thinks a lot and is calm. And kind. He thinks before he speaks, not so much Mum and Nanna," She paused. "Right your turn."

He took a deep breath, glanced at her for a moment and then stared straight ahead at the road. "My family live in Winchester. There's my mother, she has lived on her own since my father died about six years ago, well except for the housekeeper. He was a barrister and was keen for me to go into the family business. My granddad was in law and a judge before he retired. My older sister is a GP, married to a surgeon called Graham who you don't ever want to be trapped in a conversation with. I'm twenty seven and it's mentioned in hushed whispers that I've not settled down yet. My mother used to ask if I was one of those homosexuals she keeps reading about." He laughed out loud and Maureen joined him. "Subtle as a brick my mother." He said.

"I tell you what Timothy, when we've been to see my grandparents I'll repay the favour and come and meet your mother so she knows you like women. Whether she'll be happy to meet me is another matter."

He smiled. "Deal." He said.

"Have you not taken a girl home before then?" she asked

"Well, that's the thing." He said. "Yes and no. I'm constantly being set up at parties with people who they think I should consider. They are at my house invited, just not necessarily by me. Well at my family home. Not my own house."

"Where is your own house?"

"Winchester too. I've never gone far away except to university. It was expected I would go to Cambridge. Like everyone else in the family.

"And are you happy?" she asked.

"That's an unusual question." He said quite abruptly, as if it was not something he'd ever considered. "I'm happy to be driving with you right now. But happiness isn't something you think about really is it?"

"Sure it is." She replied. "It's everyday things, being with someone you love, buying a new book, going somewhere new, a really good cake or a smashing cup of tea. It's everywhere. And if you can't feel it you need to change what you are doing. You need the warm glow in your stomach."

He thought about what she said. He had a warm glow in his stomach being here with her, but he never said that out loud. He felt butterflies at the thought of going somewhere in her company. His mother would call it lust. Tell him to snap out of it. Want to know who this girl was and where she was from. Not the town or area, she was more interested in family blood. What the family meant. He had never ever felt more pleased to be in someone else's company and he had no intention of snapping out of anything. Even just hearing her talk about happiness made sense to him. No one in his family had asked him if he was happy doing something. He was just expected to do what was expected of him. And he was often fed up with it.

If he hadn't taken that call because someone was sick he'd have been having an expected Saturday doing neutral Saturday plans, and he would have missed her warm glow and her gentleness that was engulfing him. He had never once joined the M42 thinking such philosophical thoughts, or looking forward to driving on the motorway. She was pouring tea from her flask into the white plastic cup, squeezing the cup between her knees, trying not to spill, before screwing the stopper lid back in and putting the flask by her feet. She gently blew into the cup and took some tiny sips, the tea still steaming hot. She reached into her bag and took out the digestives, dunking and sipping as they wound their way around Spaghetti Junction. After she'd drunk her cup she repeated the knee squeezing pour and began blowing again on the hot tea.

"Here you go." She said, handing him the cup, pointing the handle towards his left hand so he could hold it as he drove. He took the cup and began slowly drinking, sharing the tea like it was the most natural thing in the world, like they had been driving together for years. She snapped a biscuit, dunked it in his tea and popped it in his mouth.

"This tea is delicious." He said.

"See, happiness in a flask." She smiled. "You can't beat a brilliant cup of tea."

"I think you might be right!" He chuckled.

They spent the journey learning about each other. They took this same journey alone and together countless times over the next forty years, but this one was his favourite. It was full of hope and laughter, learning about who she was and also the sickly sweet feeling of too many digestive biscuits. Three was the sweet spot, five too many.

By the time they knocked on the old green wooden door of the terraced cottage they knew each other quite well. The nerves of something new were taken over by the excitement of an adventure. She was sure he wasn't dodgy and dare she say, he was decent, and he was sure that she was magnificent and he felt the pain of joy in his chest that he had never experienced before. It almost hurt to swallow, he felt that excited.

She had a key but she wanted to surprise her nanna and Grandad with her being there, and they would be hugely surprised that she had brought someone home to meet them. Her and nanna giggled at each other in the doorway and squeezed each other into a hug that seemed to last forever. Maureen introduced Timothy to nanna before they even got through the door and nanna grabbed him and held him tight, hugging him close. She could see the red cheeked glow from Maureen and she assumed this young man had something to do with it.

Grandad was in the garden as usual, he was sitting at the bench stringing up onions that had been laying in the greenhouse to dry, forming their papery skins that would protect them as autumn drew on. He wiped his hands on an old rag and lifted Maureen into a hug, her slight frame not an issue for his advancing age and strong arms.

"How many onions?" She asked, she always asked.

"197 this time." He said, still proud of his stash after years of growing.

Grandad shook Timothy's hand "Good to meet you, young man." Grandad smiled, weighing up the visitor.

"You too, sir." Timothy said formally.

"Hells bells Timothy." Nanna laughed. "He's never had a sword on his shoulder, call him Grandad. And call me nanna, every bugger else does."

And the kettle was filled and boiling as bags were taken out of the car and lugged up the uneven staircase. Grandad put Timothy's bag into the spare box room, opening the window to get rid of the slightly warm, musty smell that clung to the rarely used room. He had never seen a visitor travelling with just a Burton carrier bag before and assumed it must be a last minute decision to come together. He popped Maureen's grip bag onto her bed, delighted that she had come and slightly disappointed that they would have to share her at the same time. He tutted at himself, the lad had driven his beloved girl all the way from Oxford so he should just be pleased that he'd done that. She'd never brought a lad to meet them before. Not since school.

Nanna was busy in the kitchen, buzzing about like a bee on fresh flowers, excited to have the two of them there. The tea was brewing in the pot and she was buttering bread for cheese and tomato sandwiches. Grandad had so many tomatoes they were added to anything and everything, but perfect for a buttie. The cake tin was already on the table and Maureen was putting the good cups and saucers out, she had the look from nanna to indicate that this visitor was to have the good stuff, Grandad knew that look well. Timothy was sitting at the table looking slightly bewildered at the buzzing going on around him. He kept glancing at Maureen when he didn't think she was looking and then smiling to himself. Grandad could see it all, he could see that the boy was totally smitten. Quite right too, he always said it, who could not like Maureen. She was as beautiful as she was clever and her heart was full of kindness, more importantly her belly was ablaze with fire and that meant she would put up with no nonsense and play no games. What you saw was what you got and what you got was stunning.

Maureen was filling her flask full of hot soapy water to soak and nanna was busy pouring out the tea and telling tales of familiar names who had been up to goodness knows what in the town. A new shop had opened and someone had died, Joyce down the road had had her baby boy and the postmaster had retired. Nanna kept secrets and didn't really gossip on account of the fact that they had been the subject of lots of gossip themselves over the years and it didn't feel good, but they didn't much care anymore either. Grandad held firm that, so long as they were kind and decent, everything would pass. And it usually did. He said he didn't much care to carry the weight of other people's assumptions and expectations. Maureen's favourite was when she was worried about something and he would say that worrying was like riding a wooden rocking horse, it didn't get you anywhere. If she was sitting on the sofa when she was younger, or at the kitchen table with a furrowed brow he would gently say to her: "you're not riding that wooden horse are you?"

Grandad said what was needed and spent a lot of time observing. He could see these two hadn't known each other very long, clearly smitten but carrying themselves with an awkwardness and the need to impress. It must have been the 1930s when he was in that place himself. He was still smitten with his wife, but the awkwardness had fallen away some fifty years ago, it was energy zapping to be on that much high alert. He wasn't sure these two would last the journey but sometimes travelling a while with someone was enough. Maureen didn't need to settle down, she certainly didn't need to settle, so long as she was happy, Grandad was happy.

They sat down around the table, it was three o'clock, not the usual time for lunch but the youngsters were starving, keen for full bellies. They sat next to each other at the table, chewing on their sandwiches and sipping at the tea. Nanna kept her chat up and Grandad commented occasionally with his gentle words and strong accent. He declined sandwiches himself but agreed to a slice of Victoria sponge that was sat in the cake tin, oozing homemade sticky jam and buttercream from the middle, the gentle dusting of icing sugar speckling the tip of Grandad's nose when he took a large bite. Maureen popped her hand under the table and squeezed Timothy's leg gently, this was perhaps a lot for a newcomer when they had only met yesterday. There was a lot of chatter and routine about the table, and Timothy was trying to join in and be part of it. They had their own rhythm, Maureen and her grandparents, and her mum too, when she was here. Like a perfectly in sync marching band, passing beat to beat as they spoke, they fitted together like a complete jigsaw and visitors were an add on. It was just family life, from knowing each other forever and loving each other without question. How does someone new find the beat when Timothy's own family rhythm sounded more like disjointed rock music with a first time saxophonist, rather than this gentle foot tap of a tune, found in a kitchen full of smiles? He was trying very hard to listen and join in.

"Can I take you all out for supper as a thank you for letting me stay?" Timothy asked when there was a lull in the conversation.

"You don't have to do that son." Nanna said. "I'm more than happy to cook something."

"No, really, I'd love to take you out. You choose somewhere that's good."

"Ooh what about The Oak nanna? You love it there." Maureen smiled.

It was agreed that they would head out at eight o'clock, giving the sandwiches a chance to go down. Maureen and Timothy would pop round and see if they could book a table for later and then they would have a little drive up to Loughrigg tarn while the weather was hot. Despite protests from nanna, Timothy cleared the table but then nanna said enough was enough and flicked him away with her tea towel so that she could wash the pots in peace. Grandad headed back out to the garden to carry on stringing his onions and Maureen grabbed a couple of towels from the airing cupboard for a just in case swim, she heated up the flask with hot water and brewed more tea in the pot, pouring it into the flask with a satisfying glugging noise and a flick of steam. The day had heated up nicely as it progressed and they both felt uncomfortably warm and in need of freshening up, a swim would be perfect, and hot tea was good, whatever the weather. They shouted their goodbyes at the door and climbed into the car.

"They are really welcoming." Timothy nodded as they began to drive away. "I'm not sure my family would be as welcoming, but nothing to do with you though, Maureen, they are just not as relaxed in general. Probably more formal."

"Will I be meeting them then?" Maureen asked, raising her eyebrows.

"I hope you will." Timothy replied. "If you can still put up with me after the next couple of days." There was a great deal of hope in his voice.

"Sure I can, I can just about manage to put up with you. Ok so far, unless you're holding back something menacing?" Maureen laughed loudly, tossing her head back as she pointed out directions to the tarn. She felt quite at ease, like being with him was quite normal. But really it was a very unusual situation for both of them. Relaxed as far as being on their best behaviour could be relaxed.

They parked the car at the river and walked up the steep road to the tarn. Maureen carried the towels in her rucksack, wrapped around the flask. He offered to carry the bag but she was so used to having the comfort of her provisions on her back, weighing on her shoulders, she didn't feel complete without it. He marched quickly besides her, not as fit as he should be, breathless and sweating as he tried to keep up in the heat, secretly pleased that he wasn't carrying the weight of the bag. They passed through a gate and down into the dry grass, wandering into a well worn path heading downhill. He was pleased that he could catch his breath downwards for a moment. She had barely broken a sweat, able to talk continuously as she had marched uphill, pointing out this place and that, occasionally stopping to grab a handful of early ripe blackberries, popping them into her mouth without meticulously checking for bugs. They only rule, she told him as she passed him three large, jewel-like berries, was that you always picked them above dog wee height. He let the berries roll in his mouth for a moment before chewing, letting the tiny seeds play havoc with his back teeth, feeling like they might stay in there forever. At the edge of the tarn she led him to the area with a few low trees and began to take off her clothes, throwing them on top of her abandoned bag.

"I've no trunks." He said.

"Well hopefully you've got underpants on, they'll do. I'll just be in my bra and knickers. Almost a bikini and I'm sure the sheep won't mind."

"I might just sit on the edge." He said wishing he had her freedom, or bravery, or whatever it was.

"Aren't you hot?" She asked

"Like the sun." He said, running his fingers through his thick, damp hair.

"Well don't miss this opportunity," She nodded towards the water. "I'm going in."

She stood in front of him in her black bra and knickers and turned, tiptoeing across the ragged, stony beach and into the water. His breath caught as he watched her. Who would see him? Who would judge him? Who would care? Probably only himself. He kicked off his shoes and quickly undressed to his underpants, making little high pitched shocked noises as the sharp stones attacked the softness of his feet as he edged into the water. She was standing waist deep in the water, breathing in the smell of the tarn, the scent of freshness still delighted her as well as the feeling of the sun on her body.

The water was as warm as it would ever get and she still felt as though it took her breath away. He caught up to her and stood, waiting for her next move.

"Couldn't resist eh?" She smiled at him. She took his hand for a moment and held it. "We count to three and duck our shoulders under. OK?"

The water edged to their necks as they bent their knees and they sprang back up with gasps and giggles. He grabbed her quickly as they stood together, dripping wet, and he kissed her hard until the gasps coming from them had little to do with the temperature of the water.

"Oh God." He said as he pulled away for a moment.

She pulled off her knickers and held them in her hand, easing down his underpants. They were close enough to bushes to be discreet and she wrapped herself around him, his breath caught as he found himself enjoying quick sex in the water, he tried to think about something he read once, where you could form a suction and get stuck having sex in water, but it was done magnificently quickly and there was no need to call for help. She swam away on her back, pausing to put her knickers back on. He watched her as she smiled in the water, looking at him. The last time he had been in the lakes was a teenage outward bound week with school. He didn't remember a great deal about it but this visit was much more enjoyable. It was amazing. He swam after her, pulling up his pants.

They stayed in for a few more minutes, splashing about, squinting at the reflection of the sun on the top of the water. Laughing about the cold and the weeds tickling at their feet like hands grabbing them. She looked over at the shore. "Time for a brew." She said and set off to swim back to the shore.

He was being led by her for certain, and he was more than happy to follow her lead. To sit on the edge of the water wrapped in towels, to talk about where she would take him tomorrow, where they would eat tonight, to kiss for a while and then drink tea before dressing and walking back up the grass, back down there road and finding the car by the river. They held hands this time as they walked, as if what they had done added some permanence to whatever they were. It wasn't a one time thing anymore, it was a once in Oxford and a jump in Loughrigg and who knew what tomorrow, kind of thing. He held her hand tightly, feeling that she could drift off at any moment and he would be left bereft for the rest of his life. He couldn't bear the thought that this might end. He couldn't let it.

9- morning- freedom day number three.

Maureen slept in late. It was unusual for her. She was not a good sleeper at the best of times and she was sure that this wasn't really the best of times, but there was certainly potential. Her mouth was dry and her head pounded. The light was burning through the thin curtains and traffic was beginning to move outside. It was eight o'clock, which was late for her. She had slept through and she didn't feel refreshed. She scurried to the toilet wondering how she had missed her usual two toilet visits through the night. She didn't look at her phone at first, she didn't want to know, she wanted water and paracetamol and perhaps another hour to give the headache a chance to slink away. It had been such a hot day yesterday and she probably hadn't drunk enough water, she would have to rectify that today.

Maureen tucked her mass of curls into a hair bobble she had found at the bottom of her bag, to give the air a chance to kiss at her neck. It was another warm one, she could tell that already. Stuffy and hot. She had dreamt a thousand dreams overnight, of her mum, nanna and Grandad, them, but not quite them, asking where Timothy was, but she was younger in the dream, and she felt sad. She had once loved the bones of him and she knew he felt the same, but then life happened and when she needed him to look after her he took over everything about her until she was a wrung dry flannel, numb and silent. He was not the amazed young man who promised to look after her forever, but she was not the young woman full of hope with a belly full of fire. These days belly fire was indigestion, or too much cheese, but there was fire inside her still, just one step at a time. It might be an ember, but it was there

She dabbed her face with cold water at the kitchen sink, glugging down a glass full that she could feel snake down towards her stomach. The coolness of it felt instantly better. She had a banana and 2 paracetamol and couldn't even face a cup of tea, she wanted to lie back down with a damp cloth on her head. The air in the bedroom was still and warm, the sun was claiming the day already. She lay on the bed on top of the covers breathing slowly and trying to catch the edge of sleep so that she could make it her own. It was just a case of emptying her mind, which was easier said than done. She did what her mum always said to do when she was younger, count backwards from two hundred, over and over again until the sleep came. By the time the drift came the numbers stopped and she was dreaming again, but she wouldn't remember what the dream was this time. No glimpses of her beloved relatives visiting from her subconscious when she was already full to the brim with doubts.

She woke up to her phone buzzing angrily, dancing on the bedside table, and because she was not fully conscious when she put her hands on it she answered before looking at who was calling and deciding if she wanted to speak to them.

"Hello." She rasped with her croaky, not yet spoken voice.

"Goodness Maureen, are you ok, you sound dreadful." It was Florence, Timothy's sister.

"Oh fine." Maureen coughed. "I woke early with a headache and came back to bed, my voice is still asleep that's all."

"I rang Timothy to check that there's nothing new happening on the party front and since he's got no idea about anything I got no information from him. He said you were away." Florence questioned gently.

"Yes, I'm in Ambleside at the cottage." Maureen paused, there was a long silence and she didn't know how much you say. "Nothing new on the party front, it's all sorted and should just be good to go really. This time in two weeks it'll all be over and we will be nursing sore heads."

"I'm going to ask again Maureen," Florence's voice was soft but stern. "Are you ok? I never knew you had plans to go away, it seems ages since you've been up there."

"I'm fine really." Maureen said, and she was telling the truth. "I couldn't stay in the house that's all. We had a bit of a too-do, me and Timothy, and I needed to be here. I just can't be there."

"Well good." Florence replied. "I love the old bugger Maureen, but I couldn't live with him. I'm surprised you've put up with him for this long."

Maureen laughed with relief, and felt tears spring to her eyes at the same time, her breath caught and she couldn't speak for a moment. "Oh Flo, I'm sorry." She said.

"What on earth are you sorry for?" Florence asked. "How long have we known each other and been friends? You've not been yourself for a long time, and I know you've just been quietly waiting it through. I'm glad you're there and you're having some time. It's about time."

"It's your brother though." Maureen said.

"So then I know what a bloody idiot he can be." Florence laughed. "Still a mummy's boy. You know we'll have put time, blood, sweat and tears into this party and he'll be the one taking all the thanks. Do you feel better being away, being there?"

"I really do, honestly, I feel like I'm getting myself back. I even went swimming in my bra and knickers yesterday."

"See, that's the Maureen I know." Florence laughed.

"The thing is Flo, I don't feel like I'm away, I feel like I'm home, and apart from the party I'm not going back." Maureen replied.

"That's ok." Florence said gently. "How long did I manage to stay married for? Ten years. Really you've done well being there this long. I knew as soon as you stepped through the door in those pedals pushers he was punching well above his weight. And he said so himself it was only a matter of time, until you flew. But how come now, why now?"

"God it sounds so stupid when I say it out loud. It's so many things that layered and layered on top of me but then he said this thing and it was like he'd flicked a switch inside me. Like I'd been half asleep and then I was suddenly wide awake." Maureen stopped talking and thought about his words. His silly little flimsy words were just another sentence to him, just another expectation. Of all the things he had perhaps avoided saying so that she didn't wake up he would never have expected these words to be the end of them.

"What did he say?" Florence asked, as the pause on the other end of the phone lasted too long to wait.

"He said we needed to go to the hairdresser's and get my haircut because I was looking too much like my mum." Maureen was quiet but very clear. She shifted in the bed, taking the weight off her elbow that was starting to tingle and fizz with stillness.

"Fucking idiot." Florence said through her teeth. "I'm sorry to say this about my own brother but the man gets less aware of other people the older he gets. The lights are on but he's looking at himself in the bloody mirror." Maureen laughed out loud down the telephone. Florence was a tonic. She was fiercely loyal to Maureen, distant enough to not step on toes but spot on in her observations of Timothy. "It's not his fault you know, he just never got it. He never got other people, he's always been a periphery player, and then the older he's got the less you can tell him anything. He's always bloody right. Still mother's little boy."

"I know. And I did love him so, you know." Maureen said. "I never thought I'd leave. Mind you it's only three days in, he's been on longer golf trips."

"You stick with yourself Maureen." Florence replied. "You've made a decision, don't be doubting yourself. Is it ok if I come up for a couple of days after the party?"

"That would be lovely." Maureen said. And she meant it.

After they said goodbye and made plans about where they would meet so that they could get to the ninetieth party together Maureen stayed in bed for a few minutes. She didn't have a doubt about going to her mother-in-law's birthday. She had done most of the organising with Florence and no help from Timothy at all. Julia would be expecting it. She would expect her daughter-in-law there, and so would every other guest. She had no reason to feel awkward about the situation, no one needed to know anything. Most of the people they only ever saw at funerals and christenings, so she could smile and nod at the conversation and hardly say a word. They would be well used to her fluttering around and doing, offering drinks, finding coats, those with a purpose could say less. The difference with this gathering, as opposed to the many, many others over the years was that she would not be led by Timothy, and she would certainly not leave with him, she would not hear his flirtatious efforts that once had sent excited butterflies about her stomach, but lately led to disappointment and indigestion.

Maureen had never planned or wanted to set the world on fire, she was just happy to feel the glow in her belly from the everyday, from the joys of the things she loved, but when everything happened and the glow started to fade to nothing, she thought she would stop being able to breath with the grief that held her at the back of her throat. She waited for help, support, and kindness from Timothy, but it never came and she could never get the words to say 'help me', and then she stopped trying to get help and realised this was how it was. There were other things, life to do, kids to look after, work to manage, but the fiery, confident, articulate Maureen Smith became a whisper, and then she whispered for far too long and it became who she was.

Maureen got out of bed. She felt validated after speaking with Florence. She knew she was right to leave, she knew that there was no going back, but having someone say that she should stick with herself felt like she could do this. Whatever this was. Maureen smiled recalling what Florence said about Timothy punching above his weight when they first met. It felt like a million years ago and yesterday all rolled into one, before she had lived all of this life. A million years ago that they drove back down from Ambleside after two nights with Nanna and Grandad.

Maureen had hugged them tight and promised to come up again within the next few weeks. It was early bank holiday Monday, they had sat down to a breakfast of bacon sandwiches, with fried eggs, all held together in Nanna's famous buttery fried bread. It was their bank holiday breakfast for as long as Maureen could remember. It was her favourite, especially on a Christmas morning when the sandwich would be served with a satsuma and two slices of chocolate orange.

On this 'meet the family' August bank holiday they sat around the table, a pot of tea sat in the centre on a heavily tea stained cork stand, clad in a thick, woollen tea cosy that nanna had knitted when the previous one had become too grubby for guests. The usual table cloth was topped with a white embroidered cotton cloth because there was a guest and all guests got a cotton top cloth, usually with embroidered corners and a frill about the edge. Maureen stirred her tea and bit into the sandwich causing egg yolk to dribble down her chin. She wiped out quickly with her napkin, as much as she was comfortable with Timothy, she didn't really need him to see her dribbling just yet.

They were sat in the car ready for the off by 7 am. Nanna and Grandad thought nothing of the early start, they had been early risers forever, rarely in bed past 530am. Bank holiday lunches were a routine at Timothy's family home, one o'clock on the dot the first course would be served and it was expected that Timothy would be sat ready to eat. He had rung his mother from a phone box the day before to ask if he could bring his new girlfriend for lunch, to introduce her to the family. Maureen had agreed that she would take the plunge after the sudden meeting of her grandparents and just go with it. She recalled what he said about his family being less welcoming and did not expect the excitement and homeliness of nanna and Grandad's greetings. She assumed it would be more formal but if it didn't go well it wouldn't need to be repeated.

They had spent two nights with nanna and Grandad, holding hands, cuddling up on the sofa, getting to know each other. The car was packed up with a great box of vegetables and three dozen eggs. Grandad had given her two bottles of gorse flower wine that they had tried the night before and proclaimed to be delicious, zesty and coconutty, and they had all four of them drank a little too much and giggled as they played find the lady with pack of cards that was always kept in the little drawer at the side of the dining table. It took several rounds before Timothy got the hang of it but he didn't win a game, and after four glasses of gorse flower wine he didn't care at all, and he normally liked to win.

They had taken a walk to the lake before bed and watched the stars reflected in the water, swaying as they walked back up the road to home. Timothy felt his cheeks glowing and thought it was the wine, but it was the first flushes of love too, and the new feeling of being with a family who genuinely liked each other's company, no pomp or ceremony, just conservation and a lot of laughter. He dozed off to sleep that night wondering how his family would greet Maureen. He shouldn't care as long as he was impressing her, but his guard was down, gone, the moment she looked at him, then turned her head and walked away, the guard was already gone when he chased her down the road just two days earlier. He was nervous, anxious even, not at being with her, but at the thought of not being. It was too late to play a game, play it cool, be how he normally was around women, she had caught him already and he couldn't do a thing about it.

"Bring a woman home?" His mother had exclaimed when he rang and told her that he would be bringing someone to lunch. He hadn't asked, he had said that's what he was doing. And if Mother had said no he would have stayed away too. "Who is she? You've not mentioned a girlfriend before."

"I know Mother, it's all quite new, but she is rather marvellous and I'm sure you'll love her."

"Oh, you're sure are you?" She replied with clipped tones. "Well we will see you tomorrow then."

He didn't relay any of the conversation to Maureen other than to say that his mother was really looking forward to meeting her. And she would have been very much so, but out of curiosity rather than joy, and that would have to do for now.

Between waving nanna and Grandad away and ringing the front door bell of the vast house in Winchester they stopped once for a wee and to buy crisps from a service station. They drank the tea that Maureen had packed in her flask and they ate a slice of friendship cake that nanna had packed in an old margarine tub, with the very last bits of gold writing flaking off the lid. Maureen stroked her fingers across the indentations on the lid where the name of the margarine had once been, and she smiled to herself as she thought of Nanna lining the tub with greaseproof paper before filling it up with her great chunks of cake, brown sugar rolling off the top and becoming trapped in the bottom of the tub. In the bag nanna had folded two pieces of kitchen roll into squares for them to use should they need it. Maureen rested her hand on Timothy's thigh as they drove, until her hand got too hot and she had to open the window. Her hair flapped and whipped across her face until she closed it up again and laid the seat back slightly, resting her eyes from the bright sun. She had never been to Winchester before, Timothy said that there would be lots of questions his mother would probably ask and it wouldn't do if she knew how they had met, so they agreed to say they had met in the library in Oxford where he had been following a meeting. Mother didn't even like the idea that he went into police stations, she probably couldn't cope with the idea that he picked up women there too, he had said.

It seemed strange to Maureen that they were ringing the bell of the door of his parents house, not going straight in or opening it with his own key, not as a surprise like they had done in Ambleside, but because he wasn't allowed to let himself in. When the door opened he introduced her to the housekeeper who smiled widely and gave Timothy a little pat on the arm. Maureen had her bag with her and she was gifting a bottle of

Grandad's wine for the meal. She had suggested that they brought some eggs too, but Timothy had said his mother wouldn't appreciate how tasty they were and how Maureen knew the names of the hens, so she agreed to leave them in the car. There were no coats to take as it was too hot and so Mrs Jackson showed them into the drawing room where Mother and Florence were waiting, unusually without Florence's husband, Graham. Florence stood in the bay window with a glass of wine in her hand and she glanced over the top of her glasses as Maureen and Timothy walked in.

"Crikey Timothy, I've never seen you in a pair of jeans." She chuckled. "Very casual." She looked past Timothy and smiled as she saw Maureen walk through the door, looking the exact opposite of any woman she expected to see her little brother with. She was dressed casually and did not seem in the least bit nervous. Florence noticed that Timothy kept glancing between Maureen and Mother and he did appear nervous, not his usual slightly cocky self, he must be keen on this one.

Maureen walked over to Mother and smiled, shaking her hand as Timothy introduced them. Maureen smiled warmly and felt that the size of the house warranted a curtsy, but she kept upright and kept her eyes firmly on Mother, who she was told to call Julia.

"Lovely to meet you, Julia." Maureen smiled, her northern accent standing out against the clipped tones of Julia.

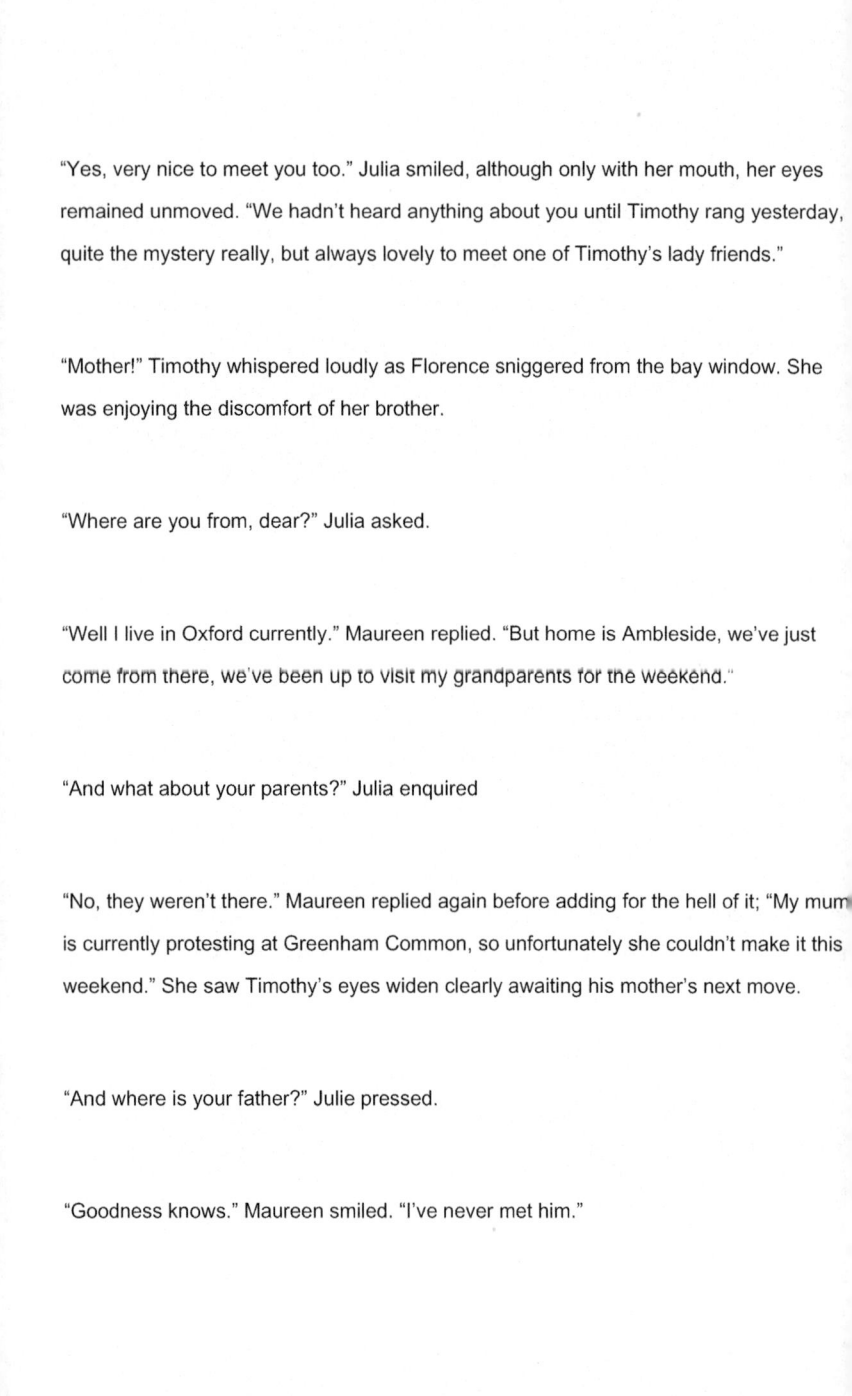

"Yes, very nice to meet you too." Julia smiled, although only with her mouth, her eyes remained unmoved. "We hadn't heard anything about you until Timothy rang yesterday, quite the mystery really, but always lovely to meet one of Timothy's lady friends."

"Mother!" Timothy whispered loudly as Florence sniggered from the bay window. She was enjoying the discomfort of her brother.

"Where are you from, dear?" Julia asked.

"Well I live in Oxford currently." Maureen replied. "But home is Ambleside, we've just come from there, we've been up to visit my grandparents for the weekend."

"And what about your parents?" Julia enquired

"No, they weren't there." Maureen replied again before adding for the hell of it; "My mum is currently protesting at Greenham Common, so unfortunately she couldn't make it this weekend." She saw Timothy's eyes widen clearly awaiting his mother's next move.

"And where is your father?" Julie pressed.

"Goodness knows." Maureen smiled. "I've never met him."

"Good grief, dear." Julia shook her head.

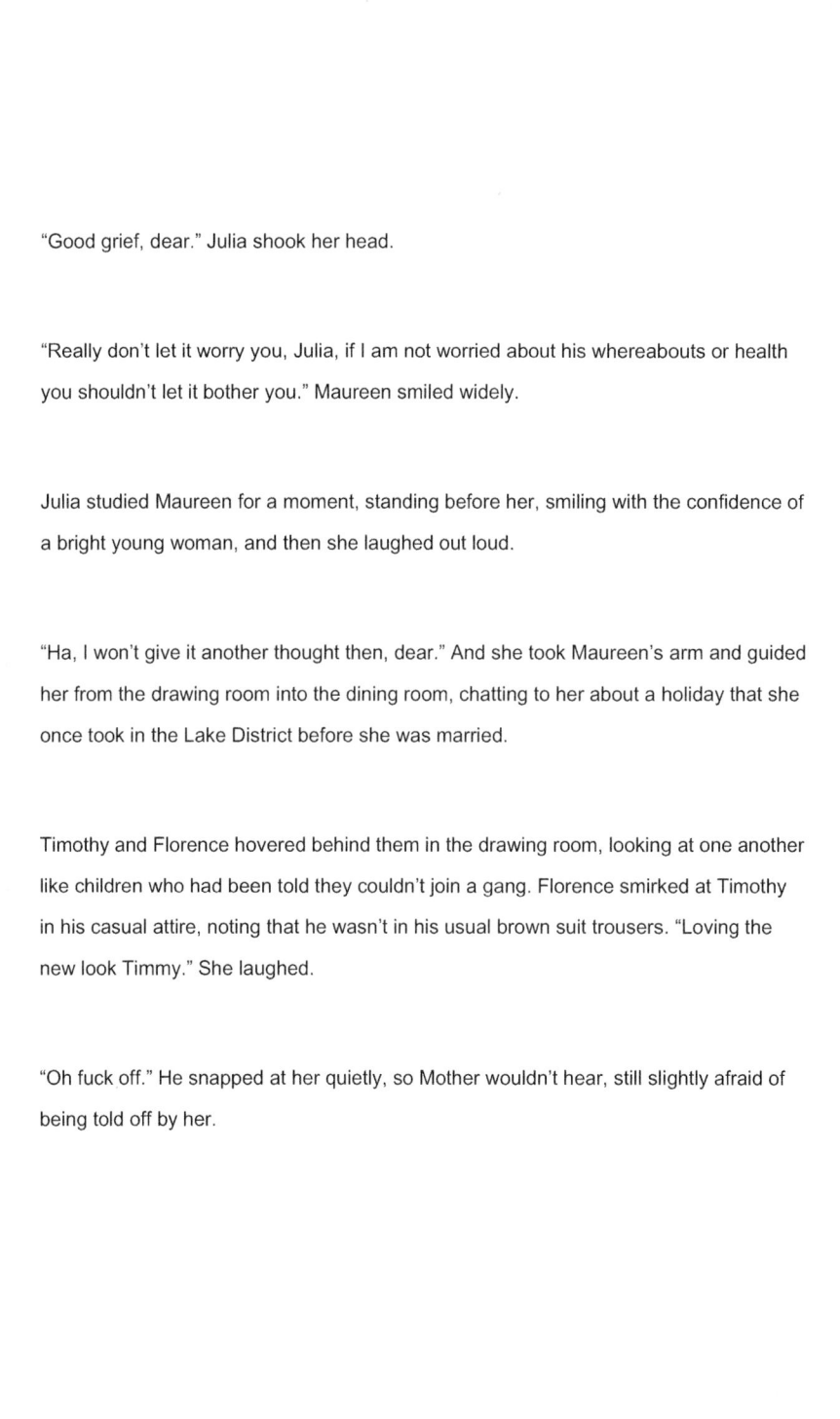

"Really don't let it worry you, Julia, if I am not worried about his whereabouts or health you shouldn't let it bother you." Maureen smiled widely.

Julia studied Maureen for a moment, standing before her, smiling with the confidence of a bright young woman, and then she laughed out loud.

"Ha, I won't give it another thought then, dear." And she took Maureen's arm and guided her from the drawing room into the dining room, chatting to her about a holiday that she once took in the Lake District before she was married.

Timothy and Florence hovered behind them in the drawing room, looking at one another like children who had been told they couldn't join a gang. Florence smirked at Timothy in his casual attire, noting that he wasn't in his usual brown suit trousers. "Loving the new look Timmy." She laughed.

"Oh fuck off." He snapped at her quietly, so Mother wouldn't hear, still slightly afraid of being told off by her.

"She's a beautiful woman, not your usual buttoned up type." Florence noted as they started walking towards the dining room.

"She's amazing." Timothy smiled into the distance. "I'm going to marry her." He said to his sister, without his usual confidence.

It was a running joke between them whenever he introduced his family to anyone, or after he had been talking to a woman at a party, or mentioned a woman at all, Florence would ask "Are you going to propose?" And Timothy would tell her where to get off. Her friends referred to him as eligible, but to her he was just her annoying brother who was her mother's little treasure, even now.

"Does she know she's marrying you?" Florence asked.

"Not yet." He replied.

They laughed together and pushed each other up the corridor like they had done when they were children elbowing and pushing each other while no one was watching, her easily the strongest until he turned twelve and became head and shoulders taller than his older sister. Then she would walk up the corridor away from him so that he couldn't send her flying. But now at the ages of twenty seven and thirty there was a gentleness to their teasing, like they had survived this house together, and yet here they were again, on their usual bank holiday formal dinner trying to trip each other up, a GP and a solicitor quietly wrestling like children, which they always became as soon as they set foot into this house. You could almost hear Mother shouting at them, telling them that it would end in tears and they should just behave. Thankfully they were too old now for a wooden spoon across their palms, but they knew a reprimand from Mother could cause them both to sting, even if their hands came away pain free.

They ate their soup and then their roast beef with Mother firing questions at Maureen which she answered with ease and then fired a question back. Mother was clearly impressed that this poor, fatherless girl had a teaching job at Oxford university. That she could speak some Latin and had made Mother laugh when she told her she had taken Timothy swimming in a tarn, although she had wisely decided to gloss over the part where they had sex in the water. Perhaps a story for another dinner party on another day, Maureen thought, causing her cheeks to flush and a smile spread across her face. Timothy glanced at her and caught her thought, losing himself in a smile too.

Maureen could see exactly why Timothy was buttoned up so tight. Why he chased her down the road. She was everything he was not, the formality of this house was something she could manage occasionally, like the dinners at university, but for this to be the place you sought shelter from the world must mean you could never breathe out. You could never wear odd socks without question because you'd lost the pair, or stay in your pyjamas on a Sunday because you'd been busy all week and the only place you were heading was the garden or the sofa. She could see why he would drive halfway across the country to relax, to collect eggs with Grandad and knead bread with nanna. This house was a place where you would be, her home was a place where you could do, where you could live and relax. She felt a little thrill in her stomach that she might represent freedom to him. He had chased her down the road and he was still chasing her now as they were sat here eating. He was across the table, there was no cosiness of a cake tin and a pot of tea, you didn't have to get up to be fed, someone in an apron was bringing and serving. You couldn't accidently brush each others knees and feel the thrill of the touch, you couldn't catch your breath as your little fingers touched while you were eating at the table, there was too much space and it would be seen by everyone, it would not be a thrill, it would be an observable act on a table this big.

"Where's Graham by the way?" Timothy asked Florence, as if he had just looked away from Maureen and realised his brother-in-law was absent from dinner.

Florence opened her mouth to speak, thinking of what she should say.

"They are getting a divorce." Julia said, without looking up from her apple pie.

Florence closed her mouth and looked away from everyone towards the window.

"Oh Flo." Timothy said, with a rare display of emotion in his voice. Florence shook her head as if she was declining any more words.

"Have you ever been to Ambleside?" Maureen quickly said, directing the question at Florence and changing the subject with welcome haste.

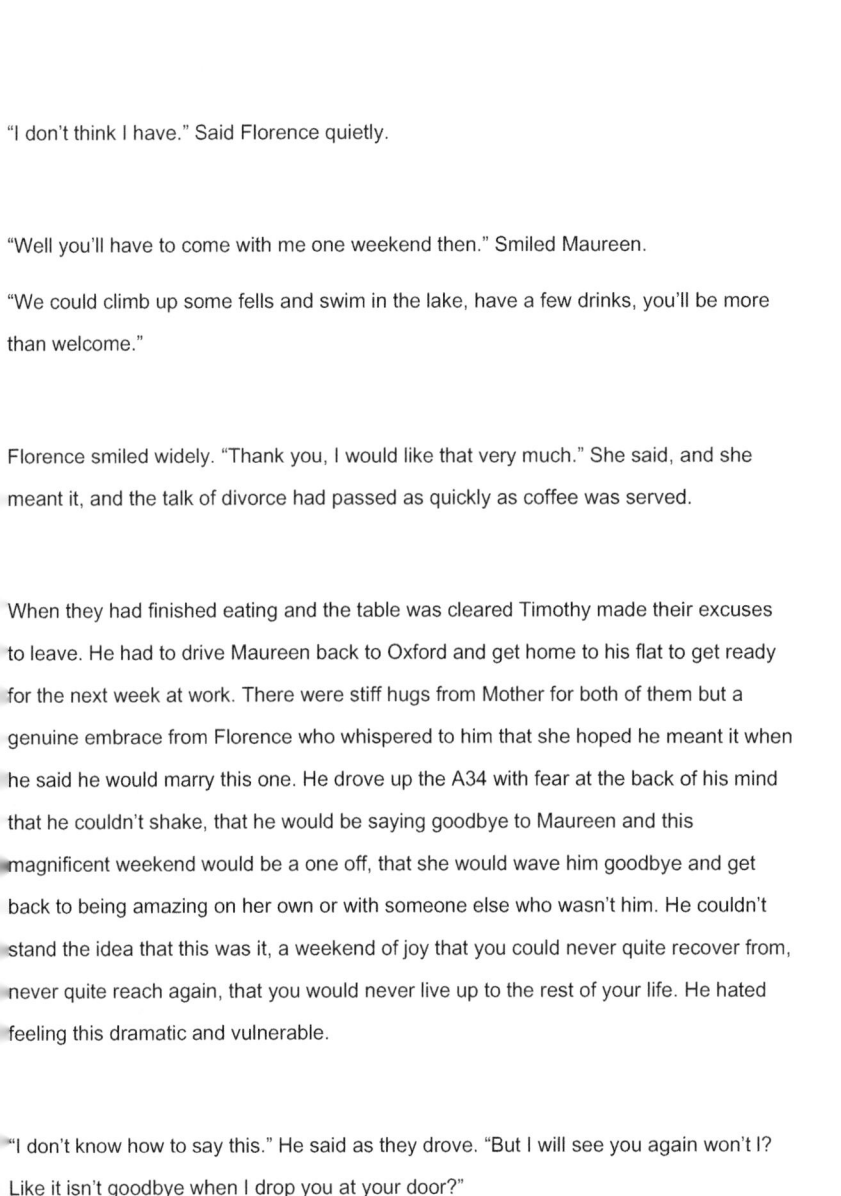

"I don't think I have." Said Florence quietly.

"Well you'll have to come with me one weekend then." Smiled Maureen.

"We could climb up some fells and swim in the lake, have a few drinks, you'll be more than welcome."

Florence smiled widely. "Thank you, I would like that very much." She said, and she meant it, and the talk of divorce had passed as quickly as coffee was served.

When they had finished eating and the table was cleared Timothy made their excuses to leave. He had to drive Maureen back to Oxford and get home to his flat to get ready for the next week at work. There were stiff hugs from Mother for both of them but a genuine embrace from Florence who whispered to him that she hoped he meant it when he said he would marry this one. He drove up the A34 with fear at the back of his mind that he couldn't shake, that he would be saying goodbye to Maureen and this magnificent weekend would be a one off, that she would wave him goodbye and get back to being amazing on her own or with someone else who wasn't him. He couldn't stand the idea that this was it, a weekend of joy that you could never quite recover from, never quite reach again, that you would never live up to the rest of your life. He hated feeling this dramatic and vulnerable.

"I don't know how to say this." He said as they drove. "But I will see you again won't I? Like it isn't goodbye when I drop you at your door?"

"You're not coming in for a cup of tea then?" Maureen laughed.

"Well yes, I should like that very much." Timothy stuttered. "But then after that, after we go about our lives and go to work tomorrow and go to bed in our separate places. I will see you again won't I?"

"Of course you will you daft apeth." Maureen replied. "I've just spent the weekend pretending you're my boyfriend, and I'm not a liar so you're going to have to be my boyfriend now."

"Oh right, great stuff." Timothy laughed nervously, tingles of sweat crawling down his back. And his shoulders relaxed a little, for now. He felt as thought he had won first prize in whatever competition this was. But he also felt like a puppy, keen to be approved of, and it wasn't a feeling he was used to. It wasn't something that was comfortable, it made him feel a bit like a child wanting to please Mother. But, God, this woman made him feel as though he could barely breathe with excitement, hope and nerves.

And that was that. They were together. He chased her down the street and wanted to impress her and he had spent forty years wanting to impress her. He just lost his way on how. What he thought she wanted and what she actually wanted for, lost somewhere, and he got muddled up with need and want and he was always trying to impress too many people at once. And too many people indicated they were impressed so he took it and forgot to be kind and caring. He thought he could get away with anything most of the time, his ego tickling away at him. And from the very moment he gave chase he hoped she would always be there, that for all his false bravado and hidden insecurities, she'd be always there, forever his, never getting away. And she almost didn't.

They spent a lot of time at each other's flats in the early days, long lazy Sundays and then a dash up or down the A34 on Monday mornings getting to work. There were more trips to Ambleside and Winchester as well as a couple of hot holidays to the seaside, where he would watch her walking across the sand, her wild hair in a bun to keep the heat from her neck as she made her way to the bar to get lemonade or beer. He couldn't believe his luck that she still walked towards him and sat beside him when she could have anyone she wanted. He finally met her mum, Coral, after they had been together about six months, she had come to stay in Maureen's flat in Oxford before she was travelling back up north. She'd been offered a job teaching in a school local to Ambleside and had come from the protest to clean up and see her girl before moving back home.

Maureen was beyond excited to spend the weekend with her mum, she told Timothy her plans. He was going to drive up on the Saturday night and take them out to dinner. Coral was sleeping at the flat for three nights and in a one bedroom flat there was no room for him to stay that weekend too, so it was their first weekend not sleeping at one or the others places. As excited as Maureen was, Timothy was not impressed. He smiled in all the right places when Maureen chatted about where she would take her mum to, where they would eat, where they might walk, but he felt pushed out, abandoned, jealous even. He wasn't Maureen's priority, he wasn't part of her plan apart from the meal, and he wasn't keen on this change of their usual weekend plans. He dangled the idea of him paying for Coral to stay in a hotel so that he could spend the full weekend with them, get to know Coral better, see more of Maureen, but Maureen wouldn't hear of her mum being anywhere but with her in the flat. It was just one weekend and it was her mum, she said more than once. He sensed a smattering if irritation in her voice when she explained for the third time that she would carry on with her plan of spending some lovely time with her mum and she would see Timothy for the meal on the Saturday, and he closed down his suggestions, parked them with his disappointment and decided that Coral seemed a bit of a nuisance, needy even. He couldn't imagine his mother expecting Maureen to take second place over her on any weekend. So he balled his annoyance and set it aside and planned to surprise Maureen with a weekend away the next month so that she would be excited to spend time with him and that would be in her thoughts. He would tell her Saturday night at dinner, impress both of them at the same time, Maureen would be impressed with the trip and Coral would be thankful Maureen had him.

He arrived in Oxford at 6pm and headed straight for the flat. He had two bunches of flowers with him, one for Maureen and one for Coral, and a bottle of good wine so that they could have a glass before they headed out. He was wearing his new jeans with a shirt and tie, his shoes polished like mirrors. He felt quite jazzy, casual and smart at the same time. His hair was longer than it had been for some time and he had grown a small beard, although it was difficult to know when the stubble stopped and the beard began. He had toyed with the idea of having his hair highlighted but he had seen too many people coming from the police stations with highlights and he didn't want to start looking like a criminal. He had mentioned it to Mother too, and she had asked him if he was a solicitor in court or one of these singers off the TV? She didn't want people to get the wrong impression about him. He was twenty eight for goodness sake. Then she spent quite a bit of time talking about Maureen and when was he going to settle down, along with a lot of other things, but he had already zoned out at that point, and put the idea of highlights to one side.

Maureen was at the door before he knocked. She knew the sound of his car and she was excited to see him and show Timothy and her mum off to each other. Two people she loved who made her feel safe finally meeting.

"Really good to meet you Mrs Allonby" Timothy said as he shook Coral's hand.

"Goodness, that's my mother, Mrs Allonby, call me Coral, please." Coral replied, leaning in and giving Timothy a hug.

Timothy was quite taken aback at how similar the two women were. Coral was just an older looking version of Maureen, she had a few more lines and some grey dancing about her hair, but there was no denying genetics with these two. He suddenly felt quite uncomfortable, like he was on the edge of things, outside the shared history of them. He handed out the flowers and gave Maureen the wine. She sensed his discomfort and gave him a tight squeeze, kissing him on the lips and stroking the back of his head gently, winking as she pulled away. He felt his breath catch in his throat and suddenly felt that he belonged with Maureen, like she could soothe him forever. He made small talk with Coral but his eyes continuously flicked towards Maureen, watching her face as she talked, smiling when she smiled and laughing as she threw her head back with laughter as she told her mum the actual true story of how they met and the quick dash north that first weekend.

Coral could see that Timothy was absolutely smitten, maybe even besotted, he could hardly take his eyes off her daughter. Maureen was clearly very keen too, perhaps not so much, but maybe Timothy was nervous meeting the mother-in-law for the first time? Coral thought that she would give him the benefit of the doubt when a but came into her mind. Maureen really likes him, but...... Timothy is polite and making conversation, but ...... Whatever it was she couldn't put her finger on it, it lay unsaid and undecipherable for the moment but it was definitely there, a ball of doubt about this one. But so long as he made Maureen smile and treated her with kindness she could set aside her doubt. Maureen had never had a serious relationship, so perhaps there was a bit of jealousy at her spreading her wings, Coral thought. She decided she would swallow it down as she would swallow down the wine that was edging its way to her from the kitchen.

They all sipped their wine in silence, Timothy juggling with what to say next in his head while Maureen applied lipstick and sprayed her hair. She looked stunning, they both did, Timothy was starving and looking forward to the meal, despite still wishing it was just the two of them, not realising Coral felt exactly the same way. Maureen floated between them both all evening, trying to include them in each other's conversation like she was a ball in an everlasting table tennis match. She could sense the caution between them both, holding back, and she wanted so much for them to like each other, for them both to see the best bits of the other one like she did.

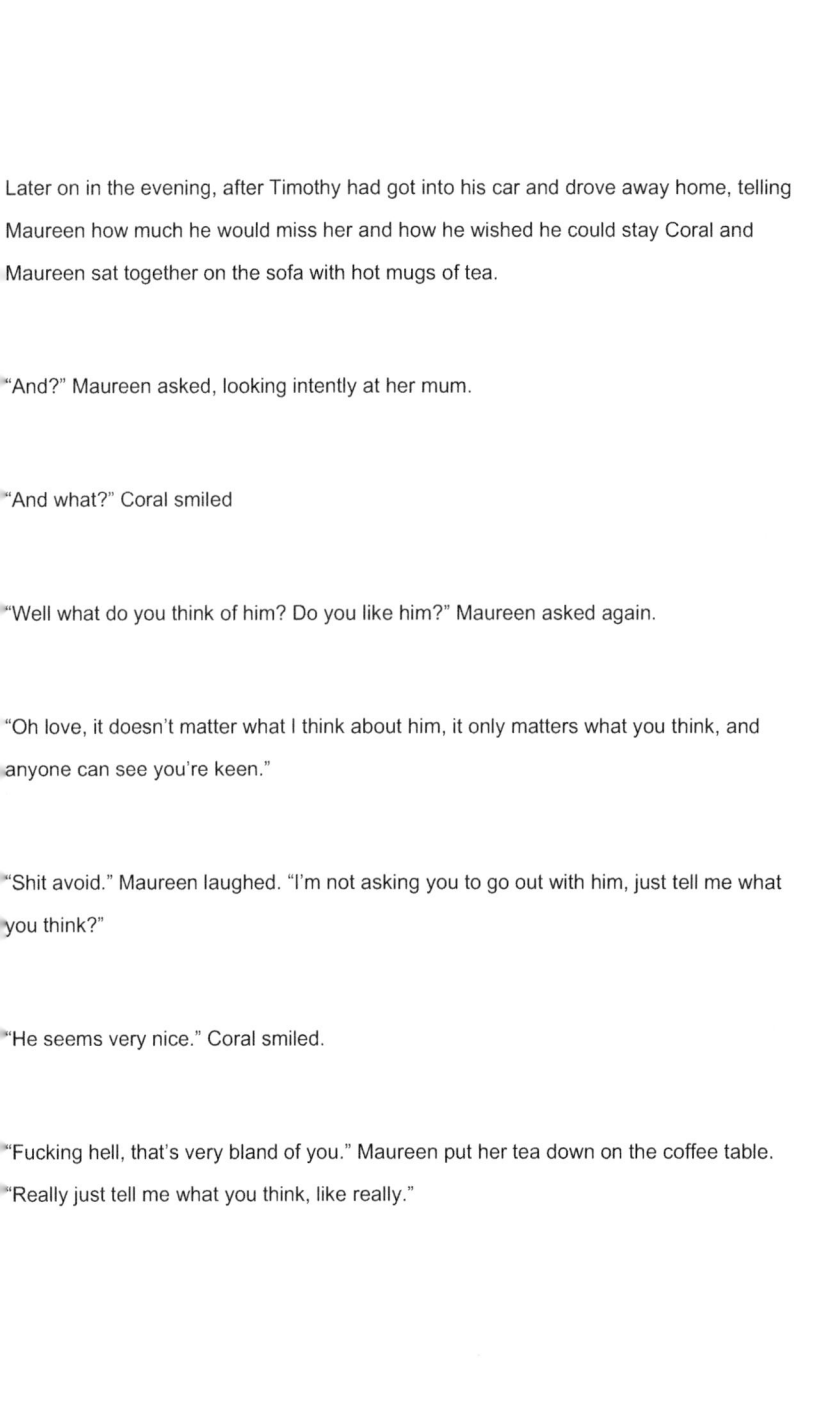

Later on in the evening, after Timothy had got into his car and drove away home, telling Maureen how much he would miss her and how he wished he could stay Coral and Maureen sat together on the sofa with hot mugs of tea.

"And?" Maureen asked, looking intently at her mum.

"And what?" Coral smiled

"Well what do you think of him? Do you like him?" Maureen asked again.

"Oh love, it doesn't matter what I think about him, it only matters what you think, and anyone can see you're keen."

"Shit avoid." Maureen laughed. "I'm not asking you to go out with him, just tell me what you think?"

"He seems very nice." Coral smiled.

"Fucking hell, that's very bland of you." Maureen put her tea down on the coffee table. "Really just tell me what you think, like really."

"Ok," Coral took a deep breath. "I think he's absolutely and utterly keen on you, more so than keen, I think he's a bit like a puppy around you. But he's a bit jealous in his keenness, I don't think he really loved seeing me here, I think he'd rather just be the two of you."

Maureen didn't try to defend him, she couldn't disagree.

"I don't think he was trying to let me know he wasn't excited with me being here, and he didn't kick me under the table or give me dead eyes or even a look, he just isn't really good at hiding his displeasure."

Maureen laughed. "Yes, that's true. I don't think he's going to make it big in poker."

"I just feel that he needs to be right, you know, that he wants people to know he knows stuff and he thinks he's right." Coral took hold of Maureen's hand. "But he's really right about you, you are amazing, and if he makes you happy and you like him then I like him too, but just with a bit of caution."

Maureen hugged her mum. "He does make me happy mum, I sort of feel safe when I know he is with me, if that makes sense."

"Absolutely, love." Coral smiled. "Just promise me you won't lose yourself with him. You'll always know your core and make sure he respects it. Don't let him twist and turn you and make you doubt yourself. Promise me that. You're a fire Maureen, a catch, a delight. Don't let anyone dampen you."

"I won't Mum, I promise." Maureen smiled thoughtfully.

10- the caught

Despite Timothy's attempts at persuasions, talks of traditions, money being no problem, what his mother might want, the wedding was quite a small affair. Maureen was insistent that it was not done in a church as she was not a believer, and it was not done in Winchester, no matter how many Smiths had married in the cathedral going back countless years. The wedding ceremony was to take place in Kendal registry office and afterwards there would be a reception, as grand as Timothy wanted, in The Globe function room in Ambleside. An open topped bus would transport guests between the two venues and if it rained, it rained.

Timothy was not happy with the lack of cooperation on Maureen's part for his family traditions and expectations and was surprised that his mother mentioned that Florence had got married in the cathedral and now she was getting a divorce so maybe somewhere else would be fine. Timothy did not share his mother's change of heart or keenness to ride around the lakes in an open topped bus where she planned on waving at tourists and imagining that she was royalty. Timothy did not share Maureen's enthusiasm that the back garden of The Globe had a lake view and that Nanna and Grandad had been there for their own wedding reception in 1936. But Timothy held his tongue as much as was humanly possible for him because above all Timothy wanted Maureen to be his wife, and if he had to bite his lip until it bled, he would do so.

As the relationship progressed Timothy could not shake the worry that at any moment Maureen would be gone. He feared that she would work out that he wasn't the enigmatic charmer he portrayed and she would become bored and move on, taking her smile and her walk, her easy laughter and joy at life with her. Timothy did not know that Maureen saw the vulnerable boy in him that hid behind his attempts at charm and she loved that boy. She loved his furrowed brow and his attempts at humour and his long talks at things he assumed she would be interested in. She loved that he tried and attempted to woo her still, she loved that he talked to Grandad in the garden even though he was not in the remotest bit interested in growing vegetables. She loved that he had bought a flask to keep in his car so that she was always in close proximity to tea. She felt a love for him that hit her in the chest when it needed to, made her heart beat fast, but never, ever took her breath away. She loved that he was stable and reliable and she knew he adored her. And on that hot day in Kendal she promised to love him forever, until death parted them, and she very much meant it at the time. But time is long and stability can be suffocating so that eventually your breath gets taken away for whole other reasons than love. But on that day she meant every word she said.

Maureen looked stunning in her cream dress, she had decided against the puffed sleeves and meringue skirt that was all the rage and opted for a simple lace floor length dress, with her curls piled on top of her head. She carried some of Grandad's roses in her hands and she wore new walking boots on her feet rather than the satin court shoes she would never, ever wear again. Around her shoulders she wore a gold shawl that nanna had crocheted with a bit of love in every stitch. Timothy wore a navy suit, bought new but with the intention of wearing it many times over at various semi-formal events. His best man was Justin from university who smelt slightly of sweat and had become a big fan of wet look gel that he had combed through his hair, ignoring the instructions which said 'use sparingly'. Justin came alone, hoping that there would be a surplus of young women keen to be wooed at a wedding. Maureen always felt he stared at her slightly too much and stood slightly too close, hence being able to smell the lack of deodorant. His grey suit appeared to reflect the sun, with its silvery aftertaste, and anyone who was prepared to dance with him at the wedding would receive an instant static shock from the next bit of metal they touched when they had the good fortune of being released from his grip. His nylon trousers rubbed together with great haste and the shock was not pleasant, no one agreed to a second dance.

There were no bridesmaids. There were a good couple of rows of Maureen's friends parked on grey plastic chairs, but she had not wanted an event with satin and pastel dresses, court shoes and netting. The simpler the better. Whatever she wanted Timothy was agreeable to, at least outwardly. Internally his smile at this unnecessary rebellion against his good ideas had long since faded, but he would smile at her for a thousand years if she was happy to stand beside him and say 'I do'.

The only person more surprised than Timothy that Maureen was agreeing to become Mrs Smith was Coral, but she did not feel herself a good judge of love. The only man she ever loved turned out to be married to someone else and by the time she realised the betrayal she was being sick most mornings and moving back home. Coral was championing the outward smile whenever Timothy was in the vicinity, although her eyes didn't agree with her mouth and failed to move. Maureen had made up her mind to love the fool and anything said on the matter would only stir up trouble between mother and daughter, and that would be something Timothy would no doubt be very keen to assist, so the smiling continued and the small talk, and laughing at another attempt at humour. Coral knew that Maureen's happiness was worth far more than her own discomfort. One day Maureen would see it all. Just not yet.

Maureen's nanna was equally enamoured by Timothy. She fussed over him with delight, making him special cake, cups of tea, saving him bottles of blackberry wine. He called her nanna, she called him son, the grandson she always wanted. And Coral was happy her mum was happy, even though she was not keen on the source. Grandad was another matter. He nodded and smiled at Timothy, chatted to him in the garden, he had occasionally taken him to the pub, but Grandad had the same still eyes throughout, no movement during a smile. Coral could see that when Timothy was chatting to someone else, or watching Maureen talk, her dad would be watching him quietly, discreetly, with a furrowed brow. If he caught Coral watching him, Grandad would nod at her, ever so slightly, as if they were both caught in the same observation with the same opinion, but until now it had gone unsaid.

The wedding breakfast, neither a breakfast or eaten in the morning, was in the function room at the back of the pub, overlooking the lake. Maureen and Timothy had chosen fish and chips to remember their first meal together and Timothy had laughed and said that the chance he took taking that food back to the flat on the first day they met was the best chance he ever took. Maureen had laughed too, saying that she didn't realise how easily led she had been when she was hungry. Everyone else had smiled at the story but Timothy's mother had let him know that it wasn't an appropriate meal for a wedding and they should have thought of the guests. Timothy had agreed with his mother wholeheartedly and they both discussed what should have been picked, which was roast beef, but this discussion was had behind closed doors, out of ear shot of Maureen. When Maureen had suggested the fish and chips to Timothy he was delighted about the romance of it all, until he spoke with Mother.

It was a beautiful sunny day, the warmth of August with the slightly cooler night promise of an edge towards autumn, first thing in the morning. It had been April that he proposed, he hadn't relaxed into the mutual glow of love, still concerned that she might leave at any moment, that she might find someone better or just decide she didn't want anyone at all. He didn't know how these things worked, relationships were more formal, stuffy affairs from what he saw. His sister and Graham always had a distance to them, but now they were on their way to divorce so that didn't say very much. He wanted to be carefree, to act on impulse, try new things, laugh with abandon, but he was serious and hemmed in with expectation. Then she came, and she shook him up and the hemming loosened, and he was terrified that she would be gone and he would spend the rest of his life not knowing she was his.

She said yes straight away when he proposed because she loved him and she was happy and she was sure that the edges that surprised her at times were just part of the difference in their upbringing, the weight of expectation on him and the lack of joy in his life. She felt, often, that she was teaching him the meaning of joy, of doing lovely things because they felt brilliant and fed the soul, rather than not doing something because 'what would Mother think?'. It felt amazing showing someone joy, feeling that moment, when your face ached from smiling and tiredness seeped into every corner of your being from just enjoying the day. She was trying to show him that joy – enjoyment- didn't have to be paid for or gained from someone doing something for you. She knew he had been buttoned up tight his whole life and she had managed to half open his top button. She loved the feeling of seeing someone excited about something they wouldn't normally be, and she hoped, on that day, on the 16th August, that it would be a life of enjoying that together. She didn't expect it to ebb away with the weight of expectations, but it didn't go with a bang, it tiptoed away quietly in the middle of the night, whispering its goodbyes distantly, so that they couldn't be heard by those distracted by life and commitment. But on the 16th August 1984 as they danced their first song on the grass as Mr and Mrs Smith there was nothing to be felt but love and joy, nothing to be seen but smiles and happiness, exactly how it should be when two people in love promise to love each other until death parts them.

Maureen and Timothy had opted to start married life in a detached house in Oxford. They had discussed where they would live at length but with Maureen not keen on driving and Timothy keen to have a little bit of distance between his family and himself they agreed that Winchester was not the place they should be. He was impressed with the house prices in Oxford being more manageable, he wasn't without means, but he didn't want to be beholden to Mother, he didn't want to ask her for money for somewhere bigger when he could be the king of his own castle without someone else claiming they could come through the drawbridge whenever they wanted. Maureen was excited to have a spare room, hoping that with the extra space nanna and Grandad might come and stay and she could show them around the city, let them have a holiday, cook them meals and take them tea in bed. She was looking forward to friends staying, entertaining, winter nights with the fire on, reading and drinking tea in bed. Being husband and wife together.

They had only been married a couple of weeks when they were at the August bank holiday roast dinner at Mother's house in Winchester. Between soup and main course Julia had suggested that it might be time to start thinking about children since neither of them were getting any younger. Maureen laughed out loud.

"I'm only twenty six Julia." She said. "Two weeks we've been married, just two weeks."

"I was pregnant from my honeymoon." Julia stated proudly.

"Well it's a bit soon for us thanks, Julia." Maureen replied. "There's loads we want to do before we have kids, isn't it Timothy?"

Timothy took a few thoughtful sips from his wine glass. They both said they wanted children and he was of the opinion that the sooner the better. He was more than happy for Maureen to give up work and he could support them both, give her some housekeeping to manage things, but he knew now wasn't the time to suggest this to anyone. "No rush." He said, smiling at both of them, trying to keep the peace between the two women who could make him very nervous.

"Do you know I'm the only one on the luncheon ladies without a grandchild?" Julia continued, ignoring anything said by anyone else.

"And I'm not getting any younger, so perhaps you should think on? It's not as though Florence is going to produce anything, now she is a divorcee in the making." She spat out the last words not looking towards Florence.

"Julia, no!" Maureen said very firmly, making Timothy turn to her wide eyed. "I can't speak for Florence but I'm the only one who has a say over my uterus, so if and when I'm ready I'll decide when the time is right."

Maureen cast a look toward Florence and saw a brief, barely there smile hit her mouth, then disappear again. She was not smiling so much of late.

Julia coughed into her glass of water as Timothy looked from wife to mother to sister, as a deafening silence filled the room. He was so far out of his comfort zone he felt like he was twelve again trying to be part of a family discussion that was going way above his head. His mouth twitched as his head tried to think of things to say to move the conversation on. Maureen read his desperation and put her hand on his knee, giving it a squeeze.

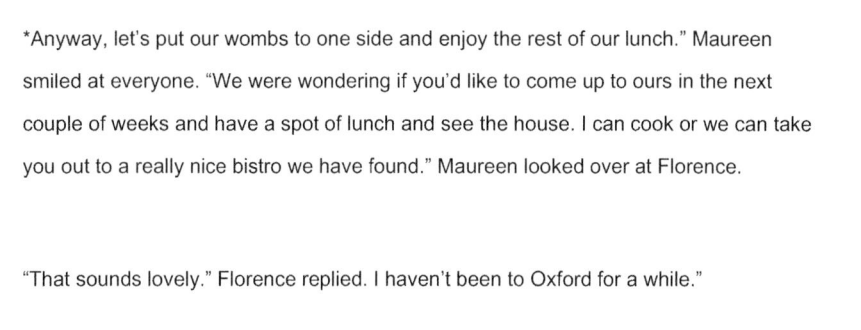

"Anyway, let's put our wombs to one side and enjoy the rest of our lunch." Maureen smiled at everyone. "We were wondering if you'd like to come up to ours in the next couple of weeks and have a spot of lunch and see the house. I can cook or we can take you out to a really nice bistro we have found." Maureen looked over at Florence.

"That sounds lovely." Florence replied. I haven't been to Oxford for a while."

"Great stuff." Maureen said. "I can show you around the university if you like Florence."

"I've been to one room, once. I think, for some conference or something. I'd love to see more of it." Florence briefly smiled at Maureen.

"You know you're welcome any time Flo, we've got a spare room and I'm more than happy to take you out bar hopping until we fall over. Timothy can come and pick us up after a girls night out." Maureen turned to Julia. "You up for a girls night out Julia? We can drink cocktails until we can't dance any more."

"Good grief." Julia exclaimed, and then added. "Well I think I should come to keep you youngsters in check. In case you make fools of yourselves."

"I feel that's a challenge then." Maureen laughed. "Let's see who keeps who in check."

And then the roast beef arrived at the table, with all of the vegetables and a big jug of thick, streaming gravy. Maureen thought of nanna, pouring her magnificent gravy onto plates straight from the green cast iron pan with the spout around the rim, drips of gravy slopping down the side of the pan. She would wonder what the point was of dirtying another dish, decanting the gravy into something else. But they would be sat eating, around the table in the kitchen, everyone pitching in with something. There wouldn't be a cook being paid in the kitchen or a housekeeper serving food. Maureen felt suddenly overwhelmed, imagining the gentleness and delight of dinner at her home. Grandad with his Sunday stubble, probably with a dribble of gravy down his shirt that would layer out, grabbing at clean cloth like a litmus paper experiment. Everyone happily chewing and talking and no one requesting Maureen change the plans of her womb to suit them. Maureen looked over at Florence who was waiting for the roast potatoes. They locked eyes for a moment and nodded gently at each other, as if knowing that their roles had been cast.

Timothy cut into his beef feeling quite pleased and relieved that the situation had been heading towards the edge of discomfort and then had sprung back to acceptable rather easily. And he hadn't had to say anything at all. His brilliant wife had caught it at the edge and like the conductor of an orchestra of disagreement she had managed to get the tune back in order with her words. She had stopped Mother, championed his sister and arranged another event before everything got out of hand. He wondered if he ought to have a word with her on the way home and ask if she could not make plans for them without asking him first, but he thought he might leave that while the going was good. He also thought she hadn't really made plans with him at all. A girls night out. With Mother? Goodness me. She could probably drink Maureen and Florence right under the table, but surely mother wouldn't go out drinking cocktails with them. Before Maureen set her line in the sand Timothy had considered discussing the child question on the way home, but he knew that was probably best left to another time, and clearly another year. He smiled to himself because he knew that there wouldn't be much space for him to say anything at all on the way home by the time Maureen had let him know what she thought, about all of it. She wouldn't go too far and say something she couldn't take back, but she would let him know that no way was she going to be told when she would be doing things. He knew there would be swearing and a mention of the year. And he would drive and agree with her, wishing that she wasn't right about Mother and her tone, and wishing that she'd stop talking about it. That was the biggest difference he had noticed between the two families. The Allonbys didn't swallow down all of their emotion until it burnt at the back of their throat and bittered their mouths.

Maureen ate her dinner quietly, pushing it about her plate, making it look more consumed than it had been. She would have them come stay in Oxford and then she would like some free weekends for a little while, maybe a trip up to Ambleside, but with the wedding and the planning and everyone knowing the far end of their plans, she wanted to enjoy her week off and just get the house straight. She would have been happy doing that today, happy with a cheese sandwich and a bag of crisps for lunch as she cleaned corners and organised kitchen cupboards, instead of driving down to Winchester to hold her breath. She felt dreadful at the thought. They had only been married two weeks and she was trying to run away from the in-laws already. Maybe she had post wedding blues or something along those lines, or maybe she was just pissed off at the assumption of it all? She wanted tea and her own sofa and a bit of quiet, she wanted to nest, but without any chicks at the moment. She would go home and tidy around a bit, write a nice letter to nanna and Grandad at the kitchen table. Have a bit of a walk somewhere green and think occasional grumpy thoughts about the oldest Smith.

At three o'clock when lunch was finished and they were drinking tea in the living room Maureen stood up. "I'm just going to nip to the loo before we head off." She said out loud to Julia whilst looking at Timothy.

He took the hint. "Oh yes, good idea, we should be heading off, we've a few things to do at home.". He stood up too and brushed biscuit crumbs off his trousers. Homemade shortbread had been resting on his saucer and he couldn't resist, despite eating a massive roast dinner and a desert of nutmeg spiced rice pudding, with clotted cream on top.

Maureen had helped clear the table despite being told not to by Julia, that Katherine the housekeeper would do it. Maureen carried on and smiled saying that she was happy to help, which made Julia a little cross, she was not used to people not doing as they were told, and her new daughter-in-law was clearly not used to being told what to do. But she liked her, she thought she would learn, eventually, and she had her son's heart, so clear the tables she would regardless of what Julia said.

Before they got in the car they said their goodbyes. Gentle cheek kisses and unusual, almost arms length hugs that Maureen had worked out was what passed for affection in the Smith big house. Florence stood back from them all with the weight of the world on her shoulders, Maureen stepped towards her and held her in a tight squeeze.

"Fuck the lot of them Florence. Fuck them to their feet. And please come and see me next week, we will have a great time." Maureen whispered into her ear.

"I will, I promise." Florence replied. "And I will fuck the lot of them."

They hugged for longer than made Timothy and Julia comfortable, but nobody said a word.

In the car on the way home few words were spoken, but an awful lot was said. As they headed off the A34 Maureen took a deep breath. "Next bank holiday is Christmas and I'll be spending that at Nanna and Grandad's, who couldn't give a shit if and when I have kids. Will you join me?"

"Well hang on a minute, Mother will be expecting us." Timothy stuttered.

He had always spent Christmas with his mother, with aunts and uncles and extended family coming for lunch.

"I think your mother is expecting a lot of things Timothy, and expectation can lead to disappointment, but what can you do?" She turned slightly in her chair to face him better, knocking her knees on the gear stick which made it tricky to change gear. "And the way she speaks about poor Florence. She has been through so much with that shite of an ex and she needs a bit of love and care, not her divorce mentioned at every opportunity. Do you think you could try and be a bit compassionate and stand up for her, like someone you love who is going through a hard time?"

He nodded as he drove and he never regarded himself as a nodder, he was a talker and a thinker. He nodded because he had no idea what to say and he knew Maureen was right, and he also knew that although he spoke for a living for much of his job he would probably say the wrong thing if he juggled for his words. He never really thought about what Florence had gone through, he was just enjoying being the good son. He wasn't sure what Graham had done to make him a shite of an ex, he just assumed they were getting a divorce because they were, clearly Maureen was aware of more. Timothy found that he was nodding for the rest of the journey, long after Maureen had ceased to converse. Once they got into the house he knew exactly what to say.

"Do you want to sit down and I'll make you a cup of tea?" He asked as he put his key in the door.

She took his hand and kissed him on the mouth wrapping her arms around him while they were still on the front path. "I would love that, thank you." She said as they moved into the house.

He might not know what to say when she dismantled his experience of family, but he knew what to say to try and make her feel better, and she loved that about him. He had an awful lot to learn about real life, and for that she didn't feel quite so delighted and full of love. He busied himself in the kitchen and made a pot of tea carrying it through to the living room on a tray with cups and milk. She was lying on the sofa with her clothes on the floor.

"Shall we give it ten minutes to brew?" she smiled, and he didn't need asking twice.

11- afternoon, freedom day number three.

In the old days, when things started to get difficult between them and Timothy seemed content to watch Maureen become lesser, and, dare it be said, more controllable, Maureen continued to love him. She would think back to when he made her stomach flutter with excitement, when he'd ask her what she thought of something and listened to her response, when he'd tell her she was the most beautiful woman he'd ever seen, and that she was amazing. One day, after she had fallen on ice and broken her flask, he came home from work with a brand new flask with a matching tin sandwich box because he knew she was sad that she had broken the flask nanna had given her when she went away to university. He had it all in a bag with a packet of digestives and a box of tea and he placed it beside her as she sat on the sofa with her sore leg resting on a stool. It was moments like that that made her love him more, and memories like that that kept her with him when the butterflies in her stomach had long since laid down and died. He wasn't the most romantic of men but he did thoughtful things, like making her a really lovely sandwich for the train when she had to go to a conference, or having tea brewing when he knew she would be coming through the front door, when he proofread a piece she was writing for a journal or drove her up to Ambleside when nanna had fallen. Sometimes she'd arrive at the station to catch a train home from Southampton or Portsmouth after visiting the university and there he would be, fresh flask made up, fish and chips wrapped in newspaper by the entrance of the station having driven down from work to get her. They would eat their chips on a road overlooking the sea, once he had a pocket full of pennies for the penny drop machines and they spent an age dropping coins as lights flashed and bells rang on the seafront at Southsea, and they spoke about brining nanna and Grandad down for a holiday before they drove back home with aching smiles and tired eyes.

These moments sustained a lot of disregard. If there was a time scale to the effort that needed to be put into a relationship before you just put up with each other, he had estimated this to be around seven years. After that it seemed that the effort diminished. He still told her he loved her and that she was amazing, but the effort and the outward indication of love didn't go beyond the words. And by that time, with two young children, there was a lot of thinking back to how he used to be, how he was demonstrative and kind, and that sustained her. After forty years there wasn't a drop of sustenance left.

When Maureen finally got out of bed and showered on that third day, with thoughts of Florence telling her that she had done the right thing firmly implanted in her head, she decided that she would have a drive out to Kendal and get to the supermarket. She would fill the kitchen with the things she needed for the next week or so and have a look in a couple of walking shops to see if there was anything she might want. Not need, but want.

There was so much she had left behind with Timothy, things that she would have taken if she had planned, if this was something that she had built up to, but running away didn't always have a big plan around it. She had entertained a flash and gone with it. She didn't want lots, but photos of the kids when they were little, and things that she had been given from nanna and Grandad or her mum, those things she needed to gather when she was back for the birthday party. She didn't want so much that she would need to hire a van, but she wanted enough that it would fill her car up.

Her cottage in Ambleside still had her family at it's very essence, the table that she sat at she had sat at her whole life held up her tea cup, the thick eiderdowns she slept on in this hot sticky weather she would climb under when the winter came were there, they were dusty and slightly musty, but they were like a hug from nanna when you needed cuddles. China from her childhood dangling off hooks on the slightly wonky dresser, mismatched and well used, meant more to her than the matching blue Denby dinner set and matching cups that she left in the big house that was not her home. She would bake and cook using the chipped enamel trays that had been used since nanna had laid money aside for them as a newlywed. She needed very little from the big house, her history books, letters that she received and never threw away, old postcards from old friends, scrapbooks of memories, and that was all. Things that Timothy called clutter because they meant nothing to him. They meant nothing to most people but they were the story of Maureen and she would have to have them. There would be more than enough space to house them in the cottage. She would speak to Florence and ask her if she would come with her to collect them so that there would be less unpleasantness. Or perhaps she would gather some gumption and just do this thing she needed to do with her own strength that, once upon a time, got her where she needed to be

Today she would focus on what she needed from town and a bit of what she wanted, and then if she wanted to nest at home for a few days it wouldn't matter at all. She tried to remember if there was a book shop in Kendal, she considered that there were fewer things better than the smell of a new book as you disappeared into the pages for however long you were able, and she could always pop to Fred's bookshop in Ambleside tomorrow, it's comforting walls stacked high with books.

She packed her purse into her bag and headed out the door, the hot air blowing over her face as soon as she stepped out of the house, uncomfortably warm up her nostrils like the air had stopped being fresh. She hadn't had lunch and she hoped to ponder over something in a cafe, sit by a window if she could and watch the world go by. She thought she might have a look in a couple of dress shops to see if there was something she could wear for the birthday party. She was done with the dresses that Timothy had picked up for her, thinking he was doing a lovely thing, but she never felt comfortable or happy in the skirts and blouses or calf length dress that shouted that she was middle aged or older than she was, even though she knew she was old enough. She didn't feel as old as she was at the moment, she had felt tired and old for so long, but these last few days she felt lighter, younger even, like there was a glimpse of opportunity on the horizon, a glimpse of choice and fresh air and room for her own thoughts and, although that horizon looked so far away, it was closer than it had been in years.

The drive to Kendal always took longer in the summer, edging through Ambleside and then again past Windermere, heading on the road to Ings. She passed the big petrol station and all of the camper vans on the forecourt shone in the sun, promising adventure for the price of a small mortgage, she craned her neck to look at the smaller ones out front with the pop tops reaching up towards the sky. She had said to Timothy as they laid side by side in a small tent in the camping field at Glastonbury before they were married that her dream was to have a Volkswagen camper, to travel over Europe and sleep by lakes and beaches and at the foot of mountains, and eat cheese and bread and pastries every day. Timothy felt the bass of the music bang on his bones and thought anything was better than this musty tent, but really he was a hotel frequenter and would rather have had a week away in a nice hotel than a month away in a camper van. Even though the adventure of being together felt good, it felt nicer to him in a hotel And in the end the camper never came, and by the time they got to travel a bit it was city weekends, which they both loved, but it wasn't quite the romantic isolation she yearned for.

Maureen passed by the campervan dealership and wondered if it was too late to still have that dream, whether she had let too much pass her by. Then she thought of her lovely mum and all that she would have loved to do. She would have to think about money, work out what she had, what was hers. She didn't have to ask anyone permission, every couple of years when Timothy had come home with a brand new car he had never asked first, discussed it, chatted about whether he should stick with the old one. His cars got bigger and more expensive and she was happy to stick with her little run around that had seen her right for a few years. It was big enough to pack up and leave a marriage with, carry her up the motorway when she thought her head would pop, so it would do for a while yet. But the thought of sleeping by lakes and at the foot of mountains lingered in her mind a while.

Maureen parked her little car in the ridiculously small spaces outside Marks and Spencer's and made her way up the high street to find a cafe. She made sure to get one on the side of the road where the sun wasn't shining hard through the window and where shade could be found, it was hot enough outside without sitting behind glass. She managed to get a seat on a table outside, shaded enough to be comfortable and warm enough to feel like she could drop off if she sat for too long. She ordered a lemonade and a sausage roll, which she regretted as pieces of flaky pastry floated from each bite and gathered on the front of her dark top and no amount of brushing could get it all away. It was delicious and warm though, and left a greasy film across her lips that was exactly what a sausage roll should do.

After her lemonade was done she ordered tea and a shortbread biscuit, which turned out to be the size of a plate with great chunks of chocolate dotted about it. She discussed with the waitress when it was delivered to the table that she would never manage to eat it all, the size it was, and then proceeded to finish off every crumb. She paid her bill and made her way back to the car via a few shops where she bought shorts and walking trousers, t-shirts, trainers, a new backpack and a book of Wainwright fells that you could tick off once you'd climbed them. She bought pens, paper and pads as well, envelopes too, in case she wanted to write letters to wherever or whoever.

At the supermarket she bought bulk tea bags and plenty of fresh fruit and veg, things for warm days, lots of cheese and crackers, things for sandwiches and lots that didn't require the oven putting on. If she wanted to stay behind the front door for the next week she wouldn't starve. She could lock the world out or lock herself in and feast like a queen. She had spent plenty, the little catch at the back of her throat kicked in as she paid at the till at all the shops she went in, she was used to justifying what she had bought when she got home, or while they were out if they were together. He wasn't a skinflint, he just wanted to know why she wanted things or why she had to get them now or wouldn't it be better to buy this instead. So it was easier to go without than have the constant discussions to justify wanting something. She knew they had the money. She had her work pension and a lump sum that remained untouched in an account somewhere, and money from her mum that sat, not needed. Accounts in her name for tax purposes he said, but she didn't need anything so they just sat there. Her mum had always said people with money keep their money because they are tight and the rest of us would like a bit more because we want to enjoy it. Maureen wanted to enjoy her money. Buying envelopes and not checking if there were any in the house first would have been met with frowns, but they were beautiful envelopes with little watercolor flowers printed in the bottom corners and embedded with seeds so that when you'd finished reading your letter you could bury them in the garden and watch your envelope grow wildflowers, the thought of it brought joy to Maureen, it made her think of Grandad and his careful collecting of seeds from his vegetables,. He dried them on chipped saucers and cups on the windowsill and then poured them into little labelled envelopes to be planted the following year. It was a delightful thought that you could send joy in the post like that, with inky thoughts scrawled across white paper for others to digest. She would send a letter to Florence when she got home.

It was moments like this, when Maureen felt joy, that she felt guilty also. She knew she was blessed, but not in the religious sense, she was not a believer, so some might call it lucky, but she didn't believe in luck either. She had money, she had a big house that she had lived in and a second house that she had been born in. She didn't have to worry about not being able to afford the heating when it was cold, there was no worry about prices going up and cutting back on food. She felt that, compared to what lots of people were going through, she had no reason to be worried or sad or feel like her life wasn't enough. They had plenty, but none of it was her choice. She had stopped being asked what she wanted, what did she want to eat or wear? Where did she want to go? And she did as she was told. She felt guilty because that had become her choice, to go along with what was expected for ease and because of fear, that she had forgotten to say 'fuck you,' when she had spent her youth being underestimated and shocking people. She had reiterated to the kids time and time again that they should move to the beat of their own drum and not be dancing for someone else, and she felt that she had let them down, becoming a puppet for someone else, when they still needed her fire. And she had let it happen to herself. The fiery twenty five year old Maureen would have shook her head with shame at who she had become, and the thirty five year old Maureen would have sat herself down and had strong words about self respect and priorities. But the forty five year old Maureen who's mum had just died, and who had lost nanna and Grandad not long before, would have just been happy that she was getting out of bed and getting the kids to school, eating bits and not crying every day. The forty five year old Maureen would have liked to lay in bed all day and sleep, and Timothy made sure she was up and doing and sorting. But the gentle direction she needed stopped being gentle direction and became forceful expectation until she just did what she was told. She should have done something sooner, gone back to work, answered back, stood up for herself. She waited to feel like her old self, to feel like she could manage life, but she kept waiting and it never came, like she was lost in her own home, unable to be found. Timothy's controlling behaviour was incremental, she didn't wake up one morning and find he was changed and she was silent, it came in layers, tiny changes, different expectations that left her deeper in her reliance on him, as she struggled with grief and loss.

Maureen drove on the winding roads back to the cottage and felt ashamed. What took her so long? How did she let all of this life pass her by so she was a beige woman by a beige wall waiting to be told what to do. She had been out adrift so long she had expected to stay there, and all of a sudden she was out, she had reached dry land, but such a lot of wasted time.

"Stop it." She said out loud to herself.

She turned radio four on to distract herself from her own narrative. She was here now. It took some time but she was here. She had woken up and stoked her fire and now it appeared to be burning just fine, after all this time. Aside from the guilt and the fury that she had wasted all that time, she was here and she was more herself than she had felt in years. She had been telling herself so many stories about herself that she believed them. She believed that she couldn't manage and she needed looking after, needed direction, needed permission, and then out of nowhere she remembered who she was and how capable she was, how fiery, how she took no nonsense and here she was with a car full of what she wanted driving back to her beautiful, slightly musty, tired and comfortable cottage making her own choices. She just needed Timothy to understand that they were done, or not even understand, just know that this was her decision and there wasn't going back. She wasn't going to lose herself again, not now. All she wanted was her pension, her mum's money and the cottage, and the sentimental things from the kids, everything else he could keep, she didn't care for it or need it.

She was startled out of her thoughts by her phone ringing through the radio. It was Lilly.

"Hello love, how are you doing?"

"Oh Mum, it's so lovely to hear your voice. I'm good. Are you ok?"

Maureen felt her eyes getting damp. "Yes love, I'm doing good. I'm just driving back home from Kendal."

"You're going back? To dad?"

"Oh sorry Lilly, I mean the cottage, I'm going back to your Nanna's." It was still Nanna's house, Nanna and Grandad's house to Maureen, nanna's house to the kids.

"Well bloody hell, I thought I was going to have to come and give you a shake, thinking you were going back to dad. How are you really doing? Are you pleased to be up there?" Lilly spoke gently, as if she was fearful her mum might break.

"Honestly Lilly I'm doing really well. I feel bloody pleased to be up here, like it's been too long, I left it too long, I should have done this before now. Sorry love, I don't mean to speak badly of your dad, but I think he's enjoyed me being not able to manage. And I'm so sorry that I haven't been what you needed for so long."

"Mum!" Lilly almost shouted. "Don't be apologising for a second. You've been the best mum ever forever. Don't think you haven't. You've just been sad for a long time."

They spoke all the way back home in the car, Lilly calling back every time the reception went and they were spat out of the call, which happened quite a bit in the rugged landscape of the lakes. They carried on talking when Maureen was parked outside the cottage, she sat in the car in the late afternoon heat with beads of sweat occasionally rolling down her face like hot, salty tears, her nose glistening despite the open window. Lilly had told her more than once over the years that she should get away, come and stay with her or go up to the cottage, or to a friend's, but Maureen always declined, she didn't want to impose or be a nuisance. Timothy overheard once and told Lilly to stop being melodramatic, stop upsetting her mother and he went on for some time that they would go away for a break together and that Maureen wasn't ill, she was tired but fine, so Lilly could drop it and stop fussing. Lilly tried to visit when she knew her dad would be away, and her mum would be more visibly relaxed and capable, laughing more freely and working on her own time scale. There was no getting up suddenly because it was Timothy's coffee time, or he would be expecting lunch, or needed a lift back from a meeting where he had drunk plenty of wine. She visited when he was there too so she could see how it was, but those visits tended to be shorter. And Maureen had been diminishing for twenty years, the quiet, mousey woman was who people knew. Timothy always knew how to put on a show in company, the gentle husband, the kindly man looking after his shy, quiet wife. There would be those who knew Maureen of old, who could hold the interest of a group of students talking about modern history, who would hold her corner in any discussion and put up with no nonsense from anyone. Her eye contact was legendary, her response when cross or crossed impeccable, her ability to manage Julia and Timothy was envied by Florence and the wider family. And then slowly, but surely, she crumbled. Until now. Those of old would recognise her now. Her mum would know her now. She knew herself again now.

It was just over a week until Julia's ninetieth birthday and Lilly and Maureen were excited to see each other there. Maureen had told Lilly that she would be going and then travelling straight back to Ambleside afterwards. She told her there would be questions, awkwardness and potential confrontation between her and Timothy, but it would be done behind closed doors, no one else at the party would need to know unless Timothy made it public, for show, and she knew he wouldn't. He couldn't bear to be vulnerable in public, or private for that matter. She knew he'd be all smiles, trying to gather her in when she was already gone. She just had to get through the party and come home. It was an awful anticipation.

Neither Lilly or Maureen knew if Marcus would be at the party, but they suspected not. He was on a dig in Mexico, Lilly said, she'd let him know that her mam had moved up to Ambleside and he'd said 'OK'. He was a man of few words, unless it was talking about an archaeological dig, then it was explanations in the minutest detail that went on for as long as time and patience would allow.

After she had said goodbye to Lilly Maureen exited the greenhouse that was her car. Her buttocks were so damp she felt like she had had an accident, but she could have talked to Lilly for hours. She started carrying the shopping into the house, walking to the back of the house to put the food into the kitchen. It had been sitting in the hot car long enough. She had to make several journeys, getting hotter with each march back to the car. She was almost done, huffing and puffing up the corridor, ready to nest in for the evening, just one bag to go, then to lock up the car and the house and get the kettle on. Her eyes were adjusting to the dark of the house and then the light of the sun and she let out a shriek as she made her way back outside towards the front door, blinking at the brightness. There he was, in the doorway, about to invite himself into the house.

"Maureen!" he said, almost shouting, almost touching her.

12- territories.

By the time Autumn fully hit Oxford in 1984, and the rainy days mushed slippery leaves onto the pavements and parks Maureen and Timothy had got themselves into a contented newly married regimen. Early mornings for Timothy, driving down to work in Winchester and later evenings for Maureen as she juggled teaching with research. She was strict with timings, Tuesdays and Thursdays she would stay in the library until nine o'clock and make sure she had crammed as much as she could into those precious hours without too much distraction. She would get home, shattered, eating toast for tea with jam or cheese and Timothy would arrive home about the same time having been to Mother's for supper, to enjoy whatever feast the housekeeper had made. He and Mother would sit a good distance apart on the giant dining table and chat formalities. Mother would always comment that Maureen should be there, or home at the very least, and Timothy would change the subject. Mother would say that surely he was making enough money for both of them, and he was. He agreed with his mother to some extent, but was also proud that he was able to tell people that his beautiful wife was doing a PhD at Oxford. He would have liked her to be at home and he would have reduced his suppers with Mother to once weekly, ideally Maureen would go with him, even though he knew Maureen would not have been excited by that idea. Mother had expectations and Maureen had no time for tongue biting. He wasn't entirely sure who made him more nervous, and so this separate visiting with a reasonable excuse suited him perfectly, his nerves were less fraught about conversation when it was only him. Occasionally there would be plenty of leftovers and it would be packed into foil for him to carefully take home on a tin plate for Maureen when she got back from work. Maureen loved those days, when she would arrive home shattered and the smell of heating food would greet her at the door, and she could forget about putting the grill on and burning the Sunblest. Although often cheese on toast and some of Nanna's chutneys hit the spot perfectly. The sweet and sour of the vinegary vegetables that had been grown by Grandad was a little tingle of home on her tongue, a taste of autumn and childhood and all that was well with the world. Nanna had posted down 2 of her latest autumn jars from granddad's glut of sun grown vegetables, wrapped in a tea towel and several layers of cardboard, and they had arrived intact. Maureen and Timothy had cut off a great hunk of cheese each and smeared a whole teaspoon of chutney across the top of it and placed it on a slice of apple. Maureen's excitement at the parcel and then the tasting was contagious, Timothy was excited to taste what was bringing his wife such delight. The day the chutney arrived they had both been home at a reasonable time and after the first taste they decided they would have cheese and biscuits for tea, with bread, salad and crisps, then they would sit on the sofa and doze in front of whatever rubbish was on, their dwindling feast laid out in front of them on the coffee table, neither of them stopping eating when they were long past full.

Every couple of weeks something would arrive in the post hidden in the porch behind a Wellington boot. Something delicious with a letter from nanna. Maureen would set-to replying and send pages of what they had both been up to, what they had eaten, where they had been. Nanna and Grandad loved getting those letters, nanna would put the kettle on and make a brew and they would sit together at the kitchen table, nanna reading aloud to Grandad, and then Grandad would read it to himself so he could see her lovely swirly writing and think of her sat scribbling, with the tip of her tongue poking out from her lips as she concentrated. She would tell them about her research and how her thesis was going, what Timothy was up to, which nanna loved but Grandad not so much, although that was never said out loud.

Sometimes Timothy would be home well before nine o'clock and she would come home to him fast asleep on the sofa with the television blasting the news. She would turn it down a bit and leave him sleeping so she could enjoy being in the house without having to chat about the whole day. She had lived alone for some time before they met and she loved the quietness of being home and just nesting amongst all of her things without having to explain anything to anyone. She enjoyed living with Timothy but it was taking a bit of getting used to not being in her own company so much. A couple of times he had been in a stag do for someone from work or an old school friend and she had revelled in the quiet of the house, eating something simple and tidying around before getting into bed with a pot of tea and a book. Once when he was away she had caught an early Saturday train up to Oxenholme and then on to Windermere and then hitched on up to Ambleside to surprise her mum, Nanna and Grandad, staying until the early train Monday morning. She loved being in the house with them, with the gentle routine and the hours sitting around the kitchen table chatting, everyone telling stories of what they had been up to, or a walk into town so that nanna could show everyone her beloved granddaughter.

Maureen felt pangs of homesickness when she was away from the cottage, even in her own house, which was her cosy home, it never had the same feel, but she knew it was about the people and not the walls. Her people were in Ambleside. She considered that Timothy was one of her people, she had married him after all, she missed him when she was away, but she always considered Oxford to be temporary, even after buying a house there.

On the weekends in Oxford Maureen and Timothy would spend a day in town, getting shopping and having a bit of lunch before Maureen would head off for an afternoon of study, and then on a Sunday it would be tea in a flask and sandwiches and a walk somewhere, even if it rained she loved to be out exploring. Timothy was less keen on rainy walks but more than happy if any walk led to somewhere they could get food, regardless of whether there was a tin of sandwiches in Maureen's rucksack. He didn't share her joy of sitting on the edges of your coat under a tree in the rain eating whatever had been packed, but he was happy to sit just to be close to her. He was happier if they were sat in a pub where there was a possibility of something covered in gravy. Of all his fine dining experiences, and the places he had been, he would rather have a pint and a Sunday pub roast any day.

Florence had been up to visit, without Mother who declined the offer of a trip but agreed she would come another time for the day. Everyone, including Julia, was relieved that Julia was not going to be in the house, she was pleased that she wouldn't have to stay and share the bathroom and possibly sit and dine in a kitchen, and everyone else was happy that there would be no air of expectation and disappointment with an array of helpful comments to sit amongst. Florence and Maureen had been on the promised girls night out, with some of Maureen's friends. They had been out to dinner and then on for cocktails and dancing. Timothy was put out that his idea of the three of them going out for dinner was turned down in preference of a night of drinking with the girls, he thought it poor taste that his thirty-two year old sister was behaving like a teenager, it didn't dawn on him that she could behave exactly how she pleased as a single woman away on a break. He was even more disgusted the following morning after he had heard Florence retching into the toilet as he was lying in bed. He woke Maureen to say he thought his sister was ill. Maureen reassured him that Florence was merely hungover and she got out of bed to check on her and get her some water and tea. Florence had let her hair down and thoroughly enjoyed herself. She had drank away the demons that were at her newly divorced door, raised a glass to Graham and his newly pregnant twenty year old girlfriend. She had shed a tear in the night club toilets, danced her legs off and would not remember very much of it at all. It was what she needed, although the full force of the beer fear that gripped her as she coughed out her insides in the bathroom for all to hear was less than welcome. Maureen took her in some tea and biscuits, orange juice and paracetamol as Florence was settling down back into bed.

"Oh God, my head is banging." Florence said, covering her eyes with her hands.

"Right then, have these and drink all of the juice and tea, have another hour's kip and you'll feel loads better when you wake." Maureen instructed, handing Florence the tablets. Maureen had only had a couple of cocktails when she saw how much Florence was drinking, she knew both of them without legs could have gone horribly wrong. As it was they had both had a brilliant night and Maureen was thankful her head was straight

Maureen took her own cup of tea back to bed, and one for Timothy who had woken in disgust at the sound of his vomiting sister and was lying on the edge of the bed. He was appalled at the state Florence had been in when she finally got through the front door last night, and he had been in the process of telling them both what he thought. Maureen had reminded him that Florence was in her thirties and did not need permission or judgement from anyone, least of all him, and he had slunk back to the kitchen to make drinks for everyone.

When they had got into bed Timothy had coughed a little. "Really Maureen, I need to tell you something."

"No you don't, you want to tell me something, and if it's about how drunk Florence is, or how late we are, or any hint at a disappointment then you can save your thoughts for yourself." Maureen said firmly.

Timothy thought for a moment as Maureen continued to look directly at him, as if she was daring him to make a comment. After a few moments he thought better of it and turned away from her to go to sleep, which took some time as he was fuming inside, but attempting to swallow it down. He had never seen a woman that drunk. He had been to his share of stag parties and seen university friends have a last Hurrah, but he couldn't imagine seeing his own sister in that state until now. He twitched on his pillow until sleep caught him but the sound of the retching and the thought of his giggling, swaying, quiet sister coming through the front door was too much first thing in the morning. He sat up as Maureen came back into the room with the tea.

"Really Maureen, I expected better from you both. Why did you not tell her to stop drinking?" he said as she handed him his cup.

"Hells bells Timothy, she's in her 30s. Her husband left her for a twenty year old who is having his baby now and she's fed up. If she needs to dance or drink it out and shake off all of that fucking expectation then good for her." Maureen was whispering loudly.

"But what must people think?" Timothy spluttered.

"What people, who?" Maureen stared at him and he didn't answer. "You mean you, what do you think? It doesn't matter what you think. How about you think 'my poor sister has been through shit and held her head high and she's let her hair down this weekend and cried and laughed and just not done what the judgement police expected and she's fabulous. And she is Timothy, she's bloody amazing and you should be supporting her a little better." Maureen sipped her tea in bed with a calmness that did not represent the anger that she was feeling inside. "I didn't even meet the man, but who judged Graham? Where was all that judgement then when he did what he did? When he left the person he promised to love forever because his ego and fuck knows what else needed stroking? I haven't known Florence long at all but she's diminished in front of us and we need to build her not take her down. Do you understand that?"

Timothy put his cup down and leaned on his side so that he was facing Maureen. "I get it, I do." He said.

"She needs us just to be there for her, for you to see your brilliant sister and just be kind. Do you get that?" Maureen yawned.

"You should have done law instead of history you know, you'd be cracking in court. You'd win every time." Timothy laughed. She had the ability to defuse and argue at the same time.

"Well just remember that when you're trying to argue with me." Maureen laughed.

They snuggled down back into bed, the November morning was cold and there was no heating. They had an open fire with a back boiler and it wasn't lit. They had been avoiding lighting it but it was definitely time to put some heat into the house. Maureen put her cold feet onto Timothy's legs and he let her keep them there. She deserved to be warm after looking after his sister, she was here in bed with him and he couldn't believe his luck. He was still appalled at the sound of his sister vomiting in the toilet next to their bedroom, and he couldn't understand why she had drunk so much, but Maureen was right, she had lost her sparkle and he would try and look after her a bit better, he would take them out for Sunday dinner. He loved a roast when he'd had a few the night before, and without any questions from Mother whatsoever.

"Do you fancy a drive out later and we'll take Flo for lunch at the Kings Head?" Timothy asked.

She squeezed him tightly and told him it was a brilliant idea. "I'm going for a wee and I'm going to make another cuppa. Do you want one?" She asked.

He had never known anyone drink so much tea. When they went up to her grandparents it was a constant, the pot was always full or being refreshed, or he was being asked if he wanted the kettle putting on. And it was flasks away from home. He loved that they sat and drank tea together and just relaxed. No sitting around a long table or taking refreshments in the drawing room, just being together and chatting because that was how they did things.

"Yes please," He replied to the offer of more tea. He didn't really want another but he wanted to sit up in bed with her and chat.

"I'm going to light the fire too, it's bloody freezing." She was pulling a jumper over her head followed by some thick socks. "We need to get more blankets out for the bed, too."

She disappeared out of the bedroom door with their empty cups in her hands. He heard her quietly open the door of the spare room where Florence was sleeping and then close it again, he assumed that Florence must have been fast asleep and she was checking on her. That's what Maureen did, he thought, she looked after people. She looked after nanna and Grandad, making sure to write letters and send them things and visit regularly. She even looked after Mother, taking her things that she thought she might like. Even when Maureen felt that she had been insulted or Mother had been her usual undiplomatic self, Maureen still sent her things or sent him down with something. She looked after her people and he was her people too. He felt pleased with himself. He felt certain she would look after him too. It didn't really dawn on him that he should go out of his way to look after her as well, beyond the surface mutual reciprocation, but really look after this woman who he loved beyond measure. He didn't quite know how.

It was agreed that their first Christmas as a married couple would be spent in Ambleside, much to the disgust of Julia, who normally catered for festivities and bank holidays. Although the thought hadn't crossed Timothy's mind, Maureen was mindful that Florence was potentially being left to the wolves, to have her choices and plans picked through at the Smith's annual festivities that would take place on boxing day evening, when family gathered at Winchester and put on their best clothes and best faces and competed with each other as to who had had the most successful year, and if someone could be picked apart the outer regions of the family would swarm.

Florence was not an easy target, she was comfortable, she was a doctor, she was bright and normally could hold her own, but she was also recently betrayed and the Smith family gatherings were not the place for sympathy. The previous year, when Maureen was new to the family and the gathering was on new year's eve, the impending divorce was not yet common knowledge, Maureen had heard people discussing that Timothy was going out with a northerner that no one had heard of. Where had she come from? Was she after the money? Maureen had laughed out loud and turned to the accusers who were not aware she was in ear shot and told them she was able to answer all of their questions if they asked her directly, but nothing was asked and she laughed to herself as she walked away.

Maureen agreed they would go up to Ambleside on the twenty second of December, and leave early on boxing day to drive straight down to Winchester. If the roads were quiet and the weather on their side they might just make it for one o'clock, they could have lunch, exchange gifts and get ready for the evening party. She longed to be sat around her grandparents kitchen table, peeling sprouts that had been carefully planted and picked by Grandad. There would be homemade stuffing, chopped within an inch of its life by Nanna, honey glazed carrots, crispy roast potatoes, mashed potatoes, turkey and beef, Yorkshire's, parsnips, pigs in blankets, carrot and turnip mash and the richest gravy that ever did enter your mouth. Maureen had spent many a happy hour sitting around the kitchen table and preparing vegetables as tea was drunk, with the occasional glass of damson gin. A Christmas record would be playing its dizzy tunes from the living room, with a slight crackle from being overplayed.

The evening of the twenty second was always the Christmas walk about, a tradition for as long as Maureen could remember, when they would don on their thick coats, gloves and boots and make their way around the streets of the big houses looking into windows at the amazing trees, beautifully decorated and glistening with their lights, bright against the dark evening. It was not lost on her that had she lived in Winchester it was likely that they would have been peeping into the vast bay window of Timothy's house, she would have been assuming as a child that the bigger the house, the greater the magic of Christmas. She had come to understand that sitting around the kitchen table with the music playing, cracking open the Christmas cheeses and opening the box of mixed crackers was where the magic was. Where her family was.

As the five of them walked round eyeing up Christmas trees and decorations after the long drive up from Oxford, Maureen wondered if it would seem odd to Timothy that they would go looking in people's windows as they walked up and down the hilly streets, ending up in the town square where the carollers would be singing, clutching candles for lights and buckets for donations. He never spoke much about Christmas traditions or what they did as a family other than the extended family get together. He said there was no opening gifts until after they had eaten lunch, even when he was very small, which Maureen told him she thought was cruel, to make a child wait for their gifts, to see what Father Christmas had brought. There was no putting out pillow cases and thick woolly walking socks on Christmas eve in anticipation for Father Christmas. Even after Maureen was well past believing, the pillow cases would still be out, with a stocking full of little treats, including chocolates and a satsuma. She knew there would be a pillow case for Timothy in Nanna and Grandad's living room come Christmas morning, whether he wanted it or not. The family would gather in the kitchen and make a tray of tea and then they would enter the lounge to see if Father Christmas had come. Even at the age of twenty six the thought of it fluttered butterflies of excitement across Maureen's stomach.

They stood in the square listening to the carollers, with rumbling stomachs, ready to go home and have a late tea of sandwiches and chips. The potatoes were cut and cooked on the stove, ready to hit the chip pan, the triangles of sandwiches were sat in the fridge under cling film, triangles because it was a special occasion, square sandwiches would not do three days before Christmas. Nanna took Timothy's arm and they walked together, chatting on their way back to the house, with Maureen, Grandad and Coral following behind. As soon as they were all in the front door the fire was lit, and they each had a small sherry glass of damson gin. The best glasses had been gathered from the display cabinet, delicate, with tiny gold leaves gathered around the top of each glass. Even the good china was being used to serve sandwiches, this was Christmas after all. They sat around the table, their cheeks rosy from going from cold to warm, listening to the fizz of the chip pan as it whispered loudly to the potatoes. This was what they did every December the twenty second, every bit of their traditions were knitted around excitement for the big day. Even when Maureen was very young and money was tight, the magic flowed and the togetherness was what it was all about for them. When the tears flowed after school because someone had made the point that Father Christmas must have put her on the naughty list, because her presents were next to nothing she sat, after school, enveloped by Nanna.

"What was your favourite thing about Christmas?" Nanna asked. "Was it getting the present off Father Christmas ?"

"Yes." Maureen sobbed, thinking of her lovely little doll. "But also dinner, and the decorations, and the crackers, and watching that film with Grandad, and the marshmallows on the fire."

"Lovely girl, Christmas is about us all being together and getting your present was just part of it. Pay no attention to those girls. The present you get isn't the mark of who you are or how good you've been, it's part of the magic of Christmas, not all of it. And we had a lovely time didn't we? With so much magic Father Christmas knows he doesn't have to leave a massive present." Nanna hugged Maureen tightly until the tears subsided and Grandad got home from work and asked if she wanted to play some snakes and ladders, which she always did.

Timothy devoured his sandwiches and chips, amazed that it tasted so good. He was used to events, sitting around a dining table and being served if it was a gathering. It hadn't dawned on him that this wasn't a gathering, it was family getting together, without formalities or expectations. It was everyone mucking in rather than waiting to be served by whoever was in the kitchen. If you wanted a drink you got up and made one, but you better ask if anyone else wanted one at the same time, he learned that pretty quickly in this house. It was not every man for himself, it was a place to share, and drown in tea. If there were leaves left in the pot, past recycling, you walked outside and tipped them onto the compost heap and started again. He liked being part of this family, but he liked waiting to be served more. This mucking in was still a novelty to him, the novelty would wear off soon.

Despite being full to the brim Nanna popped the cake tins on the table with a familiar clatter, there was an iced Christmas cake, unsliced. There was a rule in the house that you didn't cut the cake until the twenty second, even if the Queen came on the twenty first, Grandad would always laugh, that cake was not to be cut and she would have to make do with a slice of sponge.

Aside from the bright white Christmas cake there was also mince pies and ginger biscuits. The mince pies were splattered with the caramelised, sugary, mince meat juice that had made its way out of the pastry lid and spread across the edges of the pie, sweet and chewy when you sunk your teeth into it. It was a batch of a hundred and forty four mince pies that Nanna made every year for visitors, or to take to people's houses when she went. Her home made mince meat was legendary and the pies were a gift people hoped to receive, wrapped tightly in a brown paper bag, tied with string. Nanna had a jar that she kept under the sink, any change or money in pockets before washes, profits from cakes sold, wedding cakes or christening cakes, would be put into the jar for Christmas and birthdays, so there could be gifts and they could feast like kings. When Coral started teaching and paid her housekeeping money that would be popped in there too, so Nanna felt she had quite the stash at times. There was no family money passed down the generations, people paid to do things for you, it was making ends meet, mending broken things, keeping things going for another few months, like lots of other people they knew. And Maureen knew none of it because worrying about money was not something they shared with a child. The overtime Grandad had to do or odd jobs when he was out of work was not something that Maureen ever noticed, however tired he was he always had time to read Maureen a story, or fix something for Nanna, he would often sit in his chair "resting his eyes" as Nanna said, tired out from the demands on his broad shoulders.

Timothy chose a tiny sliver of Christmas cake and a mince pie. Whatever money his family had, the food he had eaten around this kitchen table over the last year and a half was the most delicious he had ever had. It was better than the banquets he had been to, or fine restaurants he had entertained people at. It was where Maureen was happiest, where he knew she yearned to be, and he was happy to be beside her, he wasn't so keen on the expectation that he would muck in with the washing up after, he would never be expected to do that at Mother's, it was someone else's job and it went on out of sight.

After everything was cleared away a big box of chocolates were placed in the middle of the table by Maureen and the playing cards taken out of the kitchen drawer ready for a game of Find The Lady or Black Jack. It was nine thirty and Maureen was yawning her way through the evening, tired after the long drive north but desperate to cram in as much family time and tradition as she could muster. She was never the first to retire but as soon as one of them stood up and said goodnight she would be off to bed straight after them. She was shattered with all of the studying she had been doing, late nights reading, timetabled lessons and looking after the house. She wasn't sure that Timothy was aware of the amount she was doing at home, he was used to people doing things for him. It was nice to be up in Ambleside for Maureen, where Nanna and Mum would fuss her and look after her. She would sit on the two seater sofa, next to her mum, lying sideways with her legs resting on Coral's knees listening to her mum tell tales about the Christmas Nativity at school, the things that had gone wrong and the teachers stifled giggles. At some point over the Christmas break Maureen and Coral would take a walk and catch up, just the two of them. Maureen had been raised by three parent figures and sometimes Coral felt a little on the side lines, as grateful as she was that her parents had done what they had to support her, enabled her to train to be a teacher when having a young child would have dictated otherwise, it was good having a little Mother and daughter time, when they got together, with maybe a glass of wine and a bag of crisps in the pub on the way home, or an early morning march with a scurry home to warm up. Coral wanted to find out how Maureen really was behind the excitement of newly wed bliss,

 They walked with the cold wind whipping at their faces, very early in the morning. It was Christmas eve and the sun was just throwing colour on the clouds, making them appear slightly lighter than the black of the rest of the sky, creeping the morning in. Maureen had left Timothy fast asleep in bed, a cup of tea beside him getting colder as he snored. He wasn't the early riser Maureen was, he was happy to stay up past midnight and then lay in as long as possible. Maureen was ready for bed at nine, and if she was asleep past six in the morning it was a lie-in.

They were heading up to Stock Ghyll Force and then through footpaths back down the Kirkstone road, if it wasn't icy, but there was no rain, just the need for gloves and a hat for the winter day. There was less talking as they walked uphill but they still got plenty of chatter in. Maureen told her mum about Florence and their night out, the expectations of Julia and her blunt inquiries.

"She infuriates me." Maureen said. "And I don't think anyone ever tells her it's not appropriate, or it's not her right to ask or know. I heard her saying to Timothy that I should be giving up my job to look after him if we didn't have any help. Like, no questions about my research or teaching or new discoveries, just is Timothy getting his tea on time?"

"And what did Timothy say to her?" Coral enquired.

"He told her he was fine." Maureen rolled her eyes. "Not that he's capable of making tea or he's a grown up, just that he's fine. But that's their normal, Mum, that's how they are, the men must be looked after. But they all need bloody looking after, she doesn't even make her own cup of tea or breakfast. To have that much money, or that little idea of life."

"So it's going well with the mother in law then?" Coral laughed, and then they both laughed together as they walked across the field with torches in their hands.

"Florence is lovely though, Mum, she's not like her mother at all. She's been through shit and she's still getting up and going to work and putting up with her bloody mother! She's got the measure of things. She works in a really rough area in Portsmouth, so she'll see a few things. Got a bit more of an idea of what life is like, more so than them."

"Them?" Coral asked. "You mean Timothy as well?"

"I love the bones of him, Mum, but yes, he doesn't really know how the other half live. There's a lot of explaining to be done, when the news is on or when there's someone begging. He's seen it all before but not really thought about it. But I guess that goes with the money and all the bloody expectations. If you're poor it's because you're not working hard enough, or you need a better job."

"But that'll be how he has been raised, us and them. You only know what you know." Coral tried to be kind.

"Well I've a lot of educating to do then Mum, good job I know how to teach." Maureen smiled. "But there is one more thing you need to know, Mum."

Coral held her breath for a moment, hoping that Maureen wasn't pregnant yet, that she could finish her research and get her PhD, her clever girl who was mocked for being a bastard. "What's that then?"

"He loves Thatcher." Maureen said loudly.

"Fuck me." Coral shouted, disgusted and relieved at the same time. "I'm not even going there, love, not this close to Christmas day." And they both trudged across the grass sniggering with each other.

By the time they got home the house was up and about, with the Christmas record playing loudly and Nanna dancing as she fried bacon in the pan. Timothy was buttering bread whilst swaying to the music and occasionally stopping to twirl Nanna as she danced, when she would laugh loudly at the delight of it all. It was a lovely scene to come home to and Maureen felt her heart could burst with love for both of them.

"Perfect timing." Nanna said as she saw them standing at the door. "I thought you'd be about an hour and a half when I heard the front door go."

"You're up early, love." Maureen said to Timothy.

"I heard the music and the pans and thought there would be breakfast cooking. You told me Christmas eve was bacon butties for breakfast and I wasn't about to miss that." He smiled.

Maureen set about laying the table and putting the kettle on. Grandad was lighting the fire in the living room, the bucket of ashes ready to go on the compost sitting by the back door. You poured the ashes with your eyes and mouth firmly closed for as long as possible. It wasn't a job that anyone enjoyed, especially on a windy day. There was a list of jobs that needed doing, collecting the vegetables that weren't in storage in the house already, getting some milk and cream and getting the meat. Maureen and Timothy volunteered to do the collecting, then the afternoon would be spent on the preparation. It was Maureen's favourite day, full of anticipation and excitement, with all of her favourite people, and the occasional black cloud thought about leaving in two days and the journey south. She would shake off the thoughts and try to be present in the moment, rather than dwell, but it was easier said than done.

13- front door.

There he was, standing in the doorway, half in and half out. He was wearing a shirt and tie with a blazer, as if he was dressed for a business meeting rather than the heat of a June day in the Lake District. There was no other version of him, other than business, something to be sorted, a problem to solve, a business to acquire. And he had driven all of this way to sort out this latest problem, the problem being Maureen. He had cancelled his meetings, his afternoon golf, his supper out in the club, or rather his assistant had, because he had a pressing engagement. He had given her more than enough time to get this silliness out of her system and he thought he better come and get her. She must be having some sort of do or breakdown and she needed his help.

She stood in the corridor, in the shadows of the house he should have insisted harder was sold long ago. She stood with her wild curly hair resting on her shoulders and stuck to her glistening face. She was wearing shorts and a t-shirt and walking boots, looking like she was just about to climb a fell rather than shop. He had watched her carry the shopping in, a lightness about her, no blouse and skirt that she had become accustomed to wearing. She looked young and so beautiful it still took his breath away, made it catch in the back of his throat and gave him butterflies and nerves, the same ones he had managed to shake off over the last few years. But they were back, making him feel vulnerable and lost and like he wasn't in control, and he needed to be in control.

"Can I come in?" He said, trying to smile, trying to remember who she was.

"No, don't come in." She said, moving towards him. The shock of seeing him there was wearing off and she found that she wasn't afraid or anxious, she was livid. "I told you not to come."

"I know, but I was worried you might be unwell, my darling, not yourself." He tried to sound caring.

She looked at him and knew the words coming out of his mouth were not what he was thinking at all. He wasn't worried about her, he was worried for himself, for his loss. "No, Timothy, I am myself." She moved closer to the door, so he could see her in the daylight. "Let me tell you this very clearly. I am completely myself. I am not ill, although I have been over the last few years, and now I am myself."

"We need to sit down and talk. See if we can't get past this week and sort it all out, put this silliness to one side." He continued to smile but his voice was getting louder. She could see a line of perspiration forming under his chest, seeping through his pale blue shirt.

"No, we don't need to sit and talk. I've told you we are done and there's nothing else to say. I will see you at your mother's birthday, as agreed, and then that's it." She was firm and clear.

He hit the door frame in frustration. "You don't get to decide all of this. This is not your decision to make. You need to come home. We can leave your car here and you can drive back with me. Like the old days. Make a flask and we can drink tea on the journey." His voice went from anger to panic. He needed her to go home with him. Today. Right now.

He leaned into the doorway and tried to take her arm, hoping to get a firm grip of her, and wanting to feel her skin in his hands at the same time. Maureen whipped her arm back, so that she was out of reach and he stepped forward into the corridor.

"Get out of my house." She said, "Get back in your car and go. I am not going anywhere with you today or ever. I can't make myself more clear. I am already home."

He looked at her, he was at a loss, she was right, she was herself. She was the woman he spent years slightly nervous around in case she saw through him, the woman he might have let disappear around the corner the first day he saw her, the woman he had managed to calm and quiet more recently. He needed her so much and she didn't need him at all anymore, she had never needed him, she wanted him, but never needed. In the last few years he thought she needed him, and she thought she did at times, but it was not her, it was temporary. He was like a magician making her think she'd seen magic when she was really just looking in the wrong place and missed the slight of hand. He almost convinced her that she couldn't be without him. Almost.

She took a couple of steps forward. "You come in this house and I will call the police, and they will make you leave."

"I can make things very difficult for you." He said, wide eyed and angry.

"You have, you have done that for years. And I'm not afraid of you at all, for a moment. You seem to forget what I can do, what I know, the people you've pissed off. I am not intimidated by you in the slightest." She lied well. "We can both play your game, you know, and you also know how hard I can play when pushed. I am myself again and you should go."

He stepped back out of the doorway, back into the front path, his eyes remained fixed on her. He knew she was finding her strength but he hoped that she had some doubt there, that she remained faded and this was bravado. He loved her so much, he couldn't function without her being with him, without knowing she was his. He was sure that all he had done was look after her, manage her when she was lost and she had finally stopped fighting against him, she had stopped arguing and saying no, and now this, this refusal to see sense and let him look after her, it was madness. He felt his breath in his chest, his heart was beating in his ears and everything seemed silent apart from the drumming.

Her car boot was open, she couldn't leave it like that. She would have to walk past him and grab the last of any shopping, lock it and get back in the house. Her mouth was dry, heat and nerves removing any moisture. Every cell in her body was fuming that he was here, it was surprising and expected in equal measure. It was proof, which she was certain she didn't need, that she had made the right decision to leave. She had her house keys in her hand with her car keys. She shut the front door behind her knowing it would lock and walked down the path giving him a wide berth, she grabbed one last bag, shut the boot, locked the car and walked back up the path. As she walked past him he reached out to try and take her hand, and for the briefest of moments the ends of his fingers grazed the back of her hand making her falter slightly. She turned to him as she pulled her hand away. "No, Timothy, not anymore." She saw the desperation and panic in his eyes, the fear that took him down this path and trapped her with it. She looked away and walked as calmly as she could to the door, opening it with a shaking hand she hoped he could not see. Any sense of anxiety would give him ammunition to think this was a temporary moment of madness on her part, rather than the clarity she had finally found. She opened the door and locked it again behind her, it was heavy and made a bang as it found its frame with more force than she was expecting. She put on the deadlock and ran to make sure the back door was locked, even though he had no way of getting into the back. Then she went upstairs to the front bedroom, taking the stairs two by two in haste. She kneeled in the shadows so he would not be able to see her but so would be able to see when he went out of the gate.

He stood in the front garden for longer than he thought he would, looking at the house, so familiar to him and yet something he was never really part of, he convinced himself he had been sat on the periphery even though he had been welcomed with open arms and been part of the joy. He knew the way her mother looked at him, as if he was a stranger in the house. She never said it with her words but her face said it all. Even twenty years dead she had an influence on Maureen that disgusted him to his core. He should have insisted this house was sold, where would she have gone then, a few nights in a hotel would have seen her back looking for the comforts of home. But this place was something else, was it possible to hate a building? And it was hers, the deeds were hers, and all of that money from her mother and her pension and his investments, just sat in an account under her name, years ago he could have sorted that, but not now, not without her being able to cause a great deal of bother for him. She didn't have a clue how much money she had, what she actually owned, that he was keeping from her. This fucking house and the bastards who had been in it, they always kept a piece of her, so she was never wholly his. He hoped they would rot in hell.

He remembered the feeling of coming here and being part of something, seeing her face beaming in the kitchen as she chatted with her Nanna, as he ate some cake, as her mother watched him, weighing him up. That joy he felt in his heart. He would burn it all down if he could, see where she would go then. He could feel his face getting hotter, his mouth dryer and he needed to go and get a drink, he was shattered, he had definitely overdone himself but, he wouldn't tell anyone else that.

The squeak of the gate opening could be heard in the front bedroom, drifting through the open window. Maureen held her breath as she watched him open the gate, which swung closed behind him. He turned and looked up at the window, as if he knew she was there, watching, but he wouldn't be able to see her. It was too bright outside and too dark in the bedroom, but either way she felt sheer panic and pulled herself further back into the shadows. He turned and walked away, down the hill, back to his car. He would tell her when things were done, she wouldn't decide their life for them, he would be in charge of what was happening, but there was no point in being here right now, he needed a drink and to drive home to get some sleep. Then he would decide what to do next, he would think of some ideas.

She watched him disappear, feeling as though she had been holding her breath the entire time she had hidden there. She was dragged back to when Timothy and the children had been up to see her and her mum when Coral didn't have much time left. She had rung and asked if he would bring Marcus and Lilly to see their Nanna while she was alert enough to talk to them for a little while, the district nurses had started coming in to help and she was receiving the drugs she needed, but could lie and chatter for a little while. Lilly said she wanted to come and see Nanna, she was only fifteen but she knew that she wanted to say goodbye. Coral didn't want to go into hospital or a hospice, she wanted to be at home. A hospital bed had been delivered, which made her look tiny, sat up on the pillow. She was in the front room at this point, with Maureen sleeping on the sofa beside her. Reading aloud, watching TV, just bringing noise into the silent moments of dying.

Timothy had brought the children, he had held Maureen tightly in the kitchen as she wept quietly into his chest. He held her so her whole weight was on him, as he had done so many times. She was shattered, physically and emotionally, and she desperately needed some sleep. Her sleep on the lumpy sofa was light, broken and frightening, she was half expecting to wake up to her mum being gone. She didn't know how much longer she could manage and felt dreadful wondering how long it would be. How long until she was an orphan- albeit a forty five year old one? In the years to come she would wish for that time again, she would wish she hadn't cared how dreadful she felt, and she would wish that she would have managed in that emotional, sleep deprived state for years to have five more minutes with her mum. To sit around the kitchen table with her and drink tea, hug each other. She felt dreadful in that sleep deprived state, but it was nothing compared to what was to come. She had purpose and routine, to keep her mum comfortable, when that went she was quietly lost.

Timothy held her tightly as Marcus and Lilly sat either side of their Nanna, holding her hands and not knowing quite what to say as she snored gently, occasionally blasting out aloud, throat catching roar, that made Marcus and Lilly look at each other and smile. Their Nanna was known to snore, it could be heard through the walls.

"Can she go into hospital?" Timothy asked quietly as they waited for the kettle to boil.

"No!" Maureen exclaimed, slightly too loudly, causing him to jump. "She wants to be here. We agreed she would stay here. I'm not letting her down now "

"But Maureen, you're shattered and it's too much for you." He replied.

"I am tired, but it's not too much, it's my mum, and it's what she did for Nanna and Grandad, looked after them, so I'm doing it." Maureen couldn't stand the idea of her mum being alone in a hospital room without anyone there. Or Maureen having to stay with her in a bare hospital room and then walk away without her at the end, how would she ever leave?

Coral's beloved friends visited regularly, her little tribe of gals, as they called each other. They would sit and take turns to give Maureen a break, but it was a couple of hours here and there, Maureen didn't want to leave her for long. Coral had been carried downstairs by two green clad ambulance crew, when the hospital bed came, and it was too big to get up the cottage stairs. The terror in her eyes thinking that she was being whisked to hospital to live out her final days in a place she didn't know was too much for Maureen to bear, she kept reassuring Coral that they were just going downstairs, that she was staying in the house. If Timothy had seen that fear he would have understood, he would have understood, even in his often emotionless state, he would have been moved, even with his obvious disregard for Coral he would have known why the hospital wasn't the place for her. She knew he was impatient, she knew he wanted her to go home, to look after the kids and to all be under the same roof, get back to normal he had said a few days ago on the phone, but there would never be a normal again. Within the last five years she had lost Nanna and then Grandad, and she had a few precious moments left with her mum, she would stay until the end. She felt as though she was losing her core, and she had always been so sure of what that was, where she was from, what she liked and what she disliked, and who was she now? Who was she without the people who were her history, who built her core?

He had walked back to the car taking the children with him, and she had waved from the front door until they had disappeared down the road. The three of them walking away, the children turning and waving, blowing kisses, but Timothy steadfastly staring forward, stepping with purpose until he was out of view. She knew she would be back with them all soon, very soon, when Mum was gone and the house empty of people and only full of things, and she would lock up and never go in again expecting to see her face, or smell her perfume, or feel the prickly itch of her home knit woolly jumper as they hugged each other. But for now she stayed, to breathe together.

She watched outside for some time, hiding in the bedroom, long after Timothy had walked angrily away, long after she had defied him, long after there was any chance of him coming back, knocking on the door again and demanding an end to the silliness. She let out a little cough of laughter. Silly was clowns and circuses, not the ending of marriages, it was face paints and balloon animals, not reclaiming the core of yourself that someone has attempted to strangle. She would speak to a solicitor and see what needed to be done to make for a more formal separation. Timothy had pissed off enough people in the legal profession to have the pick of those who would like to help his wife detangle herself from his grip, but she didn't want to humiliate him, she just wanted some peace, so she would go and see someone in town maybe, next time she was there, or perhaps she would call on someone she knew and screw the outcome? But for now she needed to put the shopping away and check the doors and the windows, and hope he was making his way back onto the M6, heading south.

She was cross with herself that she didn't have her own tribe of gals, her own tribe to call on when needed. But she had become so isolated and distant from the friends she could have called that years ago, and the wives of Timothy's business friends or golf buddies were surface friends who raised an eyebrow if you said 'shit', who enjoyed watching someone struggle because it meant nobody was judging them for a moment. They weren't people to belly laugh with and reveal that time you coughed too much and wet yourself, and then laugh together without judgement. There was no one to call her, except the kids and Florence and Maureen felt she was too old to find friends, even though that was what she needed. The daughters of her mum's tribe were once a fiercely loyal bunch, but then life got in the way, work, kids, looking after a house. Having it all just really meant doing it all, Maureen always thought, leaving yourself last, at the back of the queue.

The kettle boiled and hissed the whisper of a promise, a moment with a brew to stop and enjoy. What was the point of all of these regrets? She couldn't get to know lots of people when she was just getting to know herself again, she had to like herself first. The shopping was away and sat down at the kitchen table with her tea and a custard cream. It was a noisy house at the best of times, creaky and echoey, but every single sound made her think it was someone on the front path, Timothy deciding to take another chance at getting her to return with him. She text Florence:

'Hello Flo, hope you are ok? Really sorry to bother you but Timothy has been up to Ambleside to try and persuade me to go home with him. He's gone again now but it's put me a bit on edge. Would you be able to give him a ring just to see if he's heading back south and not waiting to come here again later? Xxx'

Half an hour and two cups of tea later Maureen's phone buzzed with a text:

'Fear not Maureen, I've spoken to him on Bluetooth and the silly old bugger is south of Manchester heading home. He never said he'd been up to Ambleside or that you'd left him, just that he was up north on business, so I don't think he'll bother you again today. Xx'

Maureen put her phone down and breathed a sigh of relief. She needed some noise to accompany her cooking tea, something to cover up the creaking. She clicked the radio on and caught the end of The Archers, as she chopped lettuce and tomatoes while a ready made quiche heated in the oven. It was always a noisy house, with busyness going on, people popping in, activities on the go. Nanna loved the television and Grandad loved the radio. He liked Derek Jameson on radio two and then Terry Wogan. But eventually it was just Mum here, and it was quieter unless they were visiting. Maureen always told her mum that she would breathe a sigh of relief when her and the children went home and she could listen to her own thoughts again, but Coral was never pleased when they left after a visit, she always yearned for their company and her grandchildren's joy. And then the house had fallen silent except for brief visits and occasional longer holidays. It stood quietly, waiting for Maureen to return, to shuffle about the house and remind it that it was a home, a lived in place, with a memory about every footstep. If the house recognised it's dwellers from footsteps it would not know who was who between Maureen, Coral and Nanna, all three of them built the same way, walking about with their gentle steps and bouncing curls, giving the house rhythm.

When it was ready Maureen placed her tea onto a tray and grabbed a knife and fork, making her way into the living room to switch the television on. There was still a good couple of hours of sunlight left but Maureen closed the curtains, she knew he was gone but she wanted to feel snug and secure, away from any gaze. She put on the side lamps and sat with her tea on her knee and without much of an appetite to speak of. It had been replaced by that unignorable, uncomfortable stomach knot of anxiety that rolled across the middle of a person to remind them that they better be worried. She had been feeling safe and secure in the cottage, all of the comfort and security of being here felt a bit uncertain because he had come. She didn't expect it, he was not on his territory and he would normally not want to feel that out of control. But she knew he would be feeling dreadful, he would be watching his control crumble and he would cease to think straight. She knew him well enough to know that any anxiety that was kicking her abdomen was nothing compared to whatever was accompanying Timothy down the motorway.

Maureen took some deep breaths, in through the nose, out through the mouth, slowly. She knew there would be bumps, it wouldn't be simple, changing your life wasn't ever a smooth thing, but not doing anything would have meant the anxiety would have punched her gut forever, and this way it would eventually stop, because she was more sure than ever that she had made the right decision, there was no wobbling in that. She had been contained and controlled long enough, far too long, and whatever fear or worry or words that contained her was certainly gone now. She knew it, she just hoped Timothy knew it.

But somewhere south of Preston Timothy didn't know it. He drove at exactly seventy miles an hour, tired and frustrated, his mouth dry and clacky from too much anger and not enough to drink. His throat hurt when he swallowed and he was frustrated with it all, but he was also sad. He had held Maureen tightly, supported her these recent years when she had been lost and overcome, he had helped her to not have to make decisions when she was not capable, and now this? She had stood in that doorway looking and sounding every inch the woman he met forty years ago, the woman who took his breath away and took no nonsense from anyone. His clever wife, who he feared would leave him every single day for years finally had, just when he thought she was so reliant on him that she needed him as much as he needed her. How would he manage if she wasn't his any more? How would he get through each day without knowing where she was or what she was doing? Something had changed her, and there she was on that front step as plain as day looking like she'd just climbed a fell, no carefully selected skirt and blouse, no groomed hair, just a mass of curls on her head, bouncing in every direction. He loved her so much he felt he wouldn't be able to breathe without her. He would have to have her back, make her come home, take her home. He would have to. Or how would he get up each morning and go about his day? How would he talk to people and go to meetings knowing she was gone. It was too much, she was too much, and he was not enough. His eyes stung, he felt angry and sad and alone. His mother said he had married beneath himself, that he needed to keep her on a tight leash, that she said too much for her own good, and she was proved right again. He would not tell Mother she had gone. He would never tell her. He had plans to move him and Maureen down to Winchester to live with Mother, to stay in the house that was hers anyway, in her name, in his trust, or very nearly. He had planned to discuss it after Mother's birthday, after the party, and really he meant no discussions, it was something he and Mother had agreed and Maureen would be a great companion and helper for Mother whilst he was at work or away. They had agreed to it, Mother was looking forward to it and now this. He couldn't do it without Maureen.

He drove in the slow lane behind an Eddie Stobart truck, his emotions swinging from anger, disgust as his wife's behaviour, to distress and sadness, emotions that he did not enjoy or recognise easily. He could manage the anger, thrive on it even, it was the other ones that were not pleasant in his throat or stomach. He was a winner, competitive, and he revelled in it, and now he felt that he had lost. Timothy Smith has lost. He kept rolling the words around his head. He had the biggest house, the most money, the newest car, the best golf handicap, the most beautiful wife, the longest marriage, the most hair, all of the things that mattered in life had lined up, and he was too old to play dominoes and watch them fall down because someone decided they needed more. More than he had given? It had to be temporary madness on her part. Why would she not want everything he had, everything he could give her? It was madness. He was Timothy Smith for goodness sake. She had done well marrying him, where would she be without him? Stuck in that cottage without things, without all of the things he had given her, the opportunities, because of him. He conveniently didn't consider that his wife had a PhD in modern history that she had got on her own and could have managed life well without him. He didn't recall all of the times he had sought her opinion or advice in their younger days, or got her to look over proposals and plans more recently, could she write this or review that? That was what a wife should do, and what else did she have to do with the kids being adults and not having a job? That fucking woman, that woman. He was livid again, and he needed a wee. That fucking prostate. It was all simply unacceptable. He would not accept it.

14- back when

The gown was longer than expected, it was ankle length and had to be hoisted up when walking downstairs or upstairs for fear of feet tangling and falling. She was regretting having it on as she ran upstairs to the bathroom, shaking it off behind her, slipping it from her arms as she took the stairs two by two, letting it slither down the stairs behind her until it was sprawled across the bottom two steps, like she would have been if it had caught her feet.

She hit the bathroom door open with a panic and bent as quickly as she could, heaving her breakfast into the toilet with horror and relief in equal measure. Timothy followed through the door quickly and grabbed her hair, which had already been tainted with the vomit.

"Oh yak, it's wet." He said, letting it go quickly.

The second wave came and he forgot his own discomfort, grabbing the hair again as Maureen's stomach did its worst. She took breaths quickly and it seemed to settle things.

"This is all your fucking fault." She said lightly as she wiped her mouth on toilet roll and threw it in the toilet. "I hope that's it for today, I can't be doing this on stage." She sat on the edge of the bath, taking deep breaths until the feeling passed. "Happy graduation day to me."

"It'll be worth it in the end." He said, not really appreciating how rough she was feeling. "A tiny Timothy to cuddle." He laughed.

"It might be a girl, and we aren't calling it Timothy either way." She shot back.

"Well I'm not sure Mother would agree, it's a family tradition." Timothy regretted the statement as it fell from his mouth.

"Really?" She said, rising from the bath as her bottom became increasingly uncomfortable. "If your Mother wants to choose a baby's name may I suggest she has a baby."

He didn't reply or say anything else about it. He wasn't bothered about what the baby would be called, but he knew Mother wouldn't be pleased if it wasn't given her father's name. He was certain it wouldn't be, there would be no negotiation there from Maureen.

Maureen walked downstairs quickly and angrily. Every time she saw the woman there was mention of grandchildren, or a question about when would she give up work? Maureen changed the subject expertly every time, but it was grating, although she never showed Julia how irritated she was, that would be fuel for the fire. But over her dead body would Julia pick the name of this baby. They had been down to see her this past weekend and Maureen had had to excuse herself quickly to go and vomit in the downstairs toilet. On her return after much panting and heaving, Julia had advised: "Now dear, don't forget you are not sick, you are pregnant." Maureen had looked wide eyed over to Timothy who raised an eyebrow in support, but did not speak a word.

At the bottom of the stairs Maureen picked up her gown and laid it on the sofa beside her cap. She was going to invite her family down, but with the arrival of the vomiting she asked if she could go up and see them in a couple of weeks and go out for a nice meal to celebrate her graduation, although she already had the title and the job, this was just an extravagant event that she was thinking she would stay away from had it not already been planned that she would be doing a little speech for the degree graduates. If she could get through that she could come home and be safely tucked up in bed with a bucket.

"Can I get you anything?" Timothy asked as he came into the room.

"No thanks, I think it was the toast that set me off. I feel sick if I'm hungry and then if I eat it comes up anyway. I'll be ok in an hour or two." She sat on the sofa and closed her eyes. She just had to get through this and then she could come home and sleep. She had a couple of days off and she would get her energy together. "The worst thing is going off tea." She said miserably, and then gagged at the thought of it.

They'd agreed that as soon as her PhD was finished and all the research done they would start trying for a baby, not expecting it to happen straight away, but here she was, twelve weeks pregnant, ready to accept her certificate and congratulate those with degrees, where she had been a few years ago. She would do all of the reading with a watery mouth and the threat of bile rising to her throat. It was not the day she had planned but Timothy was right, it would be worth it in the end. She was certain it wasn't the last she had heard about names, from Timothy or Julia, but she wasn't going to let her mother-in-law have a say in this. She almost felt sorry for her at times, she seemed lost and didn't seem to have an understanding of what real life was about, outside her big house and her judgements, but Maureen was not going to call her child Timothy, even if it was a boy. If it was to have a family name it would be Grandad's, and that was that.

She sat on the sofa with her eyes closed and imagined eating some of Nanna's home made chips drenched in salt and vinegar, that she would manage, she would be able to eat a plate full. When they went up in a couple of weeks she would ask nanna to fire up the chip pan. It was October already, there would only be a couple of visits before they were up visiting at Christmas, and then next Christmas there would be an extra little one in the family.

The baby was due in April 1988, just before Maureen turned thirty. There had been the usual comments from friends and acquaintances asking if they were planning kids, advice not to leave it too late, they weren't getting any younger, as well as blatant demands from Julia that she was the only one without grandchildren. Maureen was adamant that she wanted to carry on working, take some time off but do some part time lecturing, maybe do some more writing, her boss was keen in keeping her and said they would always have a job for her, but currently she couldn't manage a full day at work and she was only edging out of the first trimester. The glow of pregnancy was just a myth. Surprisingly Timothy was an excellent support , she was not her usual self, her usual feisty self was vomiting too much to argue with anything, except perhaps name suggestions. He took charge, advised, helped out more. When Maureen thought about doing something, or going out, he would remind her why it was safer that she stayed at home, if she was planning on going out without him he would take extra care and drive her places so that she wasn't on her own. She was so pleased with how attentive he was, ever present, full of suggestions. Even when she was planning to catch the train up to see her mum and grandparents he insisted on her taking a shorter trip so that he could drive her. Coral said that she would come and pick Maureen up, but Timothy said it was too much for her when he could do it.

When the twelve week scan came around they were informed that there were two heartbeats and Maureen was having twins. It explained why she was feeling so poorly, and she sobbed with happiness and distress, how would she manage two small babies? Julia suggested they use a good nanny, and she happily wrote down the number of the agency that she knew. Maureen declined and said that she would not need someone else to look after her babies for her, even though she knew she would probably need help sometimes, it was the principle of the thing. At week twenty when she was tossing and turning overnight, and had fainted twice at work, it was with a heavy heart that, after much negotiation, Timothy persuaded her that she should give up work.

'I make more than enough for both of us, I can give you housekeeping and a little allowance, you don't need to worry about money." He reassured her.

'But it won't be my money, I'd have to ask you for it." Maureen explained, imagining she'd have to explain every spending decision she made.

Timothy spent a good hour reassuring her that it was fine, that it was their money, not just his, he would leave the money in an envelope each week and they would use it for shopping, anything she needed for the house or the babies when they came. It would be theirs, they were married, he said. He asked what was more important, her and the babies health or having her own income? So she had no choice, she needed to be able to rest and she trusted Timothy. She absolutely trusted him. She knew she wouldn't have to justify her spending to him, or remind him that her money wasn't there in the envelope, she knew he would be as good as his word. But she was wrong.

Because she couldn't carry heavy bags he was with her when they shopped, or he went on his own when she was resting. If she was having a good day and feeling well and wanted a walk into town or to the shops, there was often nothing there, no money, so she took to keeping some back from the previous week and leaving it in her purse or drawer to make sure she had a few pounds for when she needed it, so she could get stamps or send little gifts to Nanna and Grandad like she always did. She felt like the dynamic had changed slightly because she was more reliant on Timothy, but then again, she thought she might be feeling a bit more sensitive, and without as much to occupy herself with she ruminated more. When she cried because she missed her mum, Timothy took offence, although he did try to hide it a little, just a little. Why did she need her mum when he was doing all of this for her, sorting out money, taking her out and about, doing extra in the house, was he not enough? She was too tired to argue that she just wanted her mum, but she made sure not to mention it again, because he was doing so much for her, and she wasn't able to do very much at all.

One Thursday she rang her family and ended up quietly crying on the telephone to Coral, telling her how fed up and lonely she felt, and the next day her mum turned up for a surprise visit, she had taken the afternoon off work and had arrived by five thirty Friday afternoon. Timothy said how kind it was that she had come all of this way to see them both and there was absolutely no need, and Maureen cried with relief that her mum had come and she felt that everything would be ok while she was there. And it was. Timothy objected to Maureen going into town with Coral and insisted he came too to make sure that Maureen was OK, but Coral said how tired he looked and how he could do with a rest too, he was just to relax at home, and Timothy, the professional arguer, was unable to disagree with his mother-in-law, who appeared unmoved by his protestations. Every excuse he came up with Coral just looked at him without response until he became quiet and looked away. She had been in teaching long enough to know when to allow child-like behaviour to burn itself out. After he'd stopped speaking she merely said. "Right then, we'll be off, just the two of us, like I said." And there was nothing more to discuss.

He fumed in the house on his own, walking from room to room wondering how that woman had the audacity to ignore him in his own home, when he had been looking after Maureen so well, when he had been seeing to her every need. Fucking Coral. He wanted to tell her to leave, that they could manage on their own, but Maureen would be cross, distressed even, and he was trying to walk the line, trying to look after her the best way he could, and he didn't want her getting upset and unwell. He enjoyed knowing that Maureen was at home whenever he finished work, that he didn't have to wait for her to come in or get a call saying she was nipping out for drinks with friends, or helping a student. He wanted her to be in when he was in or waiting for him when he was out, but he knew better than to say that out loud. He also knew that this reliance on him might be temporary, but he suspected with two young babies it would carry on for some time yet.

He had come home a few times since she gave up work to find her with a friend, chatting, drinking tea now that the sickness was long gone. He would make more tea for them, offer to drop the friend back home, join in and chat, and try hard not to show them that he was cross, that there was company in the house and he didn't have Maureen to himself. When they had gone he would reclaim his space and let Maureen know that she shouldn't be overdoing it and she should take things easy, not get overwhelmed or over excited.

Maureen laughed. "Over excited, sitting or lying on this sofa talking to someone. It's hardly over excited Timothy, it's not even excited, it's just company."

"You know what I mean!" He hissed back.

"Yes, I know what you mean but I'm still here, I may be looking after the babies, resting and cooking them, but I'm still Maureen, with a need for company and conversation that doesn't begin and end with you." She said sternly, keeping her frown fixed on his face until he had to look away. He nodded and said nothing else. He didn't agree for a moment, but he swallowed it down because there was no point in starting something that she might try and make a point on.

And now Coral was here, and he'd lost the argument on that too. They were off in the city somewhere, cafe hopping and shopping, no doubt. The reality was there was no hopping anywhere and they had got a cup of tea and a sandwich and Maureen was ready for a lie down again, so they drove out of the city and sat with blankets on their knees in the car, because Maureen just wanted to be out of the house for a bit, just a change of scenery and no fuss or explanation, and she could sit quietly with her mum and have no expectations.

They sat quietly in the car for an hour, Maureen with her head nodding, the occasional snore catching in the back of her throat and making her eyes open. It was the end of January and it was chilly and when their teeth started chattering they admitted that they had been out of the house for long enough and they headed home to see what they should do for tea. Timothy was in the house when they returned, full of smiles, asking if they had had a nice time, he didn't want Coral to know for a moment that she had irritated him, he would play the devoted son -in-law even if it choked him slightly. Maureen had brought him back a cake from the cafe which he sank his teeth into with a cup of tea. He cleared the pots away and put the kettle on again, shouting from the kitchen that he was going to treat them to a Chinese take away for tea as he knew that it was one of Maureen's cravings. He heard the positive response from the living room as they started talking about what they would order and he felt rather pleased with himself. He might not get any praise from Coral but he would give her no reason to criticise him in front of Maureen.

They ate their Chinese early, with Maureen yawning heavily before she'd finished half of her plate. She was tired to her bones, and she would drop off quickly in bed and then spend much of the night waking up with heartburn or waddling to the toilet to empty her increasingly flimsy bladder. Coral said that she would need to head off back home first thing Sunday morning to get ready for the week ahead and make sure that Nanna and Grandad were ok, miss the busiest of the Sunday afternoon traffic. The next morning as Maureen watched her reverse off the drive, the pair of them waving furiously at each other. Maureen's eyes stung with tears and salty blobs rolled down her cheeks as she walked back into the house, sobbing. Everything felt so raw since she had been pregnant and she felt the distance between her and her mum and grandparents now more than ever. She had asked Timothy if there was ever a chance that they could move further north, but that would stop her work at the university in the future and Timothy needed to be close to his office. Maureen felt quite lost. Like she was at home but away from home. She knew things would be different when the babies came and she was busy and distracted, but for now she wanted her mum and she was heading back up north, away from her.

The babies came five weeks early on the ninth of March 1989. Leaving them in the hospital and coming home while they were in the neonatal unit was distressing and heart-breaking, and at the time seemed to take forever. They were soon home and it was chaotic, tiring and magnificent. Julia said having twins would be easier because they could play with each other and look after each other, but at four weeks old there was very little sign of that. Maureen had softened when she saw Timothy holding his son and shedding a tear and had agreed that his middle name could be Timothy, which Julia seemed to accept graciously. She had actually caught the train from Winchester to Oxford to visit the babies in hospital, first class of course, but nevertheless quite a thing for her to do alone.

The lack of sleep was quite something and Maureen felt like a zombie most of the first few months. Coral came to stay a good few times and she would take the babies out walking so that Maureen could sleep. Timothy told Maureen every single day how tired he was and how the babies were disturbing his sleep, but Maureen was not aware of any time he stopped snoring when they needed something in the night, she expected he would sleep through a brass band in the bedroom, and she knew that she would be the one to do it all. She wasn't working, this was her job. They didn't stay tiny for long, and Maureen developed a routine, out for walks in the morning, stopping at a cafe for tea or a hot chocolate, occasionally attending a baby group or meeting up with friends and former colleagues. A couple of times a month she would walk up to the university and have lunch with her old colleagues, hoping that she would be going back when childcare allowed. She missed the discussions and the reading. When the babies were heading towards their first birthday she had been asked to join the lecturing pool for as-and-when lecturing, as well as doing some proofreading for articles and department information which meant she had a little of her own income. Not much, not enough to live on certainly, but something of her own that she didn't need to ask for. It felt liberating. Timothy was working more hours than ever and away overnight at times, so they agreed another car was in order so that Maureen could get out and about a bit easier. They had to find one that was big enough to fit a double pushchair in the boot and reliable enough to make sure she wasn't stranded with small children. Her suggestion that Timothy get a small car for work and she use his big car was met with disdain. What would people think if he turned up in a little car, looking dishevelled? Maureen laughed wondering how you got dishevelled in a small car, and who was monitoring car sizes, but apparently it was a thing.

Maureen was more than satisfied with her ten year old Austin Maxi that had been meticulously taken care of by one owner who had driven it to town and back twice a week. It was bright white with brown interior that she had been reliably informed could fold down and become a double bed. She had huffed and puffed with the seats on the drive to show Timothy the amazingness of it, and she felt that she could go anywhere. She got herself a little wooden box and put some tea bags in it alongside her old Trangier stove and some biscuits and water and felt like she almost had a caravan. Almost. Once she had the car Maureen felt quite free, like she wasn't stuck in the house in bad weather or battling a rain cover over the pushchair when the heavens opened. To maintain fairness once a week she would drive down to Winchester to see Julia for a couple of hours and have tea while Julia held the babies. The first time she did that Timothy's face beamed when she told him when she got in from work, that she had driven all that way with the babies and spent time with his mother made his heart feel joyful. When she explained she was planning to do the same thing the following week but in the opposite direction he was not so impressed.

"It's a long way to drive on your own with two babies." He frowned.

"Well feel free to join me." She said, knowing he wouldn't.

"What if you break down or have an accident?" He said. "And I'll have to come home to an empty house."

"We'll be fine." She replied. "You'll be fine, you're a big boy now." She laughed. He scowled at her, not appreciating the joke. "And besides I have a plan. I'm going to travel up Sunday after tea and then I can drive while they sleep. And mum is going to come down on Saturday on the train and travel back up with me so I won't be on my own."

"Oh, so I'm the last to know then? It's all arranged no matter what I say?" He sulked.

"Yes Timothy it is, because I'm a big girl and I don't need your permission. Plus I'll have a break and more sleep up there."

She stared at him until he looked away, defeated. "I just worry about the three of you, that's all." He said, but really he just wanted to know that she would be at home. He had hoped that her need to see her family would lessen now that they had their own family. He felt that the monthly visits from Coral were too much, even though she often came when he was away and it gave Maureen a break, he felt that he should be enough, he should be who she needed. He had no idea that it was perfectly normal to want your mum when you'd had a baby, let alone two. He had no idea that if he did a bit more or was home more reliably Maureen wouldn't rely on someone else so much. He didn't want to do more, but he didn't want Maureen to want more. He wanted her to be around whenever he was and the thought of her being miles away made him feel rejected, although he was thinking about the extra sleep he might get. It crossed his mind to take a day off while she was away and just lie in and please himself.

The journey up with Coral went smoothly, and it felt like something Maureen could manage on her own. By eleven o'clock they were finishing off a cup of tea at Nanna and Grandad's kitchen table whilst there was a baby being held by each great-grandparent. The babies were sleeping having had their final milk and everyone else was yawning and edging towards bed.

Grandad had moved Maureen's bed and pushed it against the wall with a homemade bolster filling the small gap between the wall and the mattress so that Maureen could sleep with the babies in her big bed without worrying they would fall. It was November and they were both chubby at eight months old and sleeping better than they had done when they were new. It felt easier in the cottage with all of the extra hands, not helping because they felt they ought to, but because they were desperate to hold the babies and help their beloved granddaughter. Nanna and Grandad walked the babies around the village to show them off to anyone they knew while Maureen got her head down for an extra couple of hours of sleep. There was someone to entertain them while she had a bath, she got to drink tea while it was still hot, and there was no juggling making tea and getting the babies ready for bed. It felt lovely and she was sad to go back home where she was on her own with two little ones so much. She decided that she would do the journey once a month, she only needed to stay two or three nights if Timothy was objectionable, but it felt like she had enjoyed a really good rest and she knew that her mum, nanna and grandad had loved seeing the babies. She had managed to get some bits of work done while she was there too, so that was a bit more of a relief. She felt guilty at being sad to go home, like it was a bit of a betrayal of Timothy that she had enjoyed being away so much, but it was the help and the break and being somewhere so comfortable that she would miss, although she had missed Timothy while she was north.

She set off back early Friday morning, the babies had been awake early and had breakfast and by seven they were on the road with the radio on and the babies strapped in. The journey was smooth and Lilly slept a good couple of hours while Marcus napped and gurgled beside her. Maureen felt that it was a doable journey on her own, that getting out of Oxford was easier than ever, now that she had her car. She felt less isolated and constrained. She was back home well before Timothy got back from work and was able to tidy round and wash the pots that had been left to fester. Why, when all he had to do was look after himself did he not do that, knowing she was coming home? She wanted to talk to him about it when he got home, but the amount of sulking that would accompany her discussion would render it pointless, so she tidied up and swallowed it down, even if it left a bitter taste in her mouth. He was late home and she had the house spick and span and the babies bathed and fast asleep by the time he arrived. He had said to her on the phone the previous evening that he would bring a Chinese home from work. She was absolutely famished and getting ready to make toast and go to bed by the time he walked through the door with the food and his apology. He looked so handsome in his suit that her stomach danced with butterflies and she took the bag from him and started plating up and then remembered that she should give him a cuddle and greet him properly.

"I have to eat." She said, pulling herself away as her stomach rumbled and he held her tighter. "Hold that thought and let me shovel some food in."

They ate quickly and she told him about her trip and easy journey between mouthfuls. She told him how easy it had been with the extra pairs of hands and how well the babies had slept.

"I missed you though." He said, putting his knife and fork down. "Did you miss me at all, or were you too busy?"

"Of course I missed you." She said.

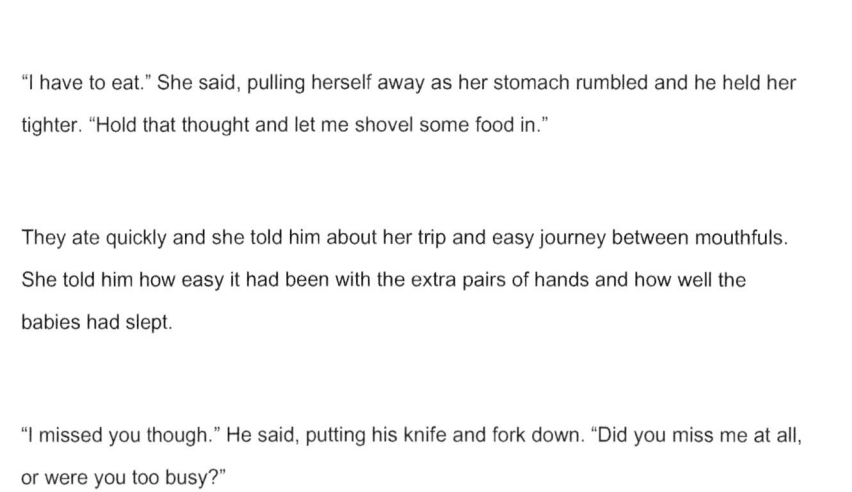

"You haven't made plans to go again before Christmas have you?" He asked, pretending it was a throw away comment rather than an expectation.

"Nope." She said, without looking up. "Next time I'm up we'll all be there together for Christmas."

He didn't reply and she knew that it was a tricky subject, spending the Christmas holidays with her family, but it was joyless at Julia's, no laughter or relaxing and she couldn't do that to herself on her favourite day of the year. She knew Christmas wasn't something that his family counted down to, or spoke of with anticipation or excitement, it was just another day to them, with food and gifts. And it was all about the gifts, not the thought. Not carefully planned purchases or specially made chutney and the cheese Nanna and Grandad tasted on their honeymoon that she'd tracked down, or the spiced gin that Coral couldn't remember the name of. It was so full of meaning for Maureen that she couldn't spend it where the meaning didn't matter.

Eventually he said. "So that's decided then, we are going up north again this Christmas?"

"Yes, we are. It's all arranged like we discussed, and I've spoken to your Mother and she's expecting us for the new year, she wants to see in the new year with a baby in each arm." Maureen said, without hesitation because she wasn't going to change her plans, their plans, that they had already agreed on.

"Oh well, if that's what you've agreed then." He said, as if it was the first he had heard of it.

She almost caught the dissatisfaction from him, almost held it and wrestled it, chewed it in her teeth and was ready to spit it back out to dance around the edges of an argument. To tell him that they had spoken, they had agreed, she had said before, but then she swallowed down the taste of the bicker and said nothing. He had decided that he wanted to tell a fresh story, of being kept out of all discussions and she decided that she wouldn't play the game today. She wouldn't justify or plead, she would say nothing because they were just doing what they planned and that was that. She kissed him on the cheek and disarmed him. He was waiting for her discomfort and his certainty that this was worth falling out over, that her being greeted home with Chinese and chatter was simply masking his resentment that she had been away for five nights and he didn't like it. She kissed him gently on the mouth and he closed his eyes as she cleared her plate into the kitchen telling him that she was shattered and she was off to bed. He ate slowly as he listened to her scraping her plate and putting the kettle on, he heard her cleaning her teeth and having a wee, checking the babies room and the gentle click of the door as she closed it. She brought him a cup of tea when it had brewed and kissed him again and walked up the stairs to bed. He sat at the table and ruminated as he chewed. He knew she needed a rest, but he didn't like her being away and getting so much from the others. He wanted to be her all. Everything she needed and it perturbed him that he wasn't, he felt he was down the list somewhere. He had no idea at all it wasn't a competition. There was plenty of love to go round, it wasn't that he had less because she loved others. He should have sat there and delighted in the fact that his wife, shattered from caring for twin babies, had been looked after and cared for and loved and was more refreshed. And he slept better and got more work done and pleased himself for a few days. He should have been grateful that other people could look after his wife and children. But he wasn't. So he sat and sulked. Sulked and chewed, and then he fell asleep on the sofa as the television hissed, instead of sleeping next to the wife he had missed so terribly and loved so much.

And that was the tale of them as the babies grew. He sulked when he couldn't get his own way, which was certainly often. He imagined he was brooding and quiet in a charming sort of way, perhaps even in a 1950's film star kind of way, but in reality he sulked when he couldn't get his own way and Maureen saw it all and mentioned it little and swallowed quite a lot down. He was funny and charming and they chatted and laughed, except when they didn't. He was kind, except when he wasn't and Maureen skirted and danced about it, but she never, ever trod on eggshells. She allowed him his moments, but there was always more than enough fire in her belly to ignite when it all got too much and he got too troublesome and then she would tell him. She would tell him that perhaps the sulking worked on his mother but she wasn't about to start dealing with a third child and he'd better bloody well snap out of it because she wasn't about to hang around that sort of behaviour. She told him when he needed telling and always out of earshot of the children. And she had a way and a stare that made him pause for a moment and try to make her want to hang around more. To try to be better and less grumpy. But it was hard changing a lifetime of being him, being in charge and being the boss and getting other people to do things for you. But Maureen wasn't other people, she was the mother to his children, the wife he never thought he would have or deserved, the sunshine to his thunder, and he would do anything for her to be there when he went to work and there when he came home.

He was aware that some of his colleagues had wives at home that they moaned about, and different women they took away on business trips, but he was not interested in any of that because he had Maureen, and if you were lucky enough to have someone like that you didn't risk it. You did whatever was needed to hold it tight and keep it all for yourself. He knew all of these things, he knew he was lucky and he had half expected her to be gone one day, but less so now they had the twins. Some of his worry about her staying up north was that he feared she would like it better, need it more and want him less. The thought of not having her made him feel like he couldn't breathe, so he twisted things to make her feel bad for getting some help and support and a break. He wanted her to see how much he loved her, and it worked when he did this with his mother, he had done it his whole life.

When he was young and needed his mother, he would cry for her and she came. If he was fighting with Florence, Mother would hold him tight and tell Florence that she expected better from her because she was the oldest. If he felt he wasn't being seen enough or cared for enough he knew exactly what to do to swing Mother's attention straight into him, even if it meant doing something unpleasant and then crying an apology afterwards, he would get what he needed and be called a good boy for saying sorry. He was told every day how special he was. Best boy, cleverest boy, favourite boy. And when Mother was out of sorts he could always manage to cajole her into a smile. That's all he wanted, to know that he was the one to rescue Maureen, to be her go to, the person she leaned on the most. He was so focused on being her all that he wasn't pleased that this lovely woman was helped and supported by people who loved her and it didn't matter that he wasn't the only one.

Maureen decided to compromise, she carried on travelling up to see her family, and although she wanted to do it monthly she pulled it back to six weekly, even if Timothy was away and she was going to be in her own at home anyway. And when she went she agreed that she would only go for three nights instead of four or five. It was a compromise worth making to reduce the sulking. She never compromised on Christmas though. She said from the get go that she would always spend Christmas in Ambleside, and if for any reason that was not possible they would stay at home. She couldn't deal with the formality at Julia's house. She wanted to be able to get her pyjamas on before tea and lie across the floor reading a recipe book, or play cards. She wanted to be able to laugh when someone couldn't contain a post Christmas dinner fart, and giggle at the look of shock on Timothy's face when Nanna let one rip after one too many snowballs. Nobody was relaxed enough to accidently let one out when they were in Winchester, no matter how much alcohol had been consumed.

Time flew quickly and the twins starting school put pay to visiting Ambleside on weekdays outside the school holidays. Timothy and Julia had suggested that the children would benefit from attending a preparatory school, Julia discussed it over Sunday dinner, letting Maureen know that money was no object so long as it was the right place. Maureen let them both know that the children would attend the local primary school and there was no need for money to change hands. She was livid that clearly this was not the first time Timothy and Julia had had a conversation about this, but she smiled and insisted that there was nothing to discuss. In the car on the way home as the children played with newly acquired Rubiks Cubes Maureen hissed quietly at Timothy.

"If you're going to discuss our children's educational path with anyone, I suggest that you try talking to me first, rather than trying to make decisions with your mother." She kept her mouth smiling so that the children were not aware of her annoyance, but it was difficult to contain herself.

"We weren't deciding anything Maureen, Mother simply suggested something when I was at hers in the week and we thought it might be worth discussing further." Timothy smiled, playing along with the not alarming the children tone. "I really think it's worth considering."

"The discussion is closed." Maureen replied. "And really, don't make decisions that affect the kids without involving me."

He took her hand that she had rested on her knee and squeezed it gently, but she kept her hand still and didn't squeeze back. "Sorry Maureen." He said. "I got carried away with talking about it with mother. Next time I'll tell her that it's a conversation between me and you rather than me and Mother."

Maureen nodded slowly. She knew it wasn't the end of it and he was trying to placate her, and she knew that they came from different walks of life, he came from money, it oozed out of the way he spoke and the decisions he made and there were expectations. But she came from the opposite end of the money scale. She had got to where she was through hard work and encouragement and hope, there was no financial platform to jump from or being able to shake hands with the right person. She knew he was doing what he thought was best, but it was the lack of discussion that drove her to distraction. He was so used to his mother making decisions that he didn't consider the alternative. It wasn't even that he was not discussing things with her because she was a woman, it was because she was the woman he didn't think was as valid as Mother. She was there to be protected and looked after in his mind, and despite being together almost a decade he didn't learn. He said he would do anything for her. But he didn't listen or digest, he just assumed. He kept hold of her hand, and she kept staring forward and keeping her hand loose. She didn't know he'd been to look around a school with his mother, he had not divulged that, she didn't know that the head was an old friend of Julia's and the discussions about them going there had been going on since they were toddlers. She didn't hear his mother say that he would just have to put his foot down and tell her that the decision had been made. He said to Mother that he would, but he didn't. He never did. He just put his head in the sand and went along with it and then Maureen took his head from the sand, and told him no. And that was that. He spent a great deal of time wondering how things might affect him, how things made him feel, how much of his time he would need to give, rather than how they could work together to make it better for both of them.

She kept her hand loose as they drove, as his hand held hers until he needed to change gear. She wondered why he didn't just think to ask before? Why not say, 'what do you think about this idea?' Rather than losing her in someone else's plan. She wished she didn't love him so much at times, that she wasn't so understanding about his background. It was assumed by him and Julia that Maureen had gone without somehow, being without money and not having a dad, but the reality Timothy had missed out on so much joy that he seemed not to understand life at times.

The children being at school meant that Maureen could do some more work at the university, she was so passionate about her subject that she was an excellent lecturer and got brilliant feedback from the students and colleagues. If the children had been up in the night and she was shattered nobody would have guessed as she spoke at the front of the lecture theatre, telling tales, with her arms swinging across her body as she animated the discussion. She put most of her wages to one side. She had bought a greenhouse for the back garden and had plans to grow tomatoes and cucumbers come the spring, and she had turned over some soil and laid cardboard on the top. The children had helped her and Marcus had been amazed that they had found some old glass bottles and bones, which he was certain was from a dinosaur.

Occasionally when she was off she would head up to Ambleside on a Thursday after school and keep the children off on the Friday. She would load them in the car with a box of tea beside them that they could munch on the way. When they had been driving and they realised that they were not heading home the twins would cheer at the excitement of a little holiday, and the thought of seeing their Nanna's and Grandad. There would be a grumble or two from Timothy, he said that he could not condone taking the children out of school, that it was harmful for their education. He would never agree to going with them himself so they were all together, he had important meetings and visits. Maureen told him he was the boss, he could take the time off without even having to ask, and he said it was because he was the boss that he couldn't take the time off. He made it clear he didn't want the three of them to go, he said he didn't like Maureen being away, she belonged at home with him. Once, when she suggested that she might go and he said he wanted her to be at home with him she agreed to stay, and she barely saw him all weekend with work and a dinner he had to attend, so she decided she wouldn't be persuaded quite so easily next time.

Nanna and Grandad were both in their eighties when the stolen Friday trips started, the twins were seven and the terms seemed long. Nanna had slipped on black ice and fractured her wrist on a particularly icy November day. She had been crossing the road with a bag of shopping and put her arm out to stop her fall. Coral rang and told her what happened and said that Nanna was down in the dumps and in a bit of pain. Maureen packed the car up on Thursday afternoon and let Timothy know her plan. She knew there would be a time in the future, that she didn't like to think of, when Nanna and Grandad would disappear from her future plans, when they would be part of great stories of love and joy, and the thought of that made her stomach twist and her eyes sting. She needed to see more of them while she had the chance to, she needed the twins to know then and remember them, to be part of the stories, to think back to enjoying cake around the kitchen table or catch the smell of tomatoes and instantly be in their great Grandad's greenhouse popping cherry red tomatoes into their mouths and tasting the spice of them. She wanted the twins to be party to it all and that meant plenty of visits.

When they got to Ambleside, tired and hungry and Nanna heard the commotion at the door as Grandad ushered them in she squealed with delight and then cried, quite overcome that they had come all this way to see her.

"Oh Maureen, I can't believe you've driven all of this way to see us on a school day." Nanna cried. Lilly and Marcus were wrapping themselves tightly around Nanna and she tried to squeeze them with her one good arm. Big tears dripping onto their heads. "I've been a clumsy old woman." She laughed, showing them her arm in its cast, which they promised to colour in for her.

Timothy rang nine times over that weekend, asking when she would be back? Could she leave early and go and visit Julia with him on Sunday? Were the children ok with the journey? Did she know where his dark blue shirt was? Letting her know he would be away for two nights the following week. He didn't ask how Nanna was, but she told him each time he rang that she was tired and in a bit of pain, and she wasn't changing her plans, she would be leaving after lunch on Sunday. Every time the phone rang she was on tenterhooks thinking it would be Timothy, again, with another question. She knew he missed them all, his little family being so far away from him, but he also knew that Nanna had had an accident and they would be with her all weekend. She would have loved it if he said 'I'm feeling a bit lost without you all' she would have soothed him over the telephone, she knew he didn't like her being away, but he was so matter of fact, abrupt even, careless with his words. She knew she was being punished for being away, and she worried how it looked to Nanna and Grandad and her mum, but she didn't really know why she was worried. She was sure he always kept himself together when he was with her family and it seemed that his discomfort at being alone was on full show. It couldn't be about him this weekend, about his needs, it needed to be about Nanna and her discomfort, about needing to cheer her.

On Sunday morning they went out walking while Coral prepared lunch, so that the twins could burn off their energy for the journey back home. Grandad came walking with them and told them great tales of adventurers who had climbed mountains and rescued people. Of him sledging down steep slopes when he was their age, being chased by cows on summer days, catching fish in rivers and cooking them on open fires for lunch. They listened intently and he had to promise to take them fishing next time they were up for a visit. He told them they would camp in the garden and cook bacon sandwiches on a stove out the back like Maureen did when she was young, and they chattered with excitement as they walked and didn't realise how far they were going. How many times had Maureen done that at their age, moaned about walking and then been hypnotised into a world of Grandad's tales, forgetting tiredness and the steepness of a hill.

After lunch they bid teary goodbyes to each other. Maureen was caught with how small Nanna suddenly seemed to be, that she was thinner, and more frail, looking tired and pale. It caught like a pain in her stomach and caused her to shed tears on the journey home, quiet tears that she hoped the children would not see. She felt bad leaving, guilty being so far away, with anxious anticipation of how Timothy would be when they got back. She just needed him to help her feed the kids, put them to bed with her and understand her worries, cuddle away her tears, brew some tea and not expect anything from her. She felt sad to her core on the journey home. They stopped once for a wee and some crisps but she kept her foot down and they were back by half past six, to a dark house and no Timothy in sight.

Maureen threw the bags into the hall and put a video on for the children, then she opened a tin of corned beef while the kettle boiled, presenting them with corned beef sandwiches and slices of cucumber on the sofa. They ate quickly, yawning in between chews as Maureen sipped at her tea. As soon as they were done it was bath and bed and they were fast asleep before eight as she quickly tidied around and washed the pots. At eight thirty Timothy came through the door, quietly. She threw her arms around him looking for comfort and warmth and she began to sob into his shoulder. His initial annoyance that she had been away crumbled quickly and he held her tightly, leading her towards the sofa where she sat as close to him as she could without sitting on his knee and told him her worries about how frail Nanna looked.

He loved the closeness of her and her need for him. He told her that it was too much her going all that way with the kids, flogging her way up the motorway as fast as she could to look after people. It was too much, he said, more than once.

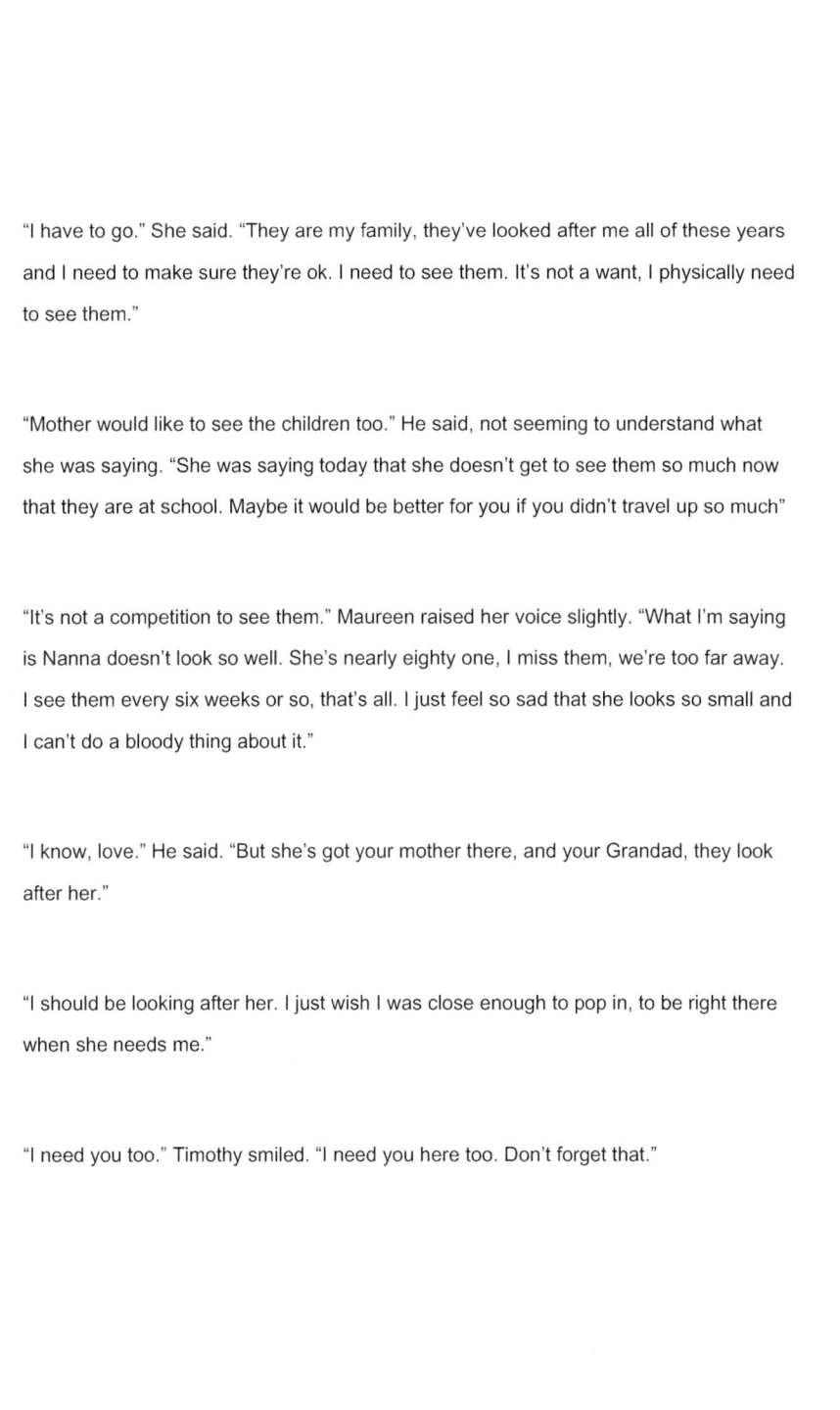

"I have to go." She said. "They are my family, they've looked after me all of these years and I need to make sure they're ok. I need to see them. It's not a want, I physically need to see them."

"Mother would like to see the children too." He said, not seeming to understand what she was saying. "She was saying today that she doesn't get to see them so much now that they are at school. Maybe it would be better for you if you didn't travel up so much"

"It's not a competition to see them." Maureen raised her voice slightly. "What I'm saying is Nanna doesn't look so well. She's nearly eighty one, I miss them, we're too far away. I see them every six weeks or so, that's all. I just feel so sad that she looks so small and I can't do a bloody thing about it."

"I know, love." He said. "But she's got your mother there, and your Grandad, they look after her."

"I should be looking after her. I just wish I was close enough to pop in, to be right there when she needs me."

"I need you too." Timothy smiled. "I need you here too. Don't forget that."

"You're thirty-seven Timothy." Maureen said, pulling away from him. "Do you not see what I'm saying? Do you not understand that I'm sad and worried? It's not about you." She looked at him for a moment and wondered if he could hear himself? If he could look at her and see what he could do to try and make her less fraught. But he couldn't. So she stood up and walked out of the room. She walked up the stairs wondering how he always appeared to be pondering how everything was affecting him. How would he feel, how would he look, who would think of him? She couldn't understand how he didn't sympathise with her, knowing that someone he loved was worried about someone they loved? But his thought was 'how do I fit into all of this.'

He sat on the sofa knowing that she hadn't listened to him, hadn't understood that there were other people to think of besides her grandparents. They had Coral to look after them, why did they need Maureen too, his mother wasn't getting any younger, she was sixty three, perhaps, somewhere around that, surely she deserved some care from Maureen too. Maureen was lucky she had her grandparents, Timothy's were long gone like this father. Surely she should be grateful for that instead of worrying about them aging, as if they were going to do anything else?

He didn't like Maureen working, he didn't need her to work, but one good thing about it was that she had to be around Oxford to do her job, and that meant less time heading north, less opportunity for running away from where she should stay. She should be home for him, not gadding about with the children. He had assumed that having the children would have rooted her to their house, the children's home, but it seemed to him that she always had one foot outside the door. She worked and she saw friends, took the children on play dates, to playgrounds. They visited Mother, but it was never there and back. It was always to this park or that park on the way, soft play, trampolining, she said that sitting in the house all afternoon with Mother was not good for them, they had to use their energy. He thought they should learn to sit quietly, learn to listen to Mother talking, and not have distractions of books or toys while they were there. Why did she have to entertain them so much, he was left to be quiet in the corner and it never did him any harm. That should be enough, she had her own family now and that should be enough.

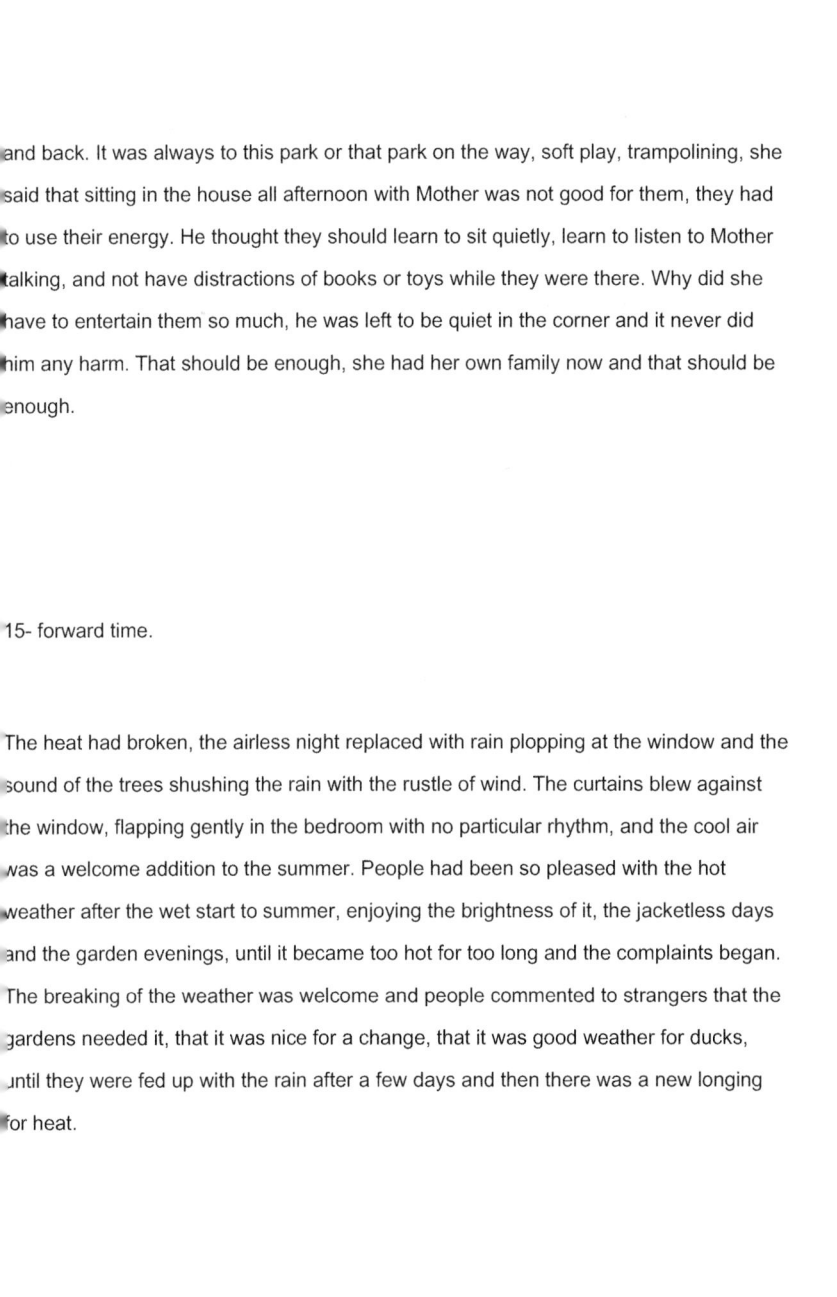

15- forward time.

The heat had broken, the airless night replaced with rain plopping at the window and the sound of the trees shushing the rain with the rustle of wind. The curtains blew against the window, flapping gently in the bedroom with no particular rhythm, and the cool air was a welcome addition to the summer. People had been so pleased with the hot weather after the wet start to summer, enjoying the brightness of it, the jacketless days and the garden evenings, until it became too hot for too long and the complaints began. The breaking of the weather was welcome and people commented to strangers that the gardens needed it, that it was nice for a change, that it was good weather for ducks, until they were fed up with the rain after a few days and then there was a new longing for heat.

Maureen laid in bed and listened to the curtains, occasionally flopping against the wall. She had got up for a wee after managing a good few hours sleep that she didn't expect. She expected to lie, feeling on edge, after Timothy's uninvited visit and his demands that life return to his normal. She expected to have one ear open and hours of restlessness, and instead she fell into a deep sleep for five full hours until her bladder reminded her that she shouldn't drink tea just before bed.

Maureen had in her head that Timothy got worse, restricted her, suffocated her, after her mum died. She could almost pinpoint the moment though, and it was when the twins went to university. Before then she was hanging on to a purpose and after that he was hanging onto her. She doubted herself so much and he filled all that doubt with talk of how she wasn't managing, how she needed to be looked after, how she was making unwise decisions and how he could steer her. So she gradually let him. She lay listening to the wind and rain and knew that he hadn't actually got worse, she had just given up the fight. She stopped saying no to him. She stopped being herself. He was always trying to look after her and steer her, even when she was able to look after herself and steer her own ship, and then one day she made him captain and sat in a corner. She should have kept saying no.

Her eyes stung with the warmth of tears and they fell down the edge of her face to the pillow. Twenty bloody years. She had been planning that awful ninetieth birthday party for months because he had asked her to, told her that no one was as good at events as she was, that she would know all the fine details, and how fond Mother was of Maureen like another daughter he said. Except she didn't want to be anyone else's daughter. Julia was rather unkind to the daughter she already had. She was only fond of Maureen when Maureen was smiling and doing what she was asked. And she did what she was asked and planned a party that was expensive and grand and in one of the halls of the house that was far too big for Julia. There were caterers and a jazz band and people were flying in from all over the world to see their oldest friend or sometime acquaintance, and Timothy would peacock throughout the whole event and tell people how they had organised the whole brilliant thing for his wonderful Mother. And Maureen would smile and nod and mingle and let Timothy hold her like a possession. He would tell her what a fine looking woman she was and how she was more beautiful now than ever. And then there would be a speech and he would call her up to stand next to him and people would clap. And she would be on the edge of a scream for the entire time, like a nodding dog, with a face full of ache from the false smile. Except now she wouldn't have to do any of that. She would not be held or pawed or applauded. She would not mingle and make small talk and take orders and have Julia tell her that something was too much or not enough. She used to love when people said she was too much, and then she stopped and tried to hide under the guidance of Timothy. It was time to be too much again.

She sat and thought about her fortieth birthday celebrations, the plan they had. Timothy had arranged a trip away, just the two of them. Coral was coming down to stay with the children, although it was tricky, Nanna and Grandad were increasingly reliant on her, although mainly Nanna, who was supported by Coral and Grandad. Unbeknownst to Maureen who had not been part of the surprise, Coral had told Timothy that it might be tricky to leave her parents for three nights. She suggested that they drive up and drop the children with her and then continue somewhere else, Edinburgh or somewhere north, but Timothy was adamant that Maureen had always wanted to go to Paris with him and that's what he really needed to do. She asked him if it was something that his mother could help with, but he said that the twins really were too much for Mother, and she knew her brilliant grandchildren would be miserable being told to be silent in a big house in Winchester, so, against her better judgement, Coral agreed to be part of the surprise and she organised for her lovely friends to spend a day each helping Grandad.

Three days before they were due to fly Coral rang to say that Nanna had been rushed to hospital with what they thought was a massive stroke and there wasn't a lot they could do for her. Maureen rang Timothy and told him that she had to go and be with Nanna. He said it was a long way to go when she might not make it and Maureen told him that she would never forgive herself if she didn't try.

"What about the children?" He asked

"You'll have to get them from school and bring them home and do tea." She said

"But..." he started to speak

"Timothy, I'm not asking you, I'm telling you what I'm doing. I'm about to get in the car. You have to pick the kids up at three thirty." There was panic in her voice.

"OK." He said quickly. "Please be careful."

She didn't say anything else, she grabbed a couple of things and threw her bag in the car, setting off on an awful journey. She drove straight to Kendal and got to the hospital too late. Nanna had already gone, peacefully and quietly without opening her eyes. Without having her hand held by Maureen and being told that she was the most wonderful human ever, the best nanna and great nanna. The best baker and cuddler. The best. A smile from Nanna as she rested her strong, thin hands on your shoulder could calm a worried soul, and the sound of her stirring the teapot was the soundtrack to Maureen's life. She had so much she wanted to tell her and she was too late.

Back at the house when they sat around the kitchen table drinking tea that was joyless, being shell shocked and quiet with an empty chair where Nanna would normally be, Coral reached over and took Maureen's hand.

"Sorry I didn't get here on time mam." Maureen whispered, her lip trembling.

"Oh love, you came, and Nanna would love that you came." Coral smiled with teary eyes.

"She would that Maureen, she would that." Grandad said, taking Maureen's other hand. "She bloody loved the bones of you, and the twins, you brought joy to her every day, even when you weren't here she was talking about you." Grandad took a sip of his tea. "She even loved Timothy." He added, winking.

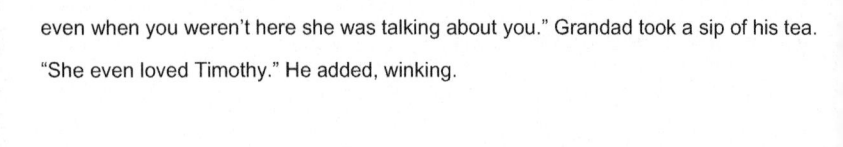

They laughed for a moment and then cried again. Maureen knew there wasn't much love lost between Coral and Timothy, and probably Grandad too, but Grandad was much more subtle, he was much more diplomatic than Coral.

"I'd better ring Timothy." Maureen said, getting up and walking to the hall where the old brown phone sat, with the turning dial.

Timothy was in the middle of trying to put the children to bed. They were ten and could shower themselves and read to themselves so there wasn't the fraught bedtimes of a few years earlier. Timothy said he was very sorry, that he loved Maureen and he was really fond of Nanna. That she was kind to him and made him the best chips and tea of anyone.

"Can I do anything?" He said.

"Just look after the children for a couple more days before I come back down." Maureen said.

"Can you come back tomorrow?" He asked.

"No, I'm going to stay a few days to help with arrangements." Maureen replied.

"But we are meant to be going away in a couple of days." He said. "We got it all sorted as a surprise for your birthday. I'm taking you to Paris."

"What?" She thought that she had heard wrong.

'Paris, for your birthday. I'm taking you the day after tomorrow. Your mother is coming down to look after the children. It's been arranged for weeks."

'No Timothy, we can't go away, Nanna has just died, we've got things to arrange and we can't have Grandad being on his own. Just no."

"It will do you good." Timothy added.

"No!" Maureen raised her voice. "We are not going away. Nanna died today. Do you hear what I'm saying?" Timothy didn't reply. "I need to speak to the kids, can you get them for me?"

Maureen spoke to the twins and gently explained what had happened, promising them that she would be back in a couple of days, she was just helping Grandad sort out some things. The twins wanted to speak to their other Nanna to make sure she was ok, so Maureen said her goodbyes and left them chatting with Coral. Maureen was seething and disappointed that Timothy would think that they were still going to go away for a couple of days after this, as if it was something that she wanted to do, or that leaving Grandad alone was an option. She couldn't hold her anger in and she let Grandad know all about it.

"The thing is love." Grandad said, putting his arm around her. "He comes from a family where it's every man for himself, survival of the fittest. They don't pull together, they compete. He won't get his head round that you look after each other just because, not because there's something in it for you. We are the lucky ones loving each other, that's why it hurts so much right now. He is bloody lucky he's got you to show him what's right."

Coral came in from the hall. "I take it you know about Paris?"

"Yes I do. And he thought we would still be going." Maureen said, with her hand on her hip.

"He thinks it'll distract you he said, but I've told him that if you've said no then it's a no." Coral explained.

"Bloody hell. He clearly didn't listen to me." Maureen rolled her eyes.

They shook their heads in unison. Maureen was distracted for a moment, with talk of Paris, and then the reality of the day crept back in and she started to cry again. It felt madness, she thought, that she would think of something else, do something, almost feel normal and then realise that this was a new normal, this sadness, this empty chair. It was nothing at the moment, early enough to pretend it wasn't happening, they could trick themselves with a short story that she was in bed or at the shops, out buying flour, they could almost play that denial game with themselves, but the reality took Maureen's breath away, took the floor from under her and left her rootless. Everything was the same for everyone except them. Life would never be the same again, and yet it carried on. The children needed her, Grandad would need her, and her mum. They all needed each other.

Coral had been doing more and more looking after Nanna, who had been diminishing with each visit north. Still full of joy and excitement, always excited and pleased to be seeing Maureen and the children, but Nanna was frail, she would sit in her armchair most of the day, using a frame to get to the toilet and get out and about. A wheelchair for longer distances out of the house. She would mix her cakes sitting at the kitchen table with Grandad doing the chopping and ingredients gathering, bending over to the oven and washing the pots after. And the cakes still tasted amazing. There would be a Christmas cake, decorated and sat in a tin the pantry for years to come, which no one would eat but occasionally smell. Nanna's little legacy, the richest fruit cake ever.

They sat round the table again, waiting for the next thing, one of them to put the kettle on, Coral to get the cake tin out, pots to be washed. They ate tiny slices of cake to make it last, Nanna's sponge cake, dusted with icing sugar that was slowly disappearing into the top layer, giving it a shine. It was only a couple of days before that she was using the old tea strainer to shake the icing sugar over the top, telling be Grandad she'd cut him a slice in a minute if he could just be a bit patient, to drink his tea and she would make him another when the cake was sliced. The difference of a couple of days. The awfulness of today. They sat quietly around the table with their cake. Eyes red from crying, stinging from salty tears that burned Maureen's cheeks. They were tired out but nobody wanted to get up and go to bed and start a new day that Nanna was not going to see. It was the twelfth of April, a day that had started well enough and then not, it had been like any other day that you might not remember and now it was a date to be brandished on their brains forever. One of them would have to get up in a minute and go to bed, to cry elsewhere, to go to a different room and be bewildered and alone until the morning. All three of them had drunk too much tea and would be back and forth to the toilet more than once in the night. Grandad would get up while it was still dark and open the back door and smell the new day, the fresh smell in the air before the day properly began. He would sling the pile of tea leaves onto the compost heap and wonder what he was doing it for really? He would sit at the table and know that it was inevitable that one of them would be sat here on their own after all of this time. He knew when you loved someone and lived with someone for that long, one of you would end up alone, and he was glad the heartache was his, because he could not bear that his beautiful and kind, beloved wife, would feel this much pain. He could not bear that for her. He was glad the pain was his. It was also Coral's and Maureen's and the twins, and he was sorry for that, but he would look after them all for as long as he could. Do his lovely wife proud.

Timothy rang the next morning to say that he loved her and missed her and understood about Paris. Was there anything he could do? He said that the children had gone to school with a few tears but he knew the distraction would do them good. He said everything that he thought he should say to make things right between them, but he still thought that going to Paris would do them both good, remind them of easier times before the children took them from each other, when they could just do as they pleased. What he thought, though, and what he said were sometimes better to be different, he knew this, but he didn't always wish to bite his tongue. He was too old to bother, or change, and too used to being in charge at work, what he said there was not open to negotiation or question. He would prefer that Maureen fell into line a bit better, but she was not afraid to pull him up and tell him what was what, and he did get an uncomfortable thrill when she put her foot down. It was like a challenge. He would store the memory of what she was objecting to and perhaps change how he said things to limit the objection, but then again perhaps not. He had long ago mastered the art of telling people what they wanted to hear. He felt that Maureen should be grateful for the amount of time she had enjoyed grandparents, there weren't many almost forty year olds who had two grandparents alive. His were long gone, so long gone he couldn't remember a lot about them, like his father. He felt that he should have some of the sympathy for his losses, over the years, he would have enjoyed his grief being soothed by Maureen. He could hear Maureen's voice 'it's not all about you Timothy,' but it never really was about him at all, he thought, it was always the kids or family, or Maureen sorting things, it wasn't often about him. He felt his mouth pout ever so slightly and he caught himself. He knew he was right. He knew he would lose Maureen to her grief for a while, she was less likely to object to things, she would be distracted, and she would need him more. He could be quite the hero under these circumstances, masterful even, saving his wife from these bad feelings, he was looking forward to being needed more. She would, no doubt, tell other people how brilliant he had been, how she wouldn't have got through it without him. She would see him in a different light. She would need him like she had never needed him before. And his greatest wish was that Maureen needed him, couldn't do without him, that she would let him look after her, take charge, do as he suggested, was his fantasy. He was a fool to fall in love with a feisty woman, but he had no choice in the matter, she had him from the very start.

She told him all she needed him to do over the next couple of days was to look after the children, to get them to school and feed them. She didn't need them all to come up Ambleside as he suggested, she said that the children needed the stability of being at home, but the reality was that she didn't need to have to look after the children and entertain Timothy all at the same time, when she just needed to focus on Grandad and the next few days. Grandad would feel this more than anyone and try to look after everyone else the most. She needed things to be as simple as possible and if Timothy and the children were here it would bring its own complications. She felt dreadful thinking it but she could manage the children no problems, they would be a delightful distraction, it was the dealing with Timothy that was not doable, not manageable. He would want to be part of it all, the centre of the loss, and she couldn't tolerate that.

"He said he would come up and help out." She said to Coral as they say drinking tea in the front room, Grandad was in the garden.

"Oh, right." Said Coral, slowly

"I said no mam, I told him to stay put. I can't be doing with him at the moment, at times like this he's not the rock you need." Maureen was trying not to be disloyal to her husband, but she could be honest with her mum.

'I suspect he'd want to suggest things and take charge, treat it a bit like we are problems to solve." Coral replied

"Yup, you've got it spot on there Mum. But I feel very disloyal saying it."

'I'm going to say this once and then I won't mention it again." Coral said, taking a moment to choose her words carefully. "But if you ever need to not be with him, you and the kids are welcome here any time, and I don't mean just for a holiday."

"Mam!" Maureen exclaimed, "I'm not leaving him." She paused for a moment, feeling foolish and like a teenager again. " I don't know how to explain myself really.   I really do love him, but sometimes I don't think I like him very much, because of his behaviour. And I try to think that it's a different upbringing, but it's hard work. Harder work than I thought it would be. But I don't want to be without him, I just need a break every now and then" Maureen took a sip of her tea and a deep breath. "I think that's normal though, show me someone who doesn't need a break from their husband occasionally and I'll show you a liar."

"Yes, I get it." Coral replied, sensing that this was not the right time to ask any more questions. "Except I've never been with anyone looking enough to need a break, although clearly they all have or I wouldn't have been single all these years."

They both chuckled. "Would you really want to settle down with someone mam?" Maureen asked.

"No, love, not now, not after all this time pleasing myself and making up my rules, I couldn't stand someone making plans for me or having expectations of me. And I'm far too old to hold farts in, for any bugger, no matter how handsome they are." Coral laughed.

Maureen caught the laughter and thought back to her and Timothy in the first flushes of love and Coral letting rip around him after a big meal. He was aghast, so much so that Maureen could barely breath with laughter, and later when they were on their own and he explained how shocked he was Maureen found herself laughing even harder and he became all flustered.

"You want what Mum and Dad have." Coral caught herself and her voice cracked. "What they had, together for 60 years and plenty of cross words, but they loved the bones of each other, and they were friends, you could tell they liked each other, wanted to look after each other. I never wanted a show boater or a wallflower, just a decent, honest person who was kind. And he never came along, but I've not got a single regret. I've got an amazing daughter, fabulous grandchildren, wonderful parents and an unusual son-in-law. What more could I want." Coral winked at Maureen.

Grandad was sat in the kitchen. He had been in the garden with a cup of tea that had long since gone cold. He sat with the newspaper, pretending to read it but really just thinking, and feeling a deep pain in his chest from sadness. He caught some sentences off the pages and then his mind would think of something else. All that there was to do to make a human disappear. He had been here before with his own parents, but many, many years ago. He felt you made someone disappear after death, you let banks know, tell the pension people, close accounts, share the news, stop the post, stop contact. No more letters through the door, just a gradual disappearing. There would be an obituary in the local paper, letting people know. They would say suddenly but peacefully. Sometimes it was after a short illness, or a long battle bravely borne, but always much loved and sadly missed. He was used to reading about people he knew, the final chapters of their stories in less than a hundred words, inside a paper that told stories of a missing cat or cars scratched maliciously in town, and the police were following leads. Near the back, before the adverts and sports, there would be the final chapter for Nanna. Once it was printed he would tear the page out of the newspaper and put it at the bottom of his old seed tin at the back of the pantry, occasionally getting it out and reading it, or just touching it gently to know that it was there.

For a while yet letters would still come with her name on them, and for a while he would receive them with a mixture of distress and joy.. Distress that she had gone and joy that she still remained, out there in the ether, still remembered by someone, even if it was requesting a charitable donation or a Christmas card from a distant relative who had not heard the news. The obituary remained in the tin on the top shelf of the pantry, right at the back. No one found it, assuming the seed tin contained only seeds and Coral and Maureen would never part with the beloved tin, even after Grandad was long gone and the garden was becoming wild.

Just as he wanted to, Timothy became quite the hero to Maureen, soothing her distress, giving her space, taking a bigger load with the children. He suggested she take some time off work and stay home a bit more and said if it was all getting too much why not have a longer break? He insisted on planning trips up to Ambleside so that she didn't have to drive alone, so that he could be with her, to make sure that she was safe and not over tired. She relied on him that little bit more and he enjoyed being needed. When she suggested, long after the funeral, months after the loss, that she would be fine driving herself up to see Grandad and Coral, he wouldn't hear of it, didn't want her to risk that journey alone, even though she had done it many, many times. His attentive nature and insistence that she needed him to go with her had had its place, it had been helpful and much appreciated, initially, she needed his company at the funeral, and then after for a while, but now if she suggested that she went up to see her mum on a Thursday, after tea, with the kids like she used to, he would suggest they went on Saturday morning so that they could all go together. The children wouldn't miss school and he could come along, and it seemed unfair if she said no. So she said yes, even when she wanted to drive up without him, and just spend the weekend with Grandad and Mum. Timothy was her hero, then her guide, then her shadow. Even on the days the sun didn't shine her shadow would be there, offering helpful suggestions, guidance, advice, poo pooing things, shortening her time away from her Ambleside home where possible. She felt suffocated.

Maureen had visited Grandad and Coral more regularly with Timothy, but for much shorter times, more often than not, just for one night. There was no time to relax, go anywhere, have an adventure, chat late into the night. And it had suited Maureen, she was ashamed to admit. Timothy being there changed the dynamic somewhat, making the hole left by Nanna not being there less of an ongoing scream and more of a breathlessness. Staring at an empty chair was harder when Timothy was requesting attention, or saying they ought to go to bed. It wasn't until spring 1999, twelve months after Nanna had died that she told him she would be going up to stay with Grandad and Coral for a week in the Easter holidays. She knew she had to bite the bullet and be in the house for a while, entertain the kids there, sit quietly, talk to Grandad without Timothy trying to guide the conversation.

"I don't think it'll be a week Maureen." He said, reaching for his diary. "I won't be able to make a full week. Maybe three nights?"

"No, I've got two weeks off with the kids and we are going for a week." She didn't look at him, just carried on doing bits around the kitchen.

"Well, like I said, we can't, I can't get the time off." He closed his diary with a bang and she felt his eyes following her about the room as she walked from counter to counter.

"I can. I have the time off, and so do the kids, so I will take them, if you want to drive up for the three nights you can make then that's smashing, but I'm going to give them a proper break, do the full week and have a little adventure." She turned to look at him.

He opened his diary again. "Four nights, I could do four nights at a push, and I mean that is stretching myself."

"That's great." Maureen replied. "So we'll only be up there the three extra nights without you." She took a deep breath, knowing what was coming.

"No, no, no Maureen." He shook his head, his voice brittle. "That is not what I mean. We can all go for the four nights, that'll be plenty. You're tired out, you've had a very stressful year, you can't be driving all of that way on your own with the kids, it won't do you any good and I don't think you're strong enough."

"Timothy, I'm not ill, or some great weakling, I'm a forty-one year old woman who is more than fucking capable of driving up there. I'm not asking your permission or for your assistance, I'm going up for a week with the kids and if you would like to come for some of it then that's great, but I am going regardless." She could feel her cheeks get hot.

"Oh Maureen, there's no reason to speak crassly all of the time. I'm not stopping you, I'm just saying that it's something you need to think about." His voice was louder than usual, and he played with the corner of his diary in annoyance.

"Well that's very thoughtful of you, I have thought about it and I am going with the kids. I need some time with Mum and Grandad and they need some time with us. We'll be away Easter weekend."

He opened his mouth to say something else. He wanted to say that Easter Sunday was his mother's day, to sit with her and have a meal, that had always been the routine since before he and Maureen had got together and he knew Maureen wouldn't have forgotten. She knew he was on the edge of annoyance and she knew she could tell him that he couldn't take control of her every action, that he would have to put up with her making decisions and doing what she thought was best, but she also knew that the frost that would hang between them would be cold and problematic and linger for days, weeks even. She would have to put on a jolly act and try to smile and be light, tread gently and dance her happy wife dance, and try and ease him out of the sulk, so she went down a different route. She walked over to him and stood behind him, wrapping her arms around his shoulders.

"I love how well you look after me, how you've taken amazing care for me since Nanna died, but it's such a lot of pressure on you and you work so hard I just want you to pull back a bit and not worry so much." She kissed his head. "So I'm going to do this because I need it and the kids need it and you need some peace and quiet at home. Come up if you can manage a couple of nights, or just chill at home."

He looked up at her and he had nothing more he could say. He had plenty more he wanted to say but he felt silenced. He couldn't respond to that, she had snuffed out the argument and he knew she had made a decision and he was back to waving her away or waiting for her to come home. He didn't want her to go on her own but he didn't really want to go either. He knew the reception he got from Coral on their whistle stop tours to Ambleside. The woman had no sense of humour, he would crack a joke and she wouldn't raise a smile, and everyone always laughed at his little jokes, especially people from work, but his mother-in-law was humourless when it came to him. Plenty of times he had seen her belly laugh with Maureen so he assumed it was plain rudeness. He just wanted Maureen to be at home, to be there when he was. It wasn't too much to ask. He just wanted Coral to have less of an influence on his wife, he should be the one influencing her, advising her, she didn't need support from Coral when she had him.

Maureen came from a tribe of friends who looked out for each other, family who championed their kin, supported decisions, ideas, choices. Timothy came from a family where it was every man for himself, the emphasis on the man. He was the star of the show because he possessed the correct genitals and no amount of female influence or parenting a daughter would change what ran through his core. He knew his life would have been far easier if he had married one of the many yes women he had been introduced to throughout his twenties. He would probably be able to be listened to in his own home and his rules would be followed, but he also knew that his breath wouldn't catch in the same way when his wife walked into a room, his heart wouldn't race when she tossed her head back and laughed from her belly, he wouldn't be sat waiting for her to come home, hoping that she would be smiling when she saw him. But he was certain he should be able to have it all. He should be able to have Maureen there all of the time and he should be her person, she shouldn't need anyone else. He didn't feel he needed anything else, except perhaps Mother in certain quantities, he needed her praise. He didn't really need Florence and he was fairly certain Mother didn't either, not like she needed Timothy.

Florence had been an open disappointment to Mother since her divorce, and that was some time ago now. He didn't understand why she never remarried, had some sort of family, just settled down. Any relationships she had she certainly didn't discuss them with her dismissive brother. She met Maureen regularly, saw her beloved niece and nephew, but any talk of love or relationships never went as far as the ears of Timothy. Any information that went that way would have been fair game to be laid out and dissected between him and Mother, like an old rat in a science lab, and Florence knew any sensitive discussions she had with Maureen would go no further. She knew Maureen did not enjoy Julia's verbal destruction of others and she would not help contribute to that in any way, and that meant Timothy could not know certain things. He was happy to share anything about anyone that would shine his light brighter towards his mother. Maureen remembered Julia's reprimanding Florence for being drunk years ago, when she was first divorced, telling her that ladies did not drink so much that they vomited, regardless of what had gone on. Maureen had flashed a look of thunder at Timothy as Julia continued to talk about what a disgraceful way Florence had behaved and what would people think?

"People won't think anything." Maureen had said, putting her tea cup into her saucer with a clatter. "And perhaps you." She said, pointing her finger towards Timothy with disgust. "Could pass by the chance of gossiping about your sister and support her for a few moments."

"Excuse me, young lady." Julia had said, quite surprised.

"No, I won't excuse you." Maureen replied. "Let's direct our disgust and anger where it is due and support those we love who have been treated appallingly. And one more thing." She said looking from Timothy to Julia. "I don't want to hear another word from either of you that is critical or disrespectful towards Florence."

Florence's eyes were wide and you could almost feel the amusement from her, that she had been defended so vigorously and that Timothy and her mother had been told off in such a magnificent fashion made her feel championed, and that did not happen often. Timothy kept his head down slightly and his eyes firmly on his cup of tea. Maureen stared hard towards Julia who looked away, not used to being challenged so fairly, and nothing more was said on the matter. At least not there, and not to Maureen or Florence, who were both certain plenty more would have been said another time when both of them were out of ear shot. And both Maureen and Florence giggled about it to each other for years to come, the finger point and the stare became the thing of legends. They would also laugh and wonder what Julia would think if she were to know that Maureen had been pursued by Timothy after he represented her following her arrest. That had never, ever been mentioned to Julia and both of them hoped that one day it would be revealed, although so far no one had dared.

16- some mild threats.

Maureen had received 5 increasingly angry messages from Timothy as the morning progressed. As the hot weather broke he was clearly hoping that Maureen's resolve would break too. The first message was quite the paragraph about how much he loved her, what a good life they had built together, how well he had provided for her and taken care of her, especially in recent years, and how he could not understand why she had decided that she would throw their life away in this fashion. These led on to messages about how she would not manage without him, how he would make sure that the house in Ambleside was sold and she would not be able to keep it, that she would be financially ruined without him.

The messages were designed to cause her fear and distress, he knew the cottage was her anchor, her home no matter where else she was, and she was doing his damnedest to make her think it would be gone from under her, that he was still in charge of her and whatever she did she had no future without him. He was clutching at straws and she knew it, but it made her heart beat quickly in her chest until she could hear it beat in her ears, and her stomach churned, thinking about what she needed to do.

There were two people she knew well, who she could call for advice, as a very last resort. She knew there would be consequences, that they would be delighted to assist her but that they may not do it quietly, although she hoped that the respect they had for her was greater than their dislike of Timothy. Douglas Scott was Timothy's former accountant who had refused to be party to some sort of transactions Timothy was planning in the last couple of years, and likewise, one of his former members is staff, who had worked with him for the best part of forty years, Michael Price, would be more than happy to assist with anything that would be of annoyance or problematic for Timothy. Both Dougie and Mick were very fond of Maureen and would be happy to help. She would never have called them or told them anything if Timothy wasn't making threats. She felt that she had no choice and she needed to get their advice to calm herself.

She made the first call at ten thirty, before she was dressed, sitting at the kitchen table with a pad and pens, tea on one side and water on the other. Mick said he was delighted to hear from her and even more delighted that she had left the old bastard and she should have done it years ago, always too good for him, he said, too kind to be part of his roughness, too classy for his rudeness. She forwarded him the messages he'd sent and asked what she should do. Unless much had changed in the last couple of years she didn't need to do anything. The house was in her name and had been passed specifically to her. Timothy had lots of properties, their own house, his mother's home was in his name and had been for many years, and that was worth goodness knows how much. If all she wanted was this house, her family home, then it was unlikely that a judge would think she was asking for too much. She said she wanted nothing else but this house, no other property.

"You know I have so much dirt on Timmy boy he wouldn't dare take this further." Mick laughed. And he meant it. Timothy would be appalled that Maureen had spoken to Mick,

He told her to fill in a legal separation form and she could do that on her own without Timothy doing it too, if she had her marriage certificate, which she did, in the files of paperwork she had taken from the safe in the bedroom, that was currently hiding under the wardrobe in her Nanna and Grandad's bedroom. She had laughed at her own paranoia when she squeezed it under there.

The next call she made was to Dougie, she had made herself a fresh cup of tea for this one and a couple of slices of toast. Dougie was in a meeting but he called her back by the time her chin was glistening from the buttery toast and the kettle was boiling again. She explained her situation again to the much more reserved man, explaining that she just wanted to make sure that she had enough money to live on, with a little comfort. She didn't need riches, she just needed to be able to pay the day to day bills, make sure she could run her car, heat the place when the cold winter hit and probably afford fish and chips once a week. She had a lot of accounts seemingly in her name, could she use some of the money? She was so used to asking for money, please could she use some for the children or the house, that she felt the need to ask permission again. She had more than enough money, he told her, she went through the bank statements she had over the phone with him and she was certain that it couldn't all be hers but it was her name on the account, would he be able to close the accounts? Dougie told her that he had been pushing money her way to be less transparent for him for years, and he couldn't get to it unless it was through other courts in divorce proceedings, but the reality was she was really very well off, Dougie said, this might seem like a fortune to Maureen but it was nothing compared to the money he had elsewhere, so if that was all she wanted no one would argue with her. She could chase lots more.

"I don't want anything else, just my house and some money to live on." She explained.

"I think that you've nothing to worry about Maureen." Dougie said. "But you know he'll be livid you've discussed this with me though. I don't think you should tell him anything, if he's not mentioned money and he can't access it, just keep carrying on until you need to go to court for anything. And I'll support you in any way I can."

It was close to noon when Maureen had finished on the phone. Still feeling anxious but calmer than before she had spoken to either of them. She knew Dougie was quiet and thoughtful and would not say a word about their discussion, but she suspected that Mick would already be informing people that she had left Timothy and word would get back to the man himself. She spent a good hour typing and deleting a message back to Timothy before she felt it was fine to send.

"Timothy, I'm sorry that you are so hurt by all of this. You have to stop sending threatening messages that are intended to cause me worry. I will not change my mind. I am filing for legal separation. I do not want anything other than this house, my car and a small amount of money to live on. I will not go after other properties, including Julia's house and properties in Winchester. I don't want the house we have been living in. I have spoken with both Mick Price and Dougie Scott for advice and they are happy to continue to support me legally and financially for advice. Please only contact me if it is something urgent that needs my immediate attention."

She sent the message and looked at her phone for some time. She checked that it had been received and read, and she saw that he was typing a reply, three dots full of potential threats, but nothing came through, so she assumed he had decided not to respond after all. At least for now. She knew he would be livid that she had spoken to Dougie and Mick, he would not have expected that at all, but if he was going to shake her she needed help to steady herself. He had spent so long trying to keep her quiet he appeared to forget how loud she could be, how strong and how fierce. She had forgotten that about herself for far too long as well, but she was just beginning to remember.

And what now? It was the wait that drove her mad, she had done this big, brave thing, taken herself back, but it wasn't over, there were legal things, financial things and even if Timothy was calm and agreeable it would still be quite a process. But he wasn't agreeable, he was kicking the edges of acceptability, but only visibly to Maureen. He would hold his resolve to anyone else, she had seen him do it a thousand times, when he was outraged or disgusted she could see tiny changes in his demeanour, but to anyone else he was calm and together. Later, out of other's view he would rage, but to anyone else he was calm, measured, Timothy.

It was a waiting game really, the decision she made a few days ago was a long time coming, it had begun to whisper in her ear and shake her from her sleep. It asked 'is this it?' in her moments alone, in her moments in company, as she sat at the golf club in the ladies bar drinking wine. She often wondered if the other women were being held hostage to their silence, in their woollen jumpers and gold necklaces. What had they swallowed down or given up to be sat in a place that acceptably separated them from the men? She felt her youthful rage bubble, then the bitterness of her fear punched it down, and she carried on sipping the wine, watching her friends. She often pondered if they were friends, would she call them in the middle of the night, tell them tales of her youth, whisper to them about her unhappiness? Would she belly laugh with them until tears rolled down her face, drink too many wines and fall off a stool without judgement? The answer to it all was no, she would not be prepared to let her smile slip for a moment with these women in the ladies bar at the golf club. She would not tell them that she felt like she had been kidnapped and turned into a silent, middle aged woman. She just assumed they all felt the same way, but none of them admitted much beyond the odd drunken slur and an eye roll, talk of an affair, too much time at work. They talked about their husband's, not about themselves, and Maureen carried on smiling and sipping her wine and being held hostage. But now she was free and now she waited, and hoped, that the glances of others would quieten Timothy, no out of place public displays. She had already googled the legal separation paperwork and that would give her a bit more of an independent standing. She would do it today. And then she would carry on with the waiting game, she was worried that fear would get the better of her, but she was excellent at this game, she had been playing it for years, she just didn't know. She had held herself firm and played the waiting game, she just didn't realise what she was playing, what she was waiting for and if it would ever end.

She checked her phone again, half expecting a message from Timothy, once he had digested her message and toyed with the taste of it. He would feel it in his throat, in his stomach and he would not be able to settle or rest until he had done something about it. But he hadn't messaged, so she assumed that he was dealing with it in some other way.

There was a short message from Florence, checking in on her, asking if she was ok. She sent a quick reply off, updating her on her morning activities. It was just over a week until the birthday party and everyone would be there, the golf women, the people from the club, friends of Julia, associates of Timothy, Florence, Lilly and her, the wife who got free.

She was dreading it. She had agreed that she would go, it would be her last appearance with them all and then she would retreat back to her cottage and be done with the whole damn charade. All that would be left would be the legal matters and someone else would help her with that. Just over a week to get herself ready and face the bloody awful music, for one night only. The thought of it made her shudder, the whole expectation and drama of it all. But she had said to Lilly and Florence that she would be going with them. She should never have agreed to it. But she should never have agreed to lots of things and she wouldn't have been in this situation, she would have been in the cottage years earlier and not having to deal with Timothy still. She should have left when the children went to university. She could have left then. But she didn't. She needed him. And he supported her every move, closing in until she couldn't breathe without him, and then suffocating her so she could barely breathe at all. She should have left sooner, but she didn't. She left when she did and if she suffocated now under the weight of regret she would waste her time and opportunity. She left now. Now is a good time. Now is the right time to leave.

"Hindsight is twenty-twenty and foresight is blurry. Stop with the regrets, we do the best we can with the information we have at the time." Grandad would say. And he was right. He was usually right. Even after Nanna died he carried on being wise, carried on giving support, quietly and thoughtfully.

"It's lovely to see you on your own." He said once, when she had stopped being escorted up to Ambleside by Timothy. "Less of a rush for you, a proper little break."

"I know. I didn't want to keep coming and dashing off again. I wanted to spend some time with my favourite Grandad."

Grandad chuckled at the table, his shoulders gently moving up and down. Coral had taken the twins to the pictures to see Stuart Little, which they both said they would see if they could have a popcorn each and not have to share, which Coral agreed to. She would let them have whatever they wanted, sweets, ice cream, fizzy pop, the works.

"And are you doing ok?" Grandad asked. "At home I mean. You don't seem to be out and about like you were before."

"Before Nanna?" Maureen said.

Grandad nodded. "You're an independent girl, always have been, always will be. Don't let anyone restrict you, love."

Maureen knew there must have been discussions between Grandad and her mum. That's where the conversation was coming from. She felt a bit embarrassed, but she was pleased they had noticed that she wasn't being paranoid that Timothy was creeping into her every move.

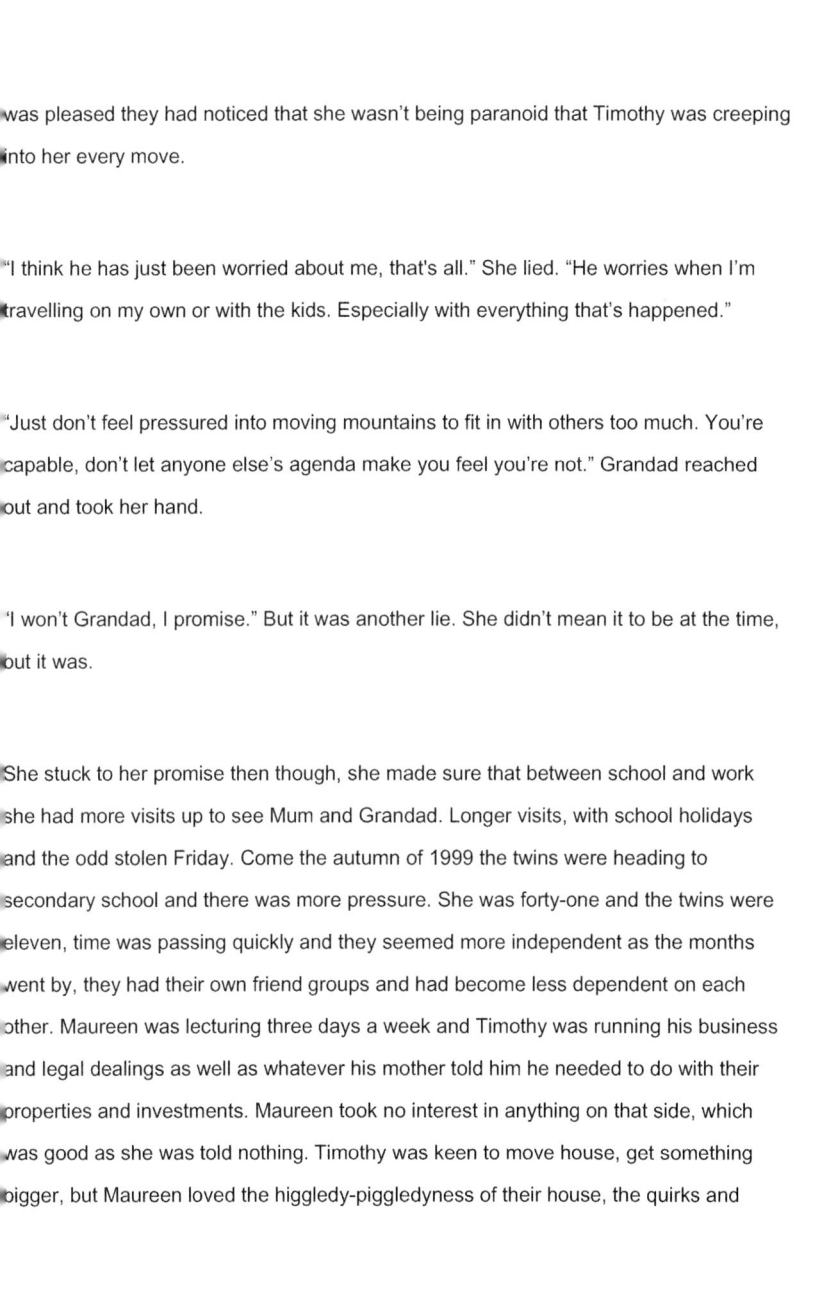

"I think he has just been worried about me, that's all." She lied. "He worries when I'm travelling on my own or with the kids. Especially with everything that's happened."

"Just don't feel pressured into moving mountains to fit in with others too much. You're capable, don't let anyone else's agenda make you feel you're not." Grandad reached out and took her hand.

'I won't Grandad, I promise." But it was another lie. She didn't mean it to be at the time, but it was.

She stuck to her promise then though, she made sure that between school and work she had more visits up to see Mum and Grandad. Longer visits, with school holidays and the odd stolen Friday. Come the autumn of 1999 the twins were heading to secondary school and there was more pressure. She was forty-one and the twins were eleven, time was passing quickly and they seemed more independent as the months went by, they had their own friend groups and had become less dependent on each other. Maureen was lecturing three days a week and Timothy was running his business and legal dealings as well as whatever his mother told him he needed to do with their properties and investments. Maureen took no interest in anything on that side, which was good as she was told nothing. Timothy was keen to move house, get something bigger, but Maureen loved the higgledy-piggledyness of their house, the quirks and uneven walls. It was where she brought her babies home to and it suited her well. It suited the children well, only five minutes walk and they were on the bus to school. Timothy wanted a new build, one of the big executive homes he spoke of, he had a stake in a building company and he could get anything built that she fancied, big rooms he said, shiny new kitchen, double garage, anything she fancied he kept saying. But she didn't fancy any of it, she liked her cosy rooms and bay window, her pantry and her old kitchen with pictures on the cupboard doors. She told him the kids needed to be settled into school before they make any changes, but she didn't want to make any changes settled or not.

She had fallen in love with this house and it reminded her of home. She was never sure why it reminded her of what it should actually be, home, but if they got a new house it would be somewhere Nanna had never visited, never sat, never looked out of the window and said what a lovely view. And for now, at the moment, she couldn't manage that. All that newness. She really wanted to fill her garden with chickens and greenhouses and vegetables, but for now getting the kids to do homework and marking papers, cleaning and doing tea was about all she could muster. But she loved a dream.

She was slowly making her way through a jar of blackberry and apple jam that she had been given to her by Coral, left over in the pantry of the cottage in Ambleside, made by the sturdy, gentle hands of Nanna, on a good day when her memory was managing, before the worst day of all. She toasted two pieces of bread in a morning and only put jam on one to stretch it out, and she didn't share it. The tartness at the back of her tongue when the jam hit her taste buds transported her to all of her autumns; the smell of the jam bubbling in the pan and the cold saucer ready to take the teaspoon of boiling liquid and test if it had hit the right point. It was the smell of autumn, the countdown to Christmas, the promise of jam tarts. The jam pan earned its keep without a doubt, and sometimes a hundred jars lined the top shelf of the pantry with Nanna's jams and chutneys. And now she was savouring this last jar, closing her eyes as she chewed her toast, sticking her nose towards the top of the jar so she could smell the sticky sweetness and pretend, for the briefest of moments, she was in that kitchen, helping. There would be no jam tarts or jam sponges this year, just her and her toast and the odd tear.

Once when the children were well settled into school, and away staying with friends, Timothy took Maureen for a drive out and a meal. They stopped at the edge of a housing development with huge, new, red brick houses with their brown window frames and high roofs. Three stories of wide windows blinking into the sun.

"What do you think?" He asked as they drove towards the show home.

"Very new and swanky." She said, before adding: "Without the s."

He looked at her and couldn't make out what she was talking about. "But what do you think for us?"

"Hmmmm, they look very new and samey." She said.

"Yes, aren't they beautiful?" He gushed. "Well made, sturdy, and a long warranty. They've got three and four bedroom ones here and further back, for us, the five bedroom ones with the bigger gardens and garages. And in the city, no more village living"

She went through the motions of looking at the show home, and it was impressive, but new wasn't for her.

"I can't see myself living there." She said as they sat down for dinner. "I like to think of the history of a place, the people who've lived there before, brought their families there. I just love an old house. New builds aren't for me, for us. It's not for us. I don't want to move out of the village, we are happy in our house aren't we?"

She tried to take his hand but he picked up his knife and fork and started eating again so she couldn't hold on.

"I love it." He said, then putting his cutlery down he went on. "Do you know of all of our circle of friends, of everyone at work, we have the smallest house? It doesn't look good. It doesn't reflect who we are. We can afford a much bigger house and we should have one."

"Timothy, we can't move the kids and leave our lovely home so that people can envy our house. No one cares." Maureen replied.

"I care. It matters to me." Timothy scowled. "What if we looked at older houses, bigger houses but with history?"

"Well there's no harm in looking but I'm more than happy where we are. I love our house." She started eating and nothing more was said on the matter for now, but there was a decided chill for the rest of the evening.

Occasionally, over the next few months, he would come home with a brochure from an estate agent and they would be off on an appointment to view a house. And some were beautiful, grand places, but he wasn't as keen because he had his heart set on a new build and that was not something she could agree with. Even Julia told him that he should get himself a grand, old house, but he wanted modern and square. And Maureen was more than happy staying where they already were, regardless of what Timothy thought others might think. The house hunting went on for a couple of years, occasional viewings, discussion and argument, and then nothing for a while. By the time the twins were teenagers their house was getting quite full, with sport equipment and musical instruments. Timothy and Maureen agreed that they would spread their net wider and look at possibilities that they both liked. In October 2001 they had found a house they both loved, old with some modern renovations and they were waiting for searches and legal issues, and it felt hopeful.

Grandad was eighty nine at the beginning of November. He looked smaller than he had, his eyes more deep set and the little hair he had was waving over his ears and neck. He had woken up every day for three years without his great love, after waking up with her each day for sixty two years. He was tired of waking up without her. He was tired of that briefest of moments when he first came too before he remembered that she had gone. The shock of it all was replaced with an empty feeling that he didn't reveal to Coral or Maureen, or anyone who greeted him as he went about his daily business. He was tired of carrying only one cup of tea up to bed and only one digestive biscuit in the top pocket of his shirt. They, whoever they were, said that it would get easier, but in the last few weeks he felt that it had got so much harder, he was tired of it all. The only time he felt better was when Maureen came to visit with the twins, and he had to put his best brave face on and pretend he was doing ok, and that seemed to chivvy him along a bit. Until she left to go back to that dreadful man who was squeezing her life away.

Grandad had made up his mind to have a bit more of a direct talk with Maureen. To tell her, in case she had forgotten, how magnificent she was, and how he felt Timothy was having too much of an influence on her decisions. How she had calmed her spark to please him, when she was the brightest spark in any place, and she should never forget that. She was due to come up for a long weekend and he would tell her then. She had been up so see him with the children in half term and he planned to speak to her then, but it wasn't quite right, and he regrettably swallowed down his words. Before Grandad spoke to Maureen, when he was eighty nine and two days old, he carried his cup of tea, slowly, up to bed. Every few steps a dribble of tea hit the wooden staircase and if he managed he wiped it up with his foot that was clad in a thick woollen sock, tutting at himself and his clumsiness. He felt tired, as though someone had sneaked extra stairs into his house, and by the time he was at the top he was wheezing a little. Coral had told him she could carry his tea up, help him up the stairs but he shrugged her off and said that he wasn't a bloody invalid. So onwards he dribbled and wiped. He placed the tea on the bedside table, along with the digestive biscuit that had survived the perilous journey in his top pocket, and he quickly lay down on the bed, fully clothed. He felt dizzy and shattered and couldn't even muster the energy to get undressed. He lay on top of the covers catching his breath, his shirt sleeves rolled up and his tank top still bearing a bit of egg yolk from his breakfast. Grandad tried to catch his breath for a short while, but his tiredness got the better of him and at eighty nine and two days old he breathed for the last time on top of the old eiderdown he had slept under for years with his beloved wife. His tea was untouched and his digestive un-nibbled.

The next morning when he was not sat at his usual seat at the kitchen table Coral climbed the stairs to check on him before heading to work and found him lying, looking comfortable but gone. She gasped, crying for her dad, kneeling by the bed and holding his hand, she knew there was nothing that could be done for him. After a short time she went to make the calls needed, turning the radio on so that the quietness of the house didn't sound so loud. She knew people would arrive soon to do what was needed and she felt as though she wouldn't be able to breathe when her dad went out of the house for the last time. She knew she had to ring Maureen. They needed each other.

It was a long journey north for Maureen, and she had made hundreds over the years. This one seemed slower and longer than ever before. She knew she'd get this call, not right now, but she knew it was coming, because she knew he was going, he had become slower and more tired, and she had told him how much she loved him every time she saw him. Things weren't left unsaid, but it was too soon. She tried to think about how lucky she was to have him. How many Grandad's in 1958 would have embraced their unmarried daughter and loved their granddaughter proudly and without judgement? She was beyond lucky that he had guided her through childhood.

Timothy held her at the door and asked if it was a good idea that she drive all that way right now, and if she waited they could all travel after school, stay a couple of nights and then come back down Sunday. She told him no. She needed to go to be with her mum without having to think about entertaining the kids or looking after anyone else. He opened his mouth to respond, thought better of it and said at least he hoped her mobile phone was charged this time. She said she would text him if she stopped on the way, and she would only do that if she needed a wee, which she would, without question. And then she set off and drove towards a changed house.

Coral boiled and re-boiled the kettle, expecting Maureen at the door at any moment. When she eventually made it through the front door they hugged each other tightly and cried great sobs together until their eyes stung and they needed to sit down, and then they sat at the kitchen table and cried a bit more. Coral relayed what she had been told, it was an unexpected death and so there would need to be a post mortem, but the doctor said that it was most likely a heart attack.

"He was shattered, poor dad." Coral said.

"I know, he looked tired and a bit fed up when we were up here last." Maureen replied.

"Aye, but he always perked up when you were here. He loved the bloody bones of you, lived to see you, you know. You were his tonic." Coral smiled sadly.

"I love, loved the bones of him too. Couldn't have asked for a better Grandad in a million years." They were crying and smiling at the same time.

Maureen stayed for a few days, looking after things, paper work, each other, walking round the garden in the morning frost to look at the sprouts and leeks he had planted for Christmas, the garlic and onions still fattening up in the cold. His mug remained on the drainer, not to be put back in the cupboard for now, and the kettle boiled constantly with visitors coming to pay their respects. It felt sadder than when Nanna died because they had both gone, but easier because they didn't have to worry about Grandad and how he would cope, they only had to worry about each other now. Poor Mum would be in the house on her own, Maureen kept thinking.

Maureen drove back down to Oxford and the four of them returned to Ambleside a week later for the funeral, staying a full week to sort things and be together with Coral. The twins looked after their Nanna, getting into bed with her in the morning with a cup of tea that they argued over who would make it. Coral smiled saying that she'd be more than happy with two cups and she didn't expect teenagers would want to snuggle down with her but who was she to argue? It felt lovely that they were all together, a fitting tribute to Grandad. And it was a lovely funeral, lots of beautiful things said about a kind, friendly man who's onions were legendary.

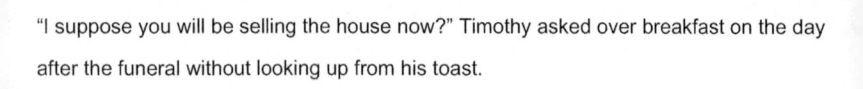

"I suppose you will be selling the house now?" Timothy asked over breakfast on the day after the funeral without looking up from his toast.

"Timothy!!!" Maureen said loudly, making him jump up with a sudden jerk.

"Why would I sell my home Timothy?" Coral asked, looking straight at him without looking away.

He paused, his toast hanging near his mouth, bending towards the table, limp and soggy. "Oh, I was just thinking that it might be a bit big and maybe you'd want something else?" He lied. He was thinking that if the house was gone, the family home, the cottage, the place she loved most, then she would not feel the need to be taking the children up the motorway every spare minute and she would be at home where she belonged.

Coral continued to look at him, making him feel uncomfortable and have to look away. "I love this house, I can't imagine living anywhere else now." She smiled, but only with her mouth.

"I don't think I could bear someone else living here." Maureen said sadly. "It's always the place I wanted to retire to, whenever that was."

Coral and Maureen shed a few tears as Timothy continued to munch his toast. The children were watching a film in the front room, out of sorts and irritable with sadness and fussing parents checking in on them every half an hour. Timothy had asked that they travel back home straight after breakfast, he had things to do, work to get on with. The weather was bad and he just wanted to be away from this awful house full of Maureen's history that didn't include him. He wanted to be back home and relaxed without feeling that Coral was watching his every move, waiting for him to say the wrong thing. She wasn't watching his every move though, she would rather not look at him at all. She wasn't waiting for him to say the wrong thing, he just managed that naturally. All of the bloody time. He just wasn't usually picked up on it, people generally didn't point out his rudeness, or ask him to think about what was said. He was a man of a certain age who had done well for himself and he didn't expect it at all.

It was Thursday and they had agreed to travel back on Friday, but Timothy had said, more than one, in private to Maureen, that they couldn't afford to stay for another day. She didn't agree, merely reiterated their previous plan. "We had better get sorted if we are leaving in the next hour." Timothy said, getting up from the table and washing the sticky jam off his hands. Shop bought.

"Tomorrow, we agreed to drive back tomorrow." Maureen said quietly.

"I know, but I said before that something has come up, an unexpected meeting and I need to be back for it." He looked around at Maureen, ignoring Coral and staring directly at his wife with a hint of annoyance in his voice.

Maureen opened her mouth to speak but Coral quickly interrupted. "I'm so grateful to you for driving these lovely people up for the funeral." She smiled. "And I know you must have missed quite a lot of work. So how about you drive back to make your meeting and I'll drive back down with Maureen and the twins on Saturday, have a spot of lunch somewhere, then that doesn't put more pressure on you Tim?"

"Oh I don't want to put you out, I can take us all today." Timothy smiled back without meaning anything pleasant at all.

"Oh nonsense, you'll get done quicker on your own, and it's not putting me out at all, we can have some music on, take a slow journey back with my favourite people. It'll be my pleasure. You'll be doing me a favour." Coral kept her voice light.

"I suppose I could miss my meeting? Wait until tomorrow?" Timothy replied.

"Goodness no, it sounded very important if you have to go back a whole day earlier than planned. You go and we'll see you Saturday." Coral folded her arms as she stood looking directly at Timothy until he turned away and thanked her.

As he left the room Coral looked over to Maureen and gave a little wink. Maureen smiled sadly back, pleased to be staying but knowing she would be enduring Timothy's annoyance at this for a few days to come yet. She heard him stomping up the stairs and walking backwards and forwards across the bedroom, gathering his things. She got up and popped her head into the front room, telling the kids that they would be staying until Saturday and asking if they wanted to go down to their favourite cafe and get a fully loaded hot chocolate once they had waved dad away. They didn't need to ask twice. It was perfect, Mum, Nanna and a gallon of hot chocolate, as well as no school.

They all stood at the door waving Timothy away as he edged his car away from the curb. He had a big bag on the back seat that was full of dirty washing and he had promised to put it in the washer as soon as he got home, and sling it in the dryer so that Maureen had less to do when he got home. He has kissed her and said not to worry, it would be the first thing on his list, but all the while he was saying he would do it he was thinking that if it was that important to her, she could get in the bloody car and come with him and do it herself. So the bag waited by the washing machine until Saturday, and he was pleased with himself every time he stepped over it.

17- a new normal

Maureen was having a lazy day, if there was such a thing on the day she filed her legal separation form and sent her three copies off, with only a couple of repeat phone calls to Mick Price for a little bit of guidance around what the hell did this and that mean? She had the back door open, blowing cold damp air through the house. She thought about her mum and what would have been different about Timothy arriving and making demands if Coral had been there. What would have been different is that he wouldn't have come in the first place. He wouldn't have thought for a second that he would drive five hours up the motorway and demand that Maureen went back to what he regarded as home. He would have used different words and held himself together if he had any kind of conversation around Coral. Maureen was so busy treading on eggshells she forgot to do what she'd been raised to do and smash them. But if Timothy felt that Coral had undetermined him or questioned him, or twisted his truth around, the victory wasn't worth more than a moment because Maureen would tiptoe about the fall out either way. She couldn't pinpoint when the tiptoeing started, and really she felt it was her own doing. If she had adopted the fierceness she had been born with and ignored the sulking and fall out from any push back he'd have learnt quickly she wouldn't put up with it. But it comes slowly, subtly, you don't wake up one day to another person who is behaving differently. She was enmeshed in being wife and mother, daughter and daughter in law, granddaughter, teacher, friend and slowly the patchwork blanket that was her became entwined into his and then the children's and she lost where she was. She could recall dates like an expert, she knew dates of deaths, meetings, holidays, wonderful events, she had studied dates for years, for her job, but the date the eggshells came remained a mystery, the date she started to disappear and stopped standing up for herself, lost in time. It made her sad, bereft at times. But the day she woke up, the day she found herself, that date would be seared across her brain with relief and celebration.

There was still a musty smell about the house from being unused for so long. It was comforting in some way, reminding her of the business of the home. Because of the age of it the threat of damp and mould had been ever present the moment it became empty, and she had paid someone she knew to do a good clean in the spring and autumn each year, air the house they called it. Then she would go several times a year and keep on top of everything once Mum had gone. It was awful going back that first time, and all of the times after, really. The house had breathed Nanna, Grandad and Mum, and then within five years they all were gone. It was a cruel grief. Talking about Nanna to Mum and Grandad kept her alive in the house, her cake tins, recipes, listening to The Archers with her, laughing about funny things she had done. Then talking about Nanna and Grandad with Coral, smiling through tears recalling a story, or a song, or the taste of something made the memories happy. Then there was no one to talk about them all with. The twins would ask and listen, Timothy at times, friends too, but Maureen had become the history keeper. The stories of her life, tales from Nanna and Grandad, all kept within her and she was the holder of it all. It was a huge, sad responsibility. The 'do you remember the time?' conversations became more recent. No one was as excited at tales about Christmas dinner from 1966 when Grandad produced the world's biggest parsnip and wrapped it up for Nanna. Or about the bike he had restored and painted for Maureen when she was ten, or the birthday cake Nanna made for her sixteenth birthday which was lemony and melted in the mouth. They were their family stories and she was the only one with them now.

It felt, often, after mum had died, that she wouldn't be able to get through the days. It wasn't sudden, it wasn't a shock, but she was surprised every single day to the point that she found it hard to breath, but she had no choice, she kept going because the twins needed her to be up and busy with them every day, they needed to be told to get ready for school, do homework, revise, wash pots, get their dirty washing, take some exercise, turn the television off. So she functioned. She felt like an orphan, like half of her life was missing, but she functioned, with numbness and panic. She had to remind herself to get on with things, sometimes at work she would sit in the toilet at lunch time and just will herself to get through the afternoon, smile in the right places and try not to cry.

When Timothy said that she looked tired and everything was getting too much for her, and she should think about giving up work she jumped at the chance, even though she had always loved her job and been fiercely independent to keep it. It was too much, smiling all day with chapped cheeks. She was cross with herself for not being able to cope but felt safer in her house and when the kids were with her. If Timothy was away Lilly would get into bed with her mum and they would drink tea together and chat like Maureen and Coral had done over the years and Maureen would feel calm and content for a short while. Maureen didn't want the twins to know she was struggling, she didn't want them to have to think about her and worry when they should be out with friends or studying or at school, so she became an Oscar worthy actress with her fake smiling and secret tears.

"I think you need to see a doctor, this has been going on for too long." Timothy said one evening when he caught her crying in the kitchen when the children were out with friends.

"I just feel sad that's all." Maureen replied. " It's not even been a year yet and I'm just sad. There's nothing you can get for grief. No magic pill. Doctors can't do anything."

"You need to stop crying all the time every time the children are out of the house. I don't want to see you crying all the time either." Timothy said, without a hint of gentleness.

"I'm not crying all of the time, I am having a few moments that's all. I've lost Nanna and Grandad and Mum in the last few years and it's devastating. It's natural to be grieving." Maureen dried her eyes, her feelings of anger rising above the sadness. "We are going to go up and stay in the house when they've finished their exams. Have a bit of a trip north. It's been a while."

"Yes well you'd do well to speak with estate agents while you're up there and get the place on the market. It's just sitting there, empty, and no doubt I'll be paying for its upkeep soon if we don't sell." He grabbed himself a mug from the cupboard.

"There's plenty of money from Mum to pay for its upkeep, as you call it." Maureen felt her anger rising. "And I'm not selling it. We've discussed this before, I want to keep it, go and stay there, maybe eventually we'll retire there?"

Timothy sighed. "It's worth a small fortune and it's empty most of the time." He stopped what he was doing and tried to take her hand, but she moved across the kitchen slightly, finding something to do to distract herself from the conversation. "Maureen, listen to me. Is it more trouble than it's worth, that house just sitting there empty making you feel you should be there? Making you fret about it?"

"No, it's the lack of people in it that's making me sad, not the house. I'd feel a bloody damn sight worse if I didn't have it, if someone else had it. Please, I beg you, don't mention about selling it again." She looked at him with her wet eyes, staring and not looking away.

His breath caught in the back of his throat. It was too much for him to see her like this, could she not see the impact she was having on him? She just had to get over this bad bit, then she could get on with being with him and not thinking about her bloody mother or that house. He had provided so much for her and her mind was elsewhere. She could smile for the children, why not for him? He didn't need to see this. "I won't mention the house again, but please, try and control your emotions a little better, it's getting too much, makes me not want to come home."

She dried her eyes and blew her nose. She resented the suggestion that she spent her days crying. She had moments, and she felt sad in those moments and that was grief. There had been a lot of it in a short space of time. Memories of cleaning her mum's face and moistening her lips with little pink sponges as she barely breathed took up a lot of her head space. They had both assumed that Coral feeling unwell and tired was the fallout from Grandad dying, the grief, her age, recovering from flu. By the time she did go to the doctor's the cancer was so far along there wasn't much to be done except comfort, and she didn't want to be anywhere but home, and Maureen didn't want to be anywhere but keeping her comfortable. That's why she had to stay away, literally torn in two by teenagers who wanted her and a dying Mum who needed her and the eggshells from Timothy in between it all.

Maureen put the tissues in the bin and started the washing up. They were still in the same house, their planned move halted after everything that had happened, but she knew Timothy was keen to get going to a bigger house. The kids were planning on A-levels and university and Timothy wanted more space. Maureen just wanted to feel a bit better, less lost, more her old fearless self, but Timothy had let her know on several occasions she was letting him down, so there was no space for talking through how she was feeling there.

She had lots of phone calls from friends, old colleagues, her mum's tribe, and she told them all she had good days and bad days and that she was getting on ok. She didn't want people to know that she had more bad days than good days some weeks, she didn't want to burden anyone. She wanted to be able to talk to Timothy and tell him what she needed, let him look after her, but he had had enough of it all. It hadn't been a year and he had had enough. She hadn't seen her mother-in-law since before Coral died. Maureen had avoided going, to avoid questions and undiplomatic conversation around everyone Julia knew who had died of cancer. She had done it when Nanna died about strokes, and again when Grandad died about anyone who had had a heart attack, and Maureen had no room left for the cancer talk. So she avoided her like the plague. Florence had been amazing, checking in, popping by, and when Maureen said she was fine Florence called her a liar and said she didn't have to pretend with her. She said "You keep saying you're fine and I'll keep asking anyway." And then she took the kids out to dinner to get them out of Maureen's hair.

The grief was ever present to Maureen, whispering at the back of her head as she went about her days. She felt that she was doing the wrong thing much of the time, never quite present in the moment. It had been a mistake to give up work. The distraction of activities got her through each day and she had less to occupy herself with. She spoke to her department head and they were having cutbacks and were not able to offer her anything other than occasional lecturing work if her specific subject came up, so she went on the lecturing bank and was occasionally back in the office. Timothy said that it was a waste of her time, the amount of preparation needed wasn't worth the money, and they didn't even need the money, he didn't understand that it was the distraction she needed, to shout louder than the whispering grief.

And so life carried on in a different way. The twins sat their exams and they enjoyed a holiday in the cottage, which felt manageable and dare she say, enjoyable. The quietness of the house was hard to swallow, but the bickering and laughter and demands of two sixteen year olds was the distraction that she needed. Then it was back to school and studying and plans for university, and in the blink of an eye she was packing them both up to go and study in different places. Lilly to do history in Manchester and Marcus to do archaeology in Cardiff. She struggled to get up to Ambleside with everything that needed doing, but Lilly would go up with her for a night or two with promises of cafe visits and a cocktail or two, once she was eighteen. Maureen struggled being in the cottage on her own, it felt so empty and quiet when she needed a hum to distract her. Florence enjoyed the odd trip up there and they had a few drinks but never repeated the drunken, vomit extravaganza of their early friendship, although they did snigger about it often, mainly the shock of Julia and Timothy at the recklessness of Florence and her gag mechanism following many, many cocktails.

Maureen felt that she was managing life a little better in the summer of 2006, not her usual self, but it was definitely less of an uphill battle every day. She smiled more easily, laughed from her belly at times, the weight of worry she had been carrying had lifted, not completely but somewhat. There was still a whispering grief at the back of her head, catching her unexpectedly at times. The noise of life drowned it out at times, but then a song or a smell or the back of someone's head bobbing along the road and she would feel her breath catch and her eyes burn. But she spoke with Florence and agreed that it was perfectly normal. With all the loss and not to mention being forty-eight, it was to be expected that she would have moments, sometimes very long ones.

September was looming large, knowing that the twins would be moving out of the house to go to university felt strange. Timothy said that they could be like newlyweds again, he said they could even have sex on the sofa again without worrying, but she didn't much fancy it. His generalized coldness towards everything didn't fill her with desire. She did hope that she might be able to communicate with him better when it was just the two of them in the house, but really she needed it to be in both directions. Lilly once told Maureen that Timothy had asked why seven times over one mealtime. She had decided to count as he kept questioning everything.

"Why did you cook the meat this way?"

"Why are you doing that?"

"Why are we listening to this music?"

"Why is there no custard?"

"Why is the window open?"

"Why is someone ringing at this time?"

"Why are we having tea and not coffee?"

It was relentless at times, he was unable to hold in his displeasure much of the time. He just didn't know how to communicate things well at home, which was amazing for someone whose job involved lots of communication. And then sometimes he would surprise her, sit her down when she got in from somewhere, bring her a cup of tea, ask her about her day, talk to her about his, and then she remembered why she'd loved him all of these years. At the time she didn't realise it was crumbs from the table, she was so happy to receive them they felt like a full meal.

After they had taken the twins to their halls of residence after a very tiring weekend, driving to Cardiff on a Saturday and Manchester on the Sunday they sat at home eating fish and chips on the sofa, and drinking tea and lemonade, tired to their bones, barely listening to the television. It was like just another day, as if Lilly and Marcus had popped out to friends, except they weren't popping back for quite some time. The quietness of the house, after the rush of getting all of their things together and making sure they had all they needed, was initially welcome, but only for the briefest period. Maureen's friends had told her about empty nesters, the feeling when the children had gone, and here she was without her chicks, and it wasn't just the nest that felt empty, she did too. The house was too quiet, so quiet you could hear the crunch of an eggshell.

She suggested to Timothy, at the end of October, that they could go and visit Lilly one Saturday and perhaps stay overnight on the way to Cardiff for the Sunday.

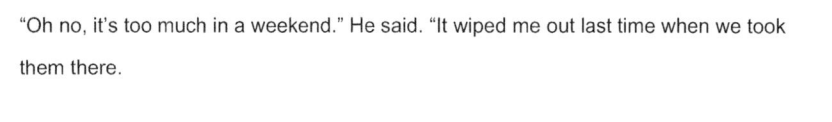

"Oh no, it's too much in a weekend." He said. "It wiped me out last time when we took them there.

"What about we do Manchester one weekend and Cardiff the next? Or the other way round. What do you think about that?" She asked hopefully.

"It's too much, two weekends, with working all week too, some of us have full time jobs you know, we can't all be ladies of leisure." He shook his head at her to make a point.

"Please come, I'm not used to traveling on my own anymore, not for the past few years. It'll be lovely, me and you on a trip, I can pack a flask, read to you, like we used to." She smiled enthusiastically.

"I told you already, it's too much, besides I want us to go to see Mother at the end of the month." He was already leaving the room. Walking away.

Maureen rang Lilly and asked if she wanted to come home for the weekend, she would send the money, but she had a part time job in a bar and was working, so then it felt like an imposition to ask if she'd be up for Maureen visiting for a couple of hours on the train. Marcus was busy too, so Maureen resigned herself to a trip to Winchester, and luckily Florence was going too. She missed her babies so much, even though they were very much not babies any more, they would always be her babies.

Timothy came home from work on the weekend of the trip that didn't happen, beaming from ear to ear, saying that he had a lovely surprise for her. Her heart leapt, she thought he must have organised something with the kids after all, and she smiled waiting for him to explain himself. He had bought her a dress. That was the surprise. He said that he knew she had been sad since the children had left, and that he had seen this in a window and knew instantly it would cheer her, that she deserved something new. He had never bought her clothes before, he had often commented that she should wear more dresses, get rid of the jeans, the phrase he used was that she should be 'more ladylike.' And she had laughed because she wasn't quite sure why anyone would strive for that? It was a flowery dress from Laura Ashley, with a full skirt and puffed sleeves, the sort of thing that might be worn at a Conservative party dinner that she had never attended. She was not, and never had been, a flowery dress kind of woman.

"Oh, I'm not sure this will suit me?" She said, trying her best to be diplomatic.

"Nonsense, my love, you will look amazing. Try it on and I'll let you know what other surprise I have for you." He was so pleased with himself.

She took her clothes off where she was and pulled the dress over her head, feeling like it might have been something Nanna would have encouraged her to wear to a party when she was about nine. To be fair to Timothy, he had got the fit just right, and she looked good in it, but it wasn't her, she would never have chosen it herself.

"Wow, you look stunning, absolutely beautiful." He said, giving her a long kiss.

She was taken aback with his enthusiasm, she felt a bit like a dressed up doll, but he was so pleased with himself, and he was so happy that she was wearing it, she felt that she had to keep it on.

"I've booked us a table at your favourite place tonight." He beamed. "I thought we could get dressed up and go out, cheer you up a bit."

"Oh lovely." She said. "I best go and have a shower then."

"Yes, good idea, I'll finish up a couple of calls I've got and you make yourself beautiful."

She felt a bit strange as she was showering, that he had come home with a dress, completely out of character, and this was his way of cheering her. She felt sad, all she really wanted to do was see the children, but she felt guilty that he was so happy to have got her a gift. She would make sure she looked amazing for him, even though the dress was not something she would have chosen. It was the small start of getting through the isolation she felt, if he was happy to spend time with her then she would wear whatever he damn well wanted. It was a really small thing, a new dress, innocent enough, she figured that he must be feeling guilty at being so distant, at not wanting to hear her tell him how she felt. It was his way of reaching out, he used to buy her gifts all the time, so it wasn't so unusual, she told herself as she buttoned it up. Then it started to become a thing, every couple of weeks or so he would come home with something for her, a new dress, a handbag, perfume, a pair of heels, a lipstick, bright red of all colours, even she never bothered with lipstick or makeup, it wasn't her thing. He was going out of his way to cheer her up, he said. He missed the mark with a lot of it, but she kept thinking that it was the thought that counted. He said the men at the golf club were saying he was showing them up with all of these presents, he said he told them that it was about time that they showed their wives a bit of appreciation.

"You've been so busy with the kids all these years, and work, and your family, it's our time now, my time to look after you, treat you." He was handing her another flowery dress, pink this time.

He had been so distant for so long it was refreshing that he was paying her so much attention, lavishing her with gifts. She told herself all of the time that she was lucky, even if it wasn't something she would choose herself, she was lucky. She would try the clothes on and he would be there, kissing her and stroking her face, and then he would take her upstairs and lie her down, telling her she was the most beautiful woman in the world, and she always had been. He said he knew it from the first moment he saw her and that he knew he'd be a fool to let her get away. He would tell her she was his and to keep the dress on as he pulled at her knickers. She was lucky, she said to herself, that he was paying her this much attention after all of this time. She felt lost and lonely without the children at home sometimes, and then he would be there with his words and distraction telling her how lucky she was, that she still had all of this, after all of these years. He said he was sorry that he didn't look after her better, but he would look after her now. Then they would go out to eat and he would hold her hand across the table as she sat in her flowery dress, with her heels digging into her and making her feet ache, but he had chosen them and told her they were to cheer her up. If he came home and she was wearing her trousers or an old top he would be frosty, he would make it known that he wanted things a bit more special, asking her if she was dressing for dinner, even if it was just at the kitchen table, and she said sure she would, because it was easier to be pinched under the arm with tight fabric as you ate pasta than it was to deal with the frost. And after everything that had gone on over the last few years, the grief and the empty nest, and the big gaping numbness in her stomach, she just didn't want to have to deal with frost.

She started clock watching and getting herself dressed when she knew he would be coming home, she'd have a shower and do her hair, put on a bit of makeup and a dress and wait to hear his car on the drive. Once when she was feeling confident and he told her how nice she looked she told him she wasn't wearing any knickers under the dress and he nearly choked on his tea, he could barely keep his eyes and hands off her, and they had sex in the kitchen, quickly and roughly, like they were twenty five again. Afterwards he told her he would prefer that they not do that again, not really very ladylike not wearing underwear. She told him she wasn't trying to be a lady, and he went and did some paperwork and left her alone for the rest of the evening. She watched television, cleared up the kitchen, and wondered if she should offer him a cup of tea but decided against it.

She was tired, and it was easier being lonely knowing Timothy was pleased with her than dealing with distance and coldness. She was lonely either way, she could be lonely with a grumpy man or lonely with a man who was brusque but affectionate, attentive but in charge. She would see friends still, but always made sure she was home in time to get herself dressed and ready for Timothy coming home. They often went out to eat, sometimes just the two of them, sometimes with a golf friend and their wife, and Maureen would be entertaining, talkative, she would laugh, she was good company. Sometimes she would feel Timothy squeeze her knee if she said too much or swore too much, so he'd have to tell her on the way home that he loved hearing her talk but Brian didn't like swearing, or Liz wasn't one for a long story, or let them get a word in next time.

Lilly said that she wasn't too sure about her mum's new look, which appeared to have manifested itself over a year or so, but Maureen appeared less stressed each time she came home from university so she didn't want to say too much. Marcus didn't notice that his mum's clothes had changed and so he didn't say anything at all. And this was how it was. The kids were buzzing with information and news about their courses and their friends and their dad didn't seem as grumpy and their mum was less sad and they came and went without much concern. Maureen was still tired and sad but it was easier to smile and ask questions about others, than ask for help, so she smiled and chatted and went through the motions of being fine. Timothy told her that she had a beautiful smile and she was still the most beautiful woman he had ever seen, and he meant it, so she smiled, wore the clothes, became good at walking in heels, listened more, swore less and cried in the bedroom in the afternoon when there was plenty of time for her eyes to dry up before Timothy came home.

Maureen was tired, but she was also very embarrassed. She wondered what Coral would think if she saw her in her dresses without her walking boots on, without her jeans, without her swear words, without her feist. She wondered how ashamed Coral would be if she saw her being quiet because Timothy said to be quiet, or if she saw her putting on eyeshadow at five o'clock in the evening, taming her curls in a bun, getting her face stroked on Wednesdays and Saturdays. So she cried in the bedroom when there was no one around because she felt lonely and lost and the fire in her belly had gone out, it had been snuffed out discreetly and carefully by someone else who knew how lonely and lost she was and took the opportunity to quiet a strong woman. That's what Coral would have seen. She would have glanced at Maureen and then set her fierce gaze on Timothy, and then she would have waited for the reigniting of Maureen Smith.

18- paperwork

In the bedroom of the great big bungalow that Maureen didn't think of as home, that smelt new and unfamiliar, even after being there a few years, was a safe. In that safe were things that Maureen kept, well, safe. She didn't think there needed to be a safe for her things, but Timothy had insisted that the world was not a safe place and documents needed locking away. In his office sat another safe for business things, that Maureen had never been in, that she did not have the code for and did not have any interest in whatsoever. She was only interested in the contents of her safe when she might need something, her passport, Nanna's rings, wedding certificates, death certificates, precious photos of the children, original photos of Nanna and Grandad and Coral from when they were young. She rarely opened the safe. Timothy went in and out, moving things about, but she just left her things in there. On the day she decided enough was enough, she gathered her things together in the bedroom, marching from drawer to wardrobe, bathroom to bedroom, getting the things that she would need to essentially run away, leave, not come back. When she was ready she had a sudden thought, and that was the contents of the safe. She had to get another bag from the top of the wardrobe, open the little metal door with her code and grab everything, all at once. She had no intention of going through the files and boxes before she bolted, so she grabbed it all.

Maureen took very little in the way of clothing with her when she left, which may have led Timothy to believe that she was taking a short trip and would be back soon. This wasn't her intention, but she was not, under any circumstance, taking any clothing with a flower on, or any heels. She was taking the few trousers she owned, t-shirts and her waterproof. She had enough money in her bank to buy more clothes, comfortable clothes, that she chose herself and that she liked. She drove away knowing she would also never, ever, wear an under-wired bra again, or any of the flimsy expensive underwear Timothy had purchased over the years. It was a mistake leaving so many clothes, only because Timothy was filled with hope, but it was not a mistake taking the contents of the safe, especially as she had taken more than her own things, she just didn't realise it at the time.

When she had found herself becoming invisible, the children had long since got their own homes and jobs, Lilly had married a lovely man who was the head teacher of where she worked. She stayed in Manchester after she graduated and did her teacher training. Marcus was off abroad most of the time, digging at dust and loving it every moment of it.

Maureen yearned to visit Ambleside, to stay in the cottage, but she found it hard on her own at first and Timothy would not go with her, even just for a couple of nights. He would ask her repeatedly to put the house on the market, to sell up and then there wasn't an old cottage two hundred and fifty miles away with the upkeep to deal with. He suggested they sell it and get a little flat nearby, something modern they could enjoy together, because as much as he had visited and stayed there over the years he hated that cottage very much. He hated going there and thinking how much Maureen loved it, how she was more her old self there, less his. She loved it so much that he felt it kept her from him, even when they weren't there. When Maureen went to visit Lilly they would often have a quick overnight stay at the cottage, where Maureen would physically relax, her shoulders would drop and she would sleep, and wake up feeling refreshed. She slept badly at the best of times but the hum of her old house made her sleep long and deep.

Timothy told her that he was fed up with old houses and one of them had to go to reduce repairs, so she agreed that her beautiful family home, where she had made her babies and raised her babies, could be sold to allow them to move into a new build. And that is how she found herself in an unfamiliar, executive, five bedroom home with a double garage, three ensuites, and the overpowering smell of plaster and plastic. To keep the cottage, to know it was there, to know that she could go and visit and sit where Nanna had sat, drink tea from the china cup and saucers that were so thin you could see the sun shine through them, she agreed to live in this awful house. She had a dressing room, full of her dresses and shoes, and whenever anyone came around the house Timothy insisted they were shown the master suite and the dressing room.

"Don't ask how much she spends on all of these bloody clothes" he would say, winking, as if he hadn't bought it all himself for his mannequin wife, as if he didn't add to the collection every couple of weeks. She showed people round her big, new bedroom and smiled, so she could lie in the old soft bed in Ambleside and smell the memories. And it was worth it.

Timothy often had to travel for a few nights, and if she knew how long he was away for, she would gather her things and go up to the cottage for a visit. That first time on her own was hard, the quietness of the house and the familiar smell mixed in with the slight sourness of damp stoking her memories, but it seemed much easier than she thought it would. She had met Lilly for a very quick lunch on the way up and they scoffed roast beef sandwiches in her forty-five minute break, eating crisps and drinking steaming tea, and then it was time for her to run back into her classes and Maureen to get back on to the motorway.

Maureen had been through the front door thousands of times, and many times since she had lost her mum, but not on her own, and the anticipation of the lack of greeting made her hold her breath, but then she was through the front door with her bag, and a carrier bag of bread and milk, bananas and tea bags. She had the kettle on before she gave herself a chance to wobble. That first cup of tea in the kitchen of her cottage on her own was the best tea she had ever tasted. She felt brave and independent, things she hadn't felt for an age. She wasn't timed, didn't have to get changed before she ate, didn't have to get up in the morning to make sure the coffee was brewing, she could lie in bed and listen to the radio or read a book. She didn't have to wash up immediately after a meal was finished or prepare a two course dinner because Timothy liked it, eat wearing lipstick and drink red wine so Timothy was not drinking alone.

On that first visit on her own Timothy messaged her throughout the day telling her how much he missed her, and she would respond quickly, making sure that her phone was irritatingly loud so she didn't miss anything, but apart from that her time was her own. She met some of her mum's friends for coffee and chatted for a good couple of hours, reminiscing and laughing, and then she went back to the cottage and felt light and free, content but sad, normal feelings when someone was in their childhood home without their childhood loved ones. She cleaned while she was there, scrubbing mould off windows and making sure the heating was set to a timer to put a bit of heat into the walls. She knew she would need to come up more, she had the twice yearly deep clean but more life needed to happen in the house. And then she was back in her big modern house, driving down the motorway the day before Timothy was due home, in case she had travel issues or was delayed somehow. She could imagine the reception she would get if Timothy got home before her and was sat waiting, and she turned up in her jeans and fleece with colour in her cheeks and freedom on her mind. There would be days of cold shoulders and things being difficult, plans being changed, no affection, no human touch, just the frost of disapproval hanging between them. She had twisted herself into someone she didn't fully recognise so that she wouldn't be hit with that frost, and it was easy, she almost had it down to perfection, so much so that she couldn't let a problem on the motorway or her car breaking down spoil it all.

She filled the house with shopping and things for a fancy tea that would take a while to cook on the day that he was coming home, his favourite food that took effort. She made sure things were spotless, the heating on to take the chill off the house, but not so hot that he would say he was in a furnace. She showered and dressed herself so that she was the version of herself she didn't know well, but he seemed to want, and then she waited. Like clockwork at six thirty his headlights shone through the kitchen window and she was at the door greeting him. He eyed her up with suspicion. She had been up to the house and she had been pleasing herself and doing her own thing, but she looked pleased to see him and had dressed how he liked it, and he was satisfied. He was pleased that the negative influence of her mother had gone, she was no longer whispering rebellious tones into the ear of his wife, taking her away, giving her options. She had been up to the cottage but had not come back hardened to him and this pleased him greatly.

"You're looking good." He said, kissing her hard on the mouth, for longer than she wanted, his breath stale from coffee and driving.

"You too." She smiled, pulling away so he didn't see that the smile didn't reach her eyes. "Come in and keep the cold out, I've made your favourite."

As they ate she asked him all about his trip and how the hotel was, how the food was, the flight, getting through the airport? He loved being asked about himself and it was easy to smooth his ego and make him the centre of everything. He was so relieved that she had gone and come back that he was slightly giddy, drank too much wine. She had chosen to come home to him, how it was meant to be. He said that he had arranged to go to Mother's the next day and take her out for lunch as he had not been able to pop in all week with him being away and Mother was really looking forward to seeing Maureen. Maureen smiled and said that would be lovely, knowing it wouldn't be lovely, or even nice, but she would go and smile and listen to tales of people Julia objected to or the latest distant relative to die. And Maureen would say 'fuck off' a thousand times in her head and smile throughout.

They had quite the gathering for Julia's eightieth birthday in 2013. Lilly and Marcus came with their respective partners, both of them twenty five, the same age Maureen had been when Timothy set eyes on her and pursued her, the same age they were when they fell in love and started their life together. Maureen was fifty five, and she had been an orphan for ten years. She wished she was organising her mum's seventy-fifth birthday, which would have been the same year, instead of fussing around with plans for this eightieth. Everything was timed to perfection, the food was perfect, the guest's many and it cost a fortune. It was formal attire and Maureen found herself in a navy blue floor length gown with her hair escaping her bun, coils of curls bouncing about as she walked around making sure that everything was as it should be. Timothy was receiving thanks from everyone for a party well planned and executed, and he took the thanks and held it for himself, telling people that it was more than worth it to see the look on Mother's face when she saw how many people were here. Florence stood by Maureen, as Timothy made a slightly too long speech, and muttered under her breath to Maureen about how he had done shit all and he was getting all the thanks. Maureen held a laugh in for too long and ended up coughing, which both Timothy and Julia frowned at. If Maureen had known she would be planning another birthday in ten years and she would be smiling without her eyes for all that time, she would have happily walked out of the party there and then, but the people she loved most in the world were in that room and she didn't want then to worry about her or fear for her, so she told them was a lovely time she was having, even when Lilly said: "For fucks sake mum, I bet he hasn't lifted a finger." Maureen smiled on.

Timothy draped his arm around the bare shoulders of his wife and told her that they were both so lucky to have each other. He was the wrong side of several whiskies and he had mingled around the room like it was his birthday and everyone was here to see him and hear him. He manoeuvred Maureen around with him at times, and she was pleased when he saw someone he needed to have a brief business chat with and he left her alone for a while. She caught up with Florence and Lilly and they shared a bottle of wine and belly laughed about the awfulness of it all, hushing each other and laughing some more. Maureen caught a frown from Timothy for laughing loudly and she tried to compose herself but there was too much wine in her stomach and she saw him shake his head at her.

"Just ignore him Mum, it's a bloody party, laugh all you want." Lilly said, staring at her dad until he looked away.

"My niece is correct." Florence smiled. "This is a very elderly party that is in need of some laughter." She topped up Maureen's glass. "Everyone is staying in the hotel, no one has to drive so just let your hair down."

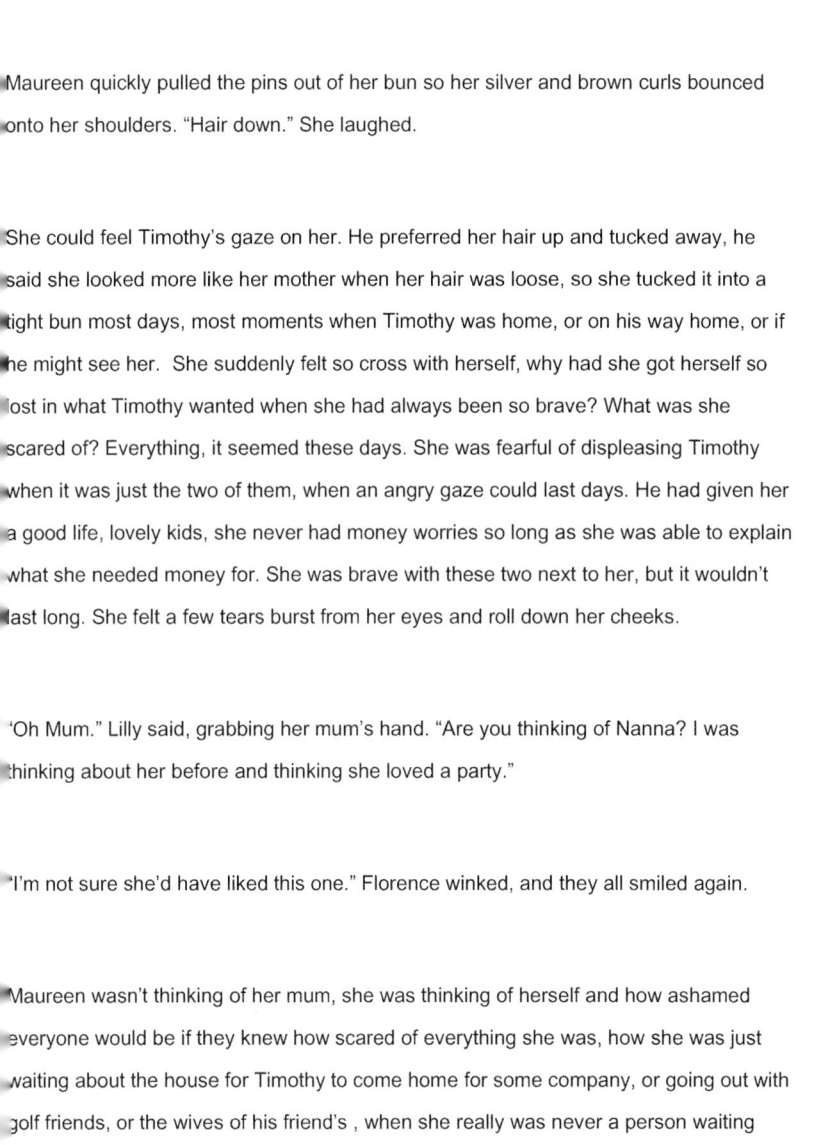

Maureen quickly pulled the pins out of her bun so her silver and brown curls bounced onto her shoulders. "Hair down." She laughed.

She could feel Timothy's gaze on her. He preferred her hair up and tucked away, he said she looked more like her mother when her hair was loose, so she tucked it into a tight bun most days, most moments when Timothy was home, or on his way home, or if he might see her. She suddenly felt so cross with herself, why had she got herself so lost in what Timothy wanted when she had always been so brave? What was she scared of? Everything, it seemed these days. She was fearful of displeasing Timothy when it was just the two of them, when an angry gaze could last days. He had given her a good life, lovely kids, she never had money worries so long as she was able to explain what she needed money for. She was brave with these two next to her, but it wouldn't last long. She felt a few tears burst from her eyes and roll down her cheeks.

'Oh Mum." Lilly said, grabbing her mum's hand. "Are you thinking of Nanna? I was thinking about her before and thinking she loved a party."

"I'm not sure she'd have liked this one." Florence winked, and they all smiled again.

Maureen wasn't thinking of her mum, she was thinking of herself and how ashamed everyone would be if they knew how scared of everything she was, how she was just waiting about the house for Timothy to come home for some company, or going out with golf friends, or the wives of his friend's , when she really was never a person waiting around to please her husband. She was ashamed to her core, but she had neither the energy or inclination to be herself again, because she'd have to tell the truth and deal with how sad she felt.

Despite Maureen's hair escaping its clips, Timothy proclaimed to her on the journey home the next day that the party had been an utter success and they had done Mother proud. He had even managed to rustle up a bit of lucrative business during the party and was feeling very pleased with himself. He suggested that they go home and spend a bit of time in bed as they had been too tired for their usual Saturday get together the night before. He stroked her face briefly as he drove and left his hand to rest on her thigh. She was shattered and his hand was hot, making her feel uncomfortable. She was queasy from the wine and hungry because she couldn't face breakfast and now she was being invited to watch him pant on top of her, although it wasn't an invite, it was what was going to happen. Her face had been stroked and her thigh touched and that was that. She closed her eyes as they drove hoping to get a few moments of sleep before the inevitable. She bit her jaw together hard to stop herself from crying, willing herself to pull herself together. It was just a moment in time, she told herself, she could manage it like all of the others. And she did manage it, she went on managing it until she felt hot inside with anger and she could no longer swallow down being quiet Mrs Smith, good old Maureen Smith, always so helpful, quiet, smiley, quite the doer. Need something done? Maureen Smith will quietly help.

One day, not long before the re-ignition, Maureen was in the ladies bar at the golf club, smiling and chatting with a white wine spritzer in her hand and a flowery dress on her shoulders. They were talking about their children going to university and the cost.

"I never went to university." Barbara said. "And it didn't do me any harm."

"I went and had to leave because I met Brian and got pregnant, so it was a wedding for me instead of a graduation." Felicity giggled.

They went around chatting about what they had done or not done at university, and Maureen remained quiet, sipping her wine and listening.

"What about you Maureen? Didn't you fancy university?" Barbara asked.

"Oh no, I went, I really enjoyed every minute of it." Maureen smiled.

"Where did you go?" Sheila asked.

"Here, Oxford. I came all the way down from Ambleside to Oxford with my mum in her old mini."

"What did you study?" Stella asked.

"History." Maureen replied. "I loved it."

"Yes but there's not much you can do with that but teach, did you teach Maureen?" Stella asked.

"Yes, I did, for a good few years, I liked that too." Maureen sipped her wine some more.

"Did you teach secondary?" Barbara asked, not imagining this quiet little woman would manage a classroom of teenagers.

"No, I taught at the university." Maureen explained.

"Well, you need more than a history degree to do that lovey." Felicity said, shaking her head.

"Oh yes I know." Maureen said, feeling annoyed at their underestimation of her. "I did my degree, then a masters, then I did a PhD. In modern history." She sipped her wine again and smiled, this time it was genuine. Her eyes lit up.

"Bloody hell, Maureen, you're a dark horse." Sheila said, louder than necessary.

"The darkest." Maureen said, and she felt a tiny ember of warmth in her stomach.

Quiet Maureen, smiling with her loud, gregarious husband, who knew she was a clever woman, clever at organising events, running a house, looking smart, blending into the background, never being too much? Clever at asking questions and getting people to talk about themselves so that they felt listened to and special, but clever at hanging back, not telling much about herself, so she didn't have to say that she was not who she really was, not a woman with a voice. She was clever at being her husband's biggest supporter and you had to be bloody clever when you supported something you started to despise, and not let anyone even notice.

On the way home, after she had revealed a brightness of herself from the shadows she took her hair down from her bun and shook it to her shoulders. That damn bum that had pulled her hair tight from her forehead and made her head ache at times. That damn bun that pleased Timothy and kept her looking 'ladylike and smart.' She took her hair down and left it down.

When she was sitting on the sofa that night, before going to bed Timothy said: "Are you going for a new look? Crazy white haired lady?"

She smiled at him and said nothing. But she kept her hair down, kept the bands and hair clips away and enjoyed the feel of her hair in her face and the frown on his. There was nothing that had changed externally, really, her need to be needed and loved, after those she loved and needed had passed, slowly edged away from her, tiptoeing out of her life quietly without so much as a goodbye. Her need for the closeness of anything, even the crumbs from Timothy, slowly whispered away. Timothy's control had crept in so slowly and quietly, it was barely noticed, and she almost welcomed it. She felt needed and could go through the motions and focus on him without needing to focus on how lost she was. And then she found herself again, one day in the middle of June, and the quietness exploded, like a sudden cough or a laugh that she didn't quite expect, like a noise she didn't recognise, until she realised it was her voice all along.

19-a good deed.

When Maureen had been through her paperwork to find her marriage certificate so that she could send her legal separation paperwork off, she emptied the contents of the bag that held the contents of the safe all over the living room floor. She knew where the certificate was and was keen to get on with the process in hand. After copying and posting and drinking a cup of tea, and then just one more cup, she sat in front of the television with a bowl of spaghetti on a stool in front of her, gently curling the pasta around her fork and slurping it in her mouth, without anyone telling her to shush. When she was feeling less ravenous she knelt on the floor stiffly, easing herself off the sofa like the white haired woman that she was.

Maureen took a deep breath and thought that it was a good idea that the paperwork wasn't stuffed back into the bag, but put away in the sideboard where all paperwork of importance had been traditionally stuffed for years. She decided as she was responsible for her own legalities, she'd go through it and know what she was dealing with. There were bank statements in her name, with quite a bit of money in, her passport that would need renewing soon, her jewellery and rings, the death certificates, folded into crisp envelopes. In one of the cardboard files were the deeds to the cottage, in her name, but the deeds to the big, new house that wasn't her home wasn't there anymore, instead, behind her cottage deeds, in the same file, was the deed to another house in her name, Quarry Road in Winchester. In her name, as the person whom it was registered to, as the owner. She couldn't believe it for a moment and she checked and double checked, laying the paper flat on the floor, staring at it in disbelief. She was the owner of her mother-in-law's house, that massive, rambling property that she neither liked nor wanted was in her name. And this was the first she'd heard of it, she had certainly not signed her name, so someone was up to no good, Timothy up to no good. He wouldn't have put this house in her name unless he was trying to hide his something from someone. The date on it was from ten months ago and enough time spent on the internet told her that she couldn't have a house put in her name without her agreement, without her signature being witnessed, and she certainly hadn't and wouldn't agree to having that house, like a chain around her neck. The only house she wanted going forward was the one she was currently sitting in, and knowing that she had these other deeds certainly gave her some leverage over negotiations. She wondered what her mother-in-law would think if she knew Maureen owned the house she lived in, that her slightly disappointing daughter-in-law held her home.

She folded all the paperwork away carefully, remembering the legal work and paperwork that was involved in sorting out the cottage when her mum died. Timothy helping with it all, guiding her through the legalities, going through probate and asking her time and time again to sell the cottage, focus on the home that they had, but she stood firm. She actually stood weeping and begged him to stop asking, she couldn't stand the idea of never being in the house again, even though she couldn't bear the thought of her mum and grandparents not being in it. He asked her repeatedly to sell it, until she agreed to the move to the 'executive house', as he called it at the time, and then he just asked periodically, when a big expense came in. It would be sold at some point, but not while there was breath in her.

She picked up her phone and sent an email to Mick, explaining what she had found and asking for his help. Just as she finished her phone pinged. "Hello mum, just checking in on you. How are you doing up there and how is the weather? I was looking at the forecast and you're due a fair bit of rain the next couple of days. Hope dad is behaving and leaving you alone? Love you." A message from Lilly. Maureen suspected her dad had spoken with her.

"All good, lovely. It's been wet today, but good, a break from the heat. Your dad drove up but he has driven back down south and I don't think he'll come up again for now. Hope you are doing ok?"

A few moments later there was another ping. "I spoke with Flo, we were saying that it might be awful for you to go to Gran's party. You don't have to go, you know."

"I know, love, but I said I'd go and she'll be expecting me. Who will she complain to about it not being right if I don't go?"

Lilly sent back a laughing face. She knew her grandmother well, she would not be satisfied unless something wasn't quite right and she could tell people she could have done better herself. She was predictably annoyed. Timothy was certainly a chip off the old block. Poor Florence didn't stand a chance, according to Julia, Florence wasn't quite right. She hadn't had children, was divorced, and didn't visit her mother often enough.

"Why the hell would I drive all that way to be told off?" Florence had said to Maureen one day when Timothy had mentioned that Mother was complaining she had not seen Florence for a month. Maureen had sniggered slightly and Timothy had given her a hard, stern look that would have repercussions for her for the rest of the weekend, long after Florence had driven home.

It was getting late and dusky outside. Maureen had been sitting for a long time, staring at the television, watching out of the window, thinking that she would get up in a minute and get to bed, but not quite having the motivation. Eventually she gave herself a good talking to and stood up. She checked the doors and windows downstairs, turned the kitchen tap tightly, after it had been dripping into the sink all evening. She hovered near the kettle but decided she would go straight up to bed without another brew, to see if she could avoid the night time toilet visits, her bladder was a cruel taskmaster. She briefly wondered what she would do with the house deeds she had found before she fell asleep soundly, listening to the rain patter its way to the window outside. She woke in the night to use the toilet, getting back in bed with a head full of thoughts, lying in the darkness with the curtains open, watching shadows dance across the ceiling. She tried to tuck thoughts away until daylight, but it was easier said than done. By the time four thirty made its way to her clock, a light hue was taking over part of the sky and she finally found a heaviness in her eyes and began to drift again.

It was taking a bit of getting used to, not hearing the alarm and jumping out of bed to put the coffee on that she would never drink herself. Maureen felt a sense of initial dread when she opened her eyes and it was later than she thought, like she would be in trouble, she was so used to being directed. The dread floated off when she came to and could lie for a moment with only her own plans to consider. She made her way down the stairs and put the kettle on, stopping for a wee on the way.

The sky was blue with grey clouds scattered about, some rain was due, but a bit of sun too. She opened the back door and breathed in the morning, watching a ginger cat disappear over her fence to a neighbours house. It was only seven fifteen, but the air was warm. She felt calm when she finished making her tea. She took a kitchen chair outside and sat in the morning freshness sipping from the hot cup. She didn't have to dash off or go anywhere, the day was her own. She had an important phone call to make, she knew that, but for now she could drink her tea and listen to the birds. She could call Timothy later, untangle herself from him after toast, when she was ready. She had an email from Mick and he was more than happy to help her.

How many times had she sat drinking tea in this garden? This calm space, even with the overgrown garden and twists of brambles she had yet to tackle, it remained a calm space. It had been cared for and molded by her Grandad, and despite becoming wilder, it was still lovely, a place of reflection. She smiled, thinking about herself in the same way. She had been molded by Grandad's calm words and presence, and despite running wild with grief and Timothy's control, here she was, settled and measured and being OK, with a steaming hot tea and a chair, there wasn't much that couldn't be soothed by a hot cup of tea and a sit down. She knew it wasn't the drink, it was the reflection and the pause, but it was reassuring and strength gathering.

She ran her plans through her mind for the day. Another cup of tea, toast, a phone call and then she would go into town, she would have some cake in a cafe, go into Fred's book shop and get a few new books that would be lying on a little table by the entrance. This call needed to be made and she needed something to look forward to afterwards. She felt refreshingly that with her plan and her feeling and belief that she was steering her own ship, she could do this. She was not the deckhand to captain Timothy any more, so she had to grab the wheel and steer, even if it was scary. Grandad used to say: "You're Maureen Allonby, you can do anything." And the name might have changed but the sentiment was still there, that spark, that ember, it was still burning inside her. She talked herself through all of the tasks as she was building up to, the one she didn't really want to do but had to. She talked herself through toast, through tea, through showering, and then it had to be done. There wasn't anything else to play with and delay.

He answered the phone quickly

"Maureen." He said sharply, but she could hear the essence of pleasure in his voice. "Maureen." He said again.

"Hello Timothy." She said and then she drew breath to say what she needed.

"Have you come to your senses?" Timothy interrupted.

"Timothy, I need you to listen to what I am saying and not interrupt. Can you just listen to me for a few moments?" She heard him sigh, with irritation and impatience, but he didn't say anything more. She could just hear the whistle from his nostrils. "I really need to explain myself. I've filled in and sent off the paperwork for a legal separation......"

"What the hell Maureen? I'm not agreeing to separate from you. We've been married for nearly forty years. I'm sixty seven. Sixty seven." He stopped, she could hear a tremble in his voice.

"Timothy, I didn't want to do this on the phone, but I can't drive down there and know you're going to be angry, I can't put myself through that, and I don't want you coming up here and getting cross. I'm not asking you if we can separate, I'm telling you that's what I've done. I've started the ball rolling and it's happening."

"After everything I've done for you, I've looked after you all of these years...."

"Timothy!" She said sternly, how she used to say it when she was herself and she needed to reel him in, let him back down to earth. "I'm not going into the you-did-I-did game. I'm not going to agree with you or you with me. We are where we are and nothing you say will make me stop what I'm planning and nothing I say will make you understand." She paused for a moment and took a sip of water, her mouth dry with anxiety and nerves. "You will get the paperwork from wherever I sent it to soon, so I don't want it to be a surprise. All I want from this is the cottage and enough money to live on. I've seen the bank statements from my safe and I know I've got plenty of money I can have access to, and I also know you will have more than enough for yourself too."

"And what if I don't agree to that, what if I want that cottage?" He spat.

"You don't Timothy, and you never did. You didn't even want me to have it to come to, that's just you being obstinate. It's in my name and it's part of any joint assets but no court will award this house to you." She lied with her confidence, she was beginning to shake, but she would not let him know. She wouldn't let him think she was close to tears or afraid of his reactions. "You can keep that big house you're in at the moment. It's worth far more than this."

She looked down at the piece of paper that she had put by the phone as a reminder and for confidence. She reached out and held the corner of it between her finger and thumb, feeling the paper. "I've got the deeds to your mother's house here." She said it quickly, hoping the weight of the sentence would get to where it needed to go. He didn't respond. "I don't know who you conspired with to put it in my name, or for what reason you needed it out of yours, but I've got it here and I've been on the internet and downloaded all of the registered bits and it's definitely mine." She paused for a moment, giving him a chance to say something, but it was just the noise from his nostrils continuing to blow down his receiver. "So I'm going to say this and hope you understand. I don't want it, I never did, and I will gladly give it to you in exchange for you agreeing that you will not even suggest that you want my cottage."

He coughed. Starting gently and ending up a hack down the phone. She held it away from her ear until he composed himself. "Maureen." He said, more gently than before. "It was just for finances that's all, I, well, I ......" And he stopped, stopped explaining himself and arguing. He trusted her completely, that she would do whatever he asked, any time He had her completely, doing as she should. He had never felt happier, more sure of himself, knowing she was at home, waiting for him, his wife, his Maureen. She was his. But she was betraying him with threats, betraying him utterly. He wanted to shout down the telephone. Get in his car and drive up there. But she had him. The quiet, agreeable bitch.

"So, Mick will sort out any paperwork associated with all of this deed mix up." She called it that, like it was an accident, like it wasn't a deliberate fraud, a financial decision, like he had made an innocent mistake. "And then we can just get on being civil, doing our own thing, separating legally."

"What about Mother?" he said. "What will she think?"

Maureen laughed momentarily, quietly so he barely heard. "I really don't care Timothy." She said quietly. "You will have to deal with your mother, like I have done, get her shopping, pay her care company, clean her house. Like I have done the past five years.

See her and help her. I'm not doing it any more. I am separating from you and from that life that I had. I'm here now."

"But her birthday?" He said, raising his voice.

Maureen paused, the dread of the journey and the false smiling, and his behaviours and reactions, driving all that way with a knot in her stomach to face them all. The anticipation was awful. "I'm not coming." She said suddenly. "I'm not coming." Her face smiled and a weight lifted from her shoulders. "I'm busy with the garden." She said, walking towards the back window to look out of the window. "I'll ring your mother and tell her, but I'm absolutely not coming, Timothy, at all. Now I'm going to have to go. Mick will be in touch and the deeds and our homes will be sorted, so keep checking your emails. Take care Timothy, and I mean that. Look after yourself."

She put the phone down, her hands shaking with relief, her mouth dry with anxiety. She put her paperwork together and put it back in the drawer. It didn't need dealing with today, Mick would do that for her as her solicitor, he had reassured her that she would be able to stay in his cottage. She put the kettle on and watched it come to the boil, thirsty for a cup of tea, and when it was ready she sat and drank it at the kitchen table with the back door open, thinking of all of her plans for the garden and house, thinking of her mum, Grandad and NannM, and smiling to herself.

She would ring Florence and Lilly, let them know what was happening, about the houses and the party, and give Florence some knowledge about all of the dealings. But for now she would drink her tea and smile because, whatever she was going to have to deal with over the next few months, she would deal with, she was Maureen Allonby afterall.

Printed in Great Britain
by Amazon